DESERT DEAD

Book #3, The Mac 'n' Ivy Mysteries
by
Lorena McCourtney

Lorena McCourtney

Desert Dead

©2019 by Lorena McCourtney
Published by Rogue Ridge Press
Cover by Travis Miles
ISBN: 978-0-578-59916-8

Scripture used in this book, whether quoted or paraphrased by the characters, is taken from the Holy Bible, New International Version®. NIV®. Copyright © 1973, 1978, 1984, 2011 by Biblica, Inc.™ Used by permission of Zondervan. All rights reserved worldwide. www.zondervan.com. The "NIV" and "New International Version" are trademarks registered in the United States Patent and Trademark Office by Biblica, Inc.™

This book is a work of fiction. Certain actual locations and historical figures mentioned in the book are portrayed as accurately as possible but used in a fictional manner. All other names, places, and incidents are products of the author's imagination. All characters are fictional, and any similarity to people living or dead is purely coincidental.

Lorena McCourtney

Psalm 46:1

God is our refuge and strength, an ever-present help in trouble.

Chapter 1

IVY

Ivy, the body was there. I *saw* it. I *touched* it. It was a dead man. But now there *isn't* a dead man! The body just disappeared."

I couldn't see her through our cell phones, but I could tell my usually unflappable friend Magnolia was definitely flapped now. I blinked and twisted my head back and forth, trying to jolt myself fully awake. I'd been napping in the bedroom of the motorhome while Mac drove, waking up only when the phone did that strange music my grandniece put on it as a ringtone. But I didn't need to come up with any brilliant comment before Magnolia hurtled on.

"It's always seemed so strange when *you* run into a dead body or a murder. So not *normal.*" Magnolia doesn't usually talk with thunderous emphasis on words, but she was certainly doing so now. "But I can see now that sometimes it just *happens.*"

"Well, yes, it does—"

"But you've never had one *disappear*, have you?"

"No, I can't say that I have." In my experience, dead bodies didn't tend to get up and wander away. "Where are you?" I asked.

"I'm not sure . . . Where are we?" Magnolia asked in a distraught aside to her husband. They were also on the road in their motorhome, and he did most of the driving. A few seconds later she said, "Geoff says we're almost back to Prosperity now—"

"Prosperity?" Neither Geoff and Magnolia nor Mac and I were lacking for enough money to get along comfortably. The good Lord provided. But none of us had ever been anywhere near *prosperity.*

"It's the name of a place. Prosperity, Arizona," she said with a bit of impatience. "But the body was out in Deadeye. Right there in the middle of the street, just outside the barber shop."

I'd never heard of either Prosperity or Deadeye. Prosperity sounded like it might be a good place to be, Deadeye not so much. Especially if there was a dead body in the street. "Surely someone else also noticed the body if it was lying there in the street. Couldn't it simply have been removed?"

"Ivy, it's a *ghost* town. Way out in the desert. Several miles off the highway. Not another soul around. We went there because I'm trying to locate someone on my mother's side of the family."

Magnolia is always on a search for members of her family tree. Husband Geoff helps with genealogical searches on the internet, but Magnolia likes to track these distant relatives down in person. I've lost count of how many she's located, but there's always another great-great-grandfather's second cousin four times removed or a great-grandmother's aunt's third cousin twice removed to search for. If aliens ever show up on earth, I'm sure Magnolia will find a genealogical connection somewhere.

Although it seemed a little odd even for Magnolia to be looking for a member of her family tree in a deserted ghost town.

But there were more important things to think about now.

"Okay, the first thing to do, even if the body has disappeared, is call 911," I said briskly. It occurred to me that a ghost town out in the desert might not have 911 coverage, but it was worth a try.

"That's what I did. I may not be as experienced as you are in these things, but I do know enough to call 911." Magnolia sounded both exasperated and mildly indignant. "I wasn't carrying my phone when I found the body, so I had to go back to the motorhome to make the call. The woman said it would take a while for someone to get there, since we were so far out."

"Where was she?"

"Yuma, I think. Though I'm not sure. We were on the highway between Yuma and Gila Bend before we turned off to go to Prosperity and then Deadeye. Anyway, I waited in the motorhome for a while but I finally went back to stay with the body until the authorities arrived." She paused. "It just didn't seem right to leave it lying out there all alone."

I've felt that way in the past too, although hanging around isn't necessarily the best idea if there's a killer lurking somewhere behind a rock or tree.

"And that was when I discovered the body was gone. I was shocked of course. Bodies don't just *disappear*. But I thought I should mark where it had been, so I could show the officers when they got there. So I went back to the motorhome again to get something to outline the spot."

This sounded more like the Magnolia I've known for years. Outlining a missing body might be a bit unusual, but she sounded calmer now, rational and in control.

"You outlined it with chalk?"

"I didn't have any chalk, and I don't think chalk would have worked very well on dirt anyway. So I used toothpaste. I used up all I had, a full tube and a half. But now I'm wondering if I got it in the right place."

I'm a strong believer that in an emergency, whether it's a cooking emergency or a hair emergency or a killer emergency, you make use of whatever is available, but I'm not sure using toothpaste in this emergency would have occurred to me. I'm also not sure it would have occurred to me to outline a non-visible body. The police don't actually outline bodies these days anyway; that's TV and movie stuff.

"Where was Geoff? Did he see the body?"

"The road out to Deadeye is really rough, dirt and gravel and ruts and potholes, and he was checking underneath to see if we'd damaged anything on the motorhome or the car. I walked through the gate into Deadeye alone."

Like most of us, Geoff and Magnolia pull a vehicle behind their motorhome for convenience in getting around while parked somewhere for a while. We tow an old Toyota pickup, but they have a classy little Subaru. Geoff is always meticulous about caring for both motorhome and car.

"The authorities never arrived?"

"Oh, yes, they arrived. Two sheriff's deputies, very nice, polite young men. After I showed them where the body had been, they had us wait in the motorhome while they spent a long time looking around. Over two hours. But they couldn't find the body, so finally they came out and suggested that perhaps I'd seen some old rags the wind had blown in and then blown away."

"Where would rags come from in a ghost town?"

"Good question."

"Was the wind blowing?"

"Yes, but I could tell what they were really thinking, which had nothing to do with wind. They thought I was a senile old lady imagining things." I could hear outrage rising in her voice.

"Magnolia, you're no more senile than I am," I assured her. Although many of us with gray hair and wrinkles sometimes do get lumped into that "s" word category. The fact that Magnolia's ever-changing hair is never gray might not keep her out of that classification in the event of a toothpaste-outlined non-body. "If you say you saw a dead body, I'm sure you did."

"Thank you, Ivy. I appreciate your confidence in me."

"Did you see a gunshot or knife wound on the body, anything like that?" I asked.

"No. But the body was all crumpled up, facedown in the dirt, not flat on the ground with arms spread out like you see in the movies. I could have missed seeing a wound or even a weapon, if it was underneath him."

"Was there blood where the body had been?"

"I didn't see any."

"Did you check for a pulse?"

"No. I just touched his hand."

I was rather at a loss where to go now, but if the body actually had a hand, it wasn't a pile of windblown rags. Finally I asked, "What about footprints or tire tracks around the body or leading away from it? Did you see anything?"

"The ground was so hard it might take dynamite to make a dent in it." She paused. "Although I guess I didn't really look for anything like that. I was quite . . . shaken."

"Did you hear anything?"

"Ivy, I'm sure you're aware dead bodies don't tend to make a lot of noise." Magnolia didn't snap at me, but she was sounding mildly exasperated again.

"I was thinking perhaps the sound of a killer running away. A car engine. Anything."

"Nothing. What I'm thinking is that maybe the deputies just didn't look thoroughly enough."

"Law officers tend to be quite thorough."

"But maybe there are hidden places where they didn't know to look. Tunnels or spaces under buildings, something like that. And maybe their minds were already made up, that there never had been a real body."

I couldn't help an additional thought: it wasn't really unreasonable the deputies might find a toothpaste-outlined, non-visible body on the street of an old ghost town a little questionable. I hesitated then. I didn't want to ask questions that might sound as if I also doubted what Magnolia said she'd seen. But still . . .

"Could he have been unconscious from some medical condition rather than dead? Or maybe inebriated from alcohol or drugs? Perhaps he simply regained consciousness and walked away."

"I'm pretty sure he was dead."

"Did his hand feel stiff and rigid? Or was there still some warmth in it?"

"Oh, Ivy, I don't know. It just felt *dead*."

I heard a hint of uncertainty creeping into her voice, as if she were beginning to have doubts herself about the deadness of the body.

"I don't know how you've managed, finding dead bodies like you do," she added.

"There haven't been all that many," I protested.

Though Mac has remarked that murder situations and I do seem to have an unlikely affinity. But then he also found a dead body not long ago, so he has a better understanding now that sometimes that just "happens."

We do know a few facts about dead bodies. The temperature of a dead body decreases at a fairly predictable rate, and rigor mortis sets in after a certain number of hours. After a further amount of time, the rigidity of rigor mortis then disappears. None of which seemed particularly helpful in this situation, so it was hard to say if the body had been there for a few minutes or a few days. If there was a body . . .

"Was there a scent? Did the body have a bad smell?" Which also might indicate something about how long it had been there.

"I didn't smell anything."

"Did you stay and look around after the deputies left?"

"They didn't run us off, but they did say that Deadeye was private property and our being there would be considered trespassing, so we left when they did."

"Was there a gate?"

"Yes, but it was standing partway open when we arrived. The officers closed it and fastened the padlock when they left."

"How about Keep Out or No Trespassing signs?"

"Well, there *were* some signs," she admitted. "But I didn't feel they applied to me. I mean, this was *family* I was looking for."

I murmured something noncommittal.

"Everything just feels so . . . unreal." She sighed deeply, and Magnolia has a generously sized lung area from which to bring up a deep sigh. "Finding a dead body is terrible enough. But then having it disappear . . . My head feels as if it might explode any minute."

There it was again, Magnolia not sounding like herself. She has never been an exploding-head type woman. I've seen her stroll through a western-themed barbecue and remain unflustered to discover a long strand of toilet tissue trailing from the cowboy spur on her heel. I've watched her prance through a chorus line performance with complete aplomb.

"Did you notice what the body was wearing?"

"A heavy, padded jacket, as if it had perhaps been colder when he was out there alive. And the same type of tan pants that Geoff likes. Chinos. With Reeboks on his feet."

Magnolia's specifics about pants and shoes boosted my confidence that she'd actually seen a dead body. And also revved what a law officer friend had once called my "mutant curiosity gene" into ready-set-go mode.

A ghost town.

A dead body.

A *missing* dead body.

I tried to throttle down the curiosity. A detour into an old dinosaur park, where we'd gone because Mac had an assignment to write a magazine article about the park, a detour further complicated by murder, had already delayed our honeymoon. We'd been planning to spend a day or two with Magnolia and Geoff in Yuma and then head across the border to Baja and the Sea of Cortez. A missing dead body was a job for the authorities, not Mac and me.

But that curiosity gene was like a burr in my bra.

"Are you going back to the RV park in Yuma?" I asked.

"I keep wondering if the body was the man I went out there to find and what happened to him. I hate to leave without knowing." Unspoken was the thought that she also hated to leave without knowing if she'd actually seen a body or if she was tottering on the edge of a senile-imagined dead man. In chinos and Reeboks.

I peered out the window of our moving motorhome. Where were we? Off to the west of the highway a scattering of black cattle grazed on hills pale green from recent fall rains. To the east lay flat agricultural land, rugged mountains in the far distance. We'd left the dinosaur park in northern California yesterday, spent a leisurely night and breakfast in a rest area, so we must be somewhere on I-5 in the middle of California now.

"Let me talk to Mac about this. Hold on." I snugged the cell phone up against my chest and repeated to my still-new husband what Magnolia had just told me.

He didn't mutter about this being none of our business or grumble about a change of plans. He didn't suggest that outlining a non-visible, perhaps non-existent body with toothpaste was a little over the top, and what Magnolia had seen probably was windblown rags. His philosophical response was one of the many reasons I love him.

"Who can resist the lure of a ghost town and a disappearing body?"

Chapter 2

IVY

Prosperity didn't exactly live up to its name when we arrived the following day.

Perhaps actual prosperity may once have been possible, but at some time a realignment of I-8, a main highway crossing Arizona, had bypassed Prosperity and doomed it to dusty oblivion. Mac braked the motorhome beside the one small store slumped behind a dusty gas station. A TV satellite dish protruded from the roof, but the only sign of life was a neon beer sign flickering in the window. Nearby, a weathered wooden Indian stood outside an antique store that looked as if, if the items inside weren't already antiques, they would be by the time anyone bought them. Two dead palm trees marked the entrance to an RV park so skimpily occupied that we had no trouble spotting Magnolia and Geoff's motorhome. Farther back on the desert among the creosote bushes and cholla cactus, an incongruous metal arch glittered in the late-afternoon sun, like the remnant of some vanished civilization.

The desert wind swirling a miniature dust storm around our motorhome smelled of dry earth and desert vegetation, maybe a long-gone mule train or two. The wind also reminded me the officers had suggested windblown rags may have given Magnolia the impression of a dead body. My own impression was that there could be any number of long-dead bodies hidden out on the desert for the wind to uncover someday.

There was no one in the peeling stucco building marked Office at the dead-palm entrance to the RV park, so we drove on in and pulled in beside Geoff and Magnolia's motorhome. They both came out to meet us.

"I'm so glad you're here!" Magnolia said.

She opened her arms for a welcoming hug. Her hair had been royal purple the last time I saw her, but it was a frosty pink now. Magnolia likes big hair, and it looks good on her. She's a generously sized lady. Mac and Geoff exchanged handshakes. Geoff was wearing tan chinos, just like Magnolia said the dead body had worn, although his feet were in Birkenstock sandals.

"Have you heard any more about the dead body?" I asked.

"Not a thing. Although we do know a little more about Deadeye. It's not exactly what I thought it was."

I could tell Magnolia was eager to tell me all about it, but Geoff suggested it would be a good idea to get our motorhome parked and hooked up in the empty space next to theirs right away. I didn't see any line of RVers eager to grab the spot before we could get it, but Geoff said that if we needed to fill our water tank we should do it now because the water supply here was a little iffy. He also said we could go up to the store and pay the park fee later.

"But not too late," he added. "I wouldn't put it past Mrs. Oldham to come gunning for you with a shotgun if she thought you were really trying to get by without paying her."

Mac and Geoff went off to get the motorhome parked and hooked up, and Magnolia pulled me toward the chairs set up on the cracked concrete that passed for a patio under their motorhome awning. There were only four other RVs in the park, two travel trailers, a fifth wheel, and one pickup-type camper sitting on blocks. They were scattered around the park as if wary of close contact with each other. No occupants were visible anywhere. Wind had swept the hard dirt of the RV park bare in places, piled desert debris in others. Mac had to dig the electrical hookup out from under some of that debris before he could plug in our electrical cord.

"Lemonade?" Magnolia asked.

"Sounds good." I dropped into one of their nicely padded outdoor lounge chairs.

She went into the motorhome and returned with two tall glasses of lemonade the same pink shade as her hair. She set them on the small metal table between the chairs and perched on the edge of the other lounge chair. She didn't waste time.

"The first thing is, Deadeye *looks* like a ghost town, but it isn't a *real* ghost town. It was built about twenty years ago as a western movie set. Several movies and a TV series were made there, but westerns have been declining in popularity for quite a while. It's all superheroes and zombies and robots now." She spoke with a hint of disapproval, as if there were something un-American about exchanging cowboys for zombies. "There hasn't been any activity out there for years."

"So an imitation ghost town turned into an actual ghost town."

"I guess you could say that. Except Mrs. Oldham, who owns Prosperity, says there are a couple of people living out there, maybe three. Lightning Langston and his brother Warren. She says there are two mobile homes, but you can't see them from Deadeye. They're stuck back behind a hill so they wouldn't show up when scenes in the town were filmed."

"Maybe that explains the disappearance of the body then." I sipped my lemonade and suggested a logical possibility. "Someone living in one of those mobile homes discovered the body after you did and moved it."

"But why?"

"Dead bodies aren't usually left just lying around." I realized that sounded a little snarky, but Magnolia didn't seem to notice.

She nodded agreement. "But it seems to me there may be something more . . . irregular, maybe even *sinister*, about removing the body in this situation. Why didn't this body-remover come out and talk to me or the deputies?"

Good question. Of course, another question was, had Magnolia found an actual dead body there in the street?

"Would someone moving the body be able to see your motorhome parked outside the gate?"

"I don't think so. The main street of the town runs crossways to the entrance gate. I went around a corner to get on the main street where I found the body."

"Does Mrs. Oldham own Deadeye too?"

"No. It's on the other side of the highway and belongs to this man named Lightning Langston." Her voice took on a hint of excitement. "That's who I'm trying to locate. Maybe you've heard of him? He was a western movie star, not as big as John Wayne or Clint Eastwood, but fairly well-known. He had a TV series too. He's part of the line descending from my great-great-great—" She paused, apparently considering how many *greats* belonged in the lineup. "I'm not sure how far back, but somewhere back there one of the great-grandfathers had a second wife, and Lightning and his brother are part of that line. My line came from the first wife."

I wondered what relation that made Magnolia and the brothers Langston, but that wasn't really important, of course. As far as Magnolia is concerned, family is family, even if the relationship is no closer than waving distance across a continent or two.

"Lightning was his professional name in the movies?"

"Yes. It came from his speed at quick-draw with a gun. He was also a trick rider, and in his TV series he was well-known for using fancy riding tricks to outdo the villain."

"I didn't know you were a western-movie and TV fan."

16

"Actually, I'm not," she admitted. "Mrs. Oldham told me about his career. She loaned me videos of his old movies and TV shows, and we watched one last night. We can watch another one tonight if you're interested."

Fine with me. Lightning Langston's name wasn't familiar to me, but I was quite enthralled with Roy Rogers and Hopalong Cassidy when I was a girl. Perhaps Lightning was more recent than my girlhood memories. Magnolia was obviously quite pleased to find a movie star, even a faded western one, in her family tree.

"Mrs. Oldham said that Lightning has hinted there may be something big going on out at Deadeye soon."

"I don't suppose the dead body was what he meant."

"I'd guess it has something to do with the movie industry or his own career." She frowned, apparently not appreciating my bit of levity. I couldn't blame her. It was a flippant remark.

I tried to make amends with a more appropriate question. "Is the brother a cowboy actor too?"

"I don't think so, but Mrs. Oldham doesn't know much about him. She says Lightning is a great guy, cheerful and friendly, always calls her his 'best gal.' But the brother, Warren, is kind of standoffish. He hasn't lived out there nearly as long as Lightning has, and he goes into Yuma or Gila Bend for groceries or anything else he needs. His daughter has also been staying out there recently. Mrs. Oldham says the brothers are about as friendly with each other as a rattlesnake and a cobra."

"Maybe the brothers had a shoot-out on Main Street and the body was one of them," I suggested.

Magnolia didn't dismiss that possibility. She nodded. "I've wondered that."

I offered a nicer possibility. "Or maybe one brother had a heart attack or some other emergency, and the other brother found him after you did and hurried him away for medical treatment. One brother taking care of the other."

"Or maybe one brother murdered the other and carried the body off to hide it," Magnolia countered darkly.

Uh-oh. Now Magnolia was into my kind of thinking. Murder had been my first thought when she said on the cell phone that she'd found a body, but I'd managed to come up with the more innocent possibility of a medical problem.

"What I want to do is go back out there and find out what's going on," Magnolia declared.

"Wouldn't that still be what the officers called trespassing?"

"Ivy, we're *family.*"

Magnolia sounded mildly exasperated with my failure to understand the importance of family, but I wasn't sure the great-great-great-grandfather thing would carry much weight in a case of "Trespassers Will Be Prosecuted." But if anyone could carry it off, it would be Magnolia. A waving-distance relative in Scotland, wary of her at first, wound up inviting Magnolia and Geoff to spend a month in his castle.

"And I need to go back out there because there *was* a body. There really was, even if the deputies didn't think so." She gave me a glance as if wondering if I had doubts too. Which, guiltily, I had to admit that I did. "But Geoff said he isn't driving the Subaru out there over that bad road, so we've been waiting for you."

I've always thought Geoff has a remarkably patient and helpful tolerance for Magnolia's enthusiasm for climbing around in her family tree, but apparently even he has his limit when it comes to the welfare of his Subaru. I wasn't interested in the genealogical aspects of Deadeye's population, but that mutant curiosity gene wasn't about to let go of a disappearing-body situation.

I figured not even an old wagon trail was beyond our tough little pickup's capabilities, although I did wonder about the logistics. We couldn't all four fit in the small cab.

After Mac and Geoff finished with the motorhome hookups and leveling, it was too late in the day to drive out to Deadeye. I walked up to the store to pay the RV space fee. I smelled onions frying from the living quarters in the back of the store, but the blind was pulled in the store window and the door locked. I knocked on the door, and after a long wait, a corner of the shade lifted and a leathery face peered out at me. The woman, apparently the Mrs. Oldham Magnolia had mentioned, didn't open the door, just pointed a bony finger at a faded handwritten notice beside the door that gave the RV park rates and instructed "Pay RV park fee here," with an arrow pointing to a slot below. The face waited to see if I paid but didn't offer thanks when I did.

After I got back to the motorhome, Mac called his son in Montana, and I talked to granddaughter Elle for a few minutes. Then I called my niece DeeAnn and grandniece Sandy in Arkansas. Family duties taken care of, Mac barbecued chicken for supper and Geoff grilled potatoes. Magnolia made salad, and I whipped up a fluffy chocolate dessert.

Afterward, with the desert evening quickly cooling, we went inside and watched Lightning Langston in something called *Ambush on the Arizona Trail*. Magnolia said it had been filmed in and around Deadeye, and there were thundering hooves and black-hatted villains, along with downing of drinks and flashes of aces in the saloon. Lightning rode a fiery black horse with the appropriate name of Thunder, and he displayed his trick-riding skills with an agile stretch along the side of his running horse and his quick-draw skills by taking out three bad guys in front of the barber shop.

I wondered if, in a touch of irony, it was his body Magnolia had found in that same spot in Deadeye.

**

The night was considerably cooler than I expected. Next morning, leaving dog BoBandy and cat Koop in the motorhome, Mac solved the space problem in the Toyota's small cab by volunteering to ride in the back of the pickup. Geoff joined him there, and I supplied an old blanket for them to sit on. I slid into the driver's seat and Magnolia sat in the passenger's seat.

"I think this is called riding shotgun, isn't it?" She sounded pleased to make the western connection. She was appropriately dressed in boots, denim skirt, and fringed jacket. Magnolia always manages to come up with clothes suitable for any occasion, from green elf outfit to exotic gypsy fortune teller. I was in old jeans and yard sale sneakers, plus a light jacket because the desert morning was still cool.

The unmarked road to Deadeye was not only rutted, washboard rough, and potholed, but, unlike the flat landscape around Prosperity, hilly, even steep in places. A line of electric poles angled across the desert in the general direction we were headed. We bounced over ruts and potholes, only the seat belt keeping my head from banging the top of the cab. Back in the pickup bed, Mac and Geoff rattled around like popcorn bouncing in a popcorn popper. I didn't expect to encounter any other vehicles, but I soon realized, from a plume of dust ahead of us, that we weren't alone on the road. One of the brothers Langston?

Then I realized there were actually two vehicles, an SUV and a pickup. The brothers, traveling separately? Both vehicles were moving faster than I was in our old Toyota, and we weren't catching up with them.

I braked once to let a snake cross the road ahead of us, and a minute later we met a roadrunner headed in that direction. I think roadrunners are quite efficient at catching snakes, but even with deadly purpose in mind, they can't help looking like the comic bird battling Wile E. Coyote in those old Looney Tunes cartoons. This one sped by us without a second glance.

I didn't spot the vehicles again, although the plumes of dust lingered in the calm desert morning. After one particularly impressive bounce through a pothole, I stopped to check on Mac and Geoff. They said they were fine, although Geoff stood and rubbed his tailbone and Mac wiped dust out of his eyes. I wondered if Geoff's tolerance for

Magnolia's genealogical zeal and Mac's tolerance for my curiosity were sagging a bit.

An SUV and a battered pickup stood outside the open metal gate into Deadeye when we arrived, three men standing just inside. The one in rough cowboy gear, boots, and white Stetson looked like an older version of the Lightning Langston we'd seen in the video last night, with the addition of grayer hair and an exuberant mustache. I guessed his age at somewhere around sixty, not a double for Sam Elliott but close to it. He also looked lean and fit, as if he might still pull off some fancy riding stunts on a horse. The other two much younger men wore jeans, too, but polo-type shirts and no hats or boots. All three turned to look at us as Mac and Geoff climbed rather stiffly out of the back of the pickup, and Magnolia and I got out of the cab.

I didn't know what to say. "Seen any good bodies lately?" didn't really seem appropriate. I let Magnolia do the talking. Lightning was, after all, her "relative."

"Mr. Langston?" she said.

"That's me, Lightning Langston," the Sam Elliott look-alike said. Which obviously meant Lightning Langston wasn't the dead body Magnolia had encountered. He gave her a friendly smile but said, "I'm busy right now, but if you'd like to wait—?" He made an expansive gesture that apparently took in all of southwestern Arizona as a waiting area. "I'll be glad to give you a photo and an autograph later. Although tomorrow might be better."

He gave the two men a quick sideways glance. Did a movie cowboy on the downside of his career actually get fans coming out to the middle of nowhere for photos and autographs? I doubted that, but I guessed that's what Lightning wanted these men to think. For the first time, under the coating of dust, I noticed the emblem on the side of the SUV. Hamilton Productions, Los Angeles, CA. Were they part of the "something big" Lightning had hinted to Mrs. Oldham?

Magnolia rose to the occasion, apparently deciding a possible boost to Lightning's career outweighed her family-link and dead-body questions. "I'd appreciate that. We've come a long way to meet you."

Lightning Langston rewarded her with a smile that probably wowed cowgirls a few decades ago and still carried a fairly high voltage.

Mac and Geoff climbed back into the pickup bed. Magnolia, before she and I got in the cab, called gaily, "Tomorrow, then," with a big wave. Lightning waved back.

So we rattled and bounced back to Prosperity.

Chapter 3

MAC

I groaned as Geoff and I climbed out of the back of the pickup. Every muscle felt stiff. Every bone bruised. Eyes and ears and all other body orifices gritty with dust. Geoff ran fingers through his sparse hair and a cloud of dust billowed around him. His eyes looked like bloodshot holes peering out of a dusty mask.

I was glad I couldn't see myself.

Ivy and Magnolia hadn't fared too well either. Enough dust had risen up through the floorboards to make them look as if they'd spent a hard day in a covered wagon.

However, after we all took showers in the limited hot water available in our motorhomes, I felt, if not good as new, reasonably revived. Ivy put her wet hair in a tidy braid and looked fresh as always. She put together ham-and-cheese sandwiches for lunch, and we took them over to join Geoff and Magnolia under their awning. Our spot lacked the luxury of their cracked-concrete patio. Magnolia had egg-salad sandwiches plus a cold pitcher of tangy gazpacho.

Afterward, I made the trek up to the store to pay for another night in the RV park. Geoff said they'd paid for a week. I considered doing that, but finally decided—hopefully—that we'd be out of here by tomorrow. I appreciate Ivy's statement that "honeymoon is a state of mind," but I still have a real honeymoon in mind and Prosperity isn't it.

Mrs. Oldham, the proprietress, had long, gray hair, leathery skin, and a body that looked as shriveled and stringy as if she'd been stranded here on the desert since Geronimo last galloped through. Perhaps she also had an eye problem because her eyelashes gave quite a flutter when she said I should call her Betsy. But she smiled a lot and was quite talkative.

She said that Prosperity had started out many years ago as someone's big dream . . . or scheme. Back in those days subdivisions in Arizona were much less regulated than they are today, and big subdivisions had blossomed in various unlikely places around the state. Some had prospered; some had disappeared back into the desert sand. Prosperity had originally been laid out as several hundred lots and heavily promoted outside the state, as many were, with high-flying plans for a club house, swimming pool, and golf course.

Hard to tell now, Mrs. Oldham reflected, if it was ever a real project or never more than a slippery scheme. Everything had been abandoned long before she and her husband bought the store and RV park.

"He's passed on now, of course, bless his heart." She handed me a cherry sucker from under the counter, and her eyelashes went into another spasm of that peculiar fluttering. I hoped it wasn't symptom of a serious eye problem.

When I got back to the motorhome, Ivy was trying to get an internet connection with the laptop and not succeeding. She wanted to find out more about Lightning Langston and Deadeye. But she was interested in my information about Prosperity too, of course. Ivy's curiosity is boundless, although what interests her can sometimes be a bit disconcerting. Does anyone else's wife keep computer files on subjects such as "Exotic Poisons" and "Unsolved Serial Murders"?

I repeated to Ivy all that Mrs. Oldham had told me along with what I'd noticed about her eye problem. "She says that big arch out back of the RV park is all that's left of the Prosperity subdivision now, but if you walk around out there you can still find some of the old survey stakes, and once someone found an arrowhead."

"Let's do it!"

Magnolia and Geoff weren't interested, but Ivy and I— remembering that snake on the road out to Deadeye—put on heavy hiking boots and, along with BoBandy, headed out to the metal arch. Up close, it was still an impressive size, but the metal was weathered and pitted, a little like shabby jewelry worn down to a cheap base. BoBandy, brown, mid-sized, and interested in everything, gave it a good sniff.

We did indeed find a number of old survey stakes, some still capped and official looking even though the lettering was gone, others just rusty metal rods sticking out of the ground. There were scattered tire tracks, as if there'd been some four-wheeling with ATVs going on out here. No doubt they were just having fun with those all-terrain vehicles, but I didn't like how they'd just smashed and crushed cactus in places. We found a crumbling old foundation of what may once have been the start of the clubhouse. Or maybe just a prop for potential buyers, something to make the grandiose plans appear legitimate.

We spotted a couple of roadrunners and a few lizards, and Ivy picked up a broken piece of braided metal. She held it up to the light, and I thought she might be imagining it was once part of a bracelet or necklace belonging to some romantic couple . . . maybe a couple like us . . . with dreamy views of a retirement home here on the desert. Although, knowing Ivy, she might instead be considering the possibility of some long-ago murder with that chain all that remained of the dead victim.

That evening we watched a couple episodes of Lightning Langston's old TV series, *Frontier Lawman*, on DVD. The man wasn't the greatest actor ever to hit the screen, but he definitely knew his way around a horse. He rode standing up on the saddle to swoop down on one villain and made a tricky move under his horse's neck to sneak up on another outlaw. He spun his gun and shot two bad guys before either one could even draw.

IVY

Next morning we headed out to Deadeye again. Magnolia had added a hat to her western outfit, and only Magnolia can carry off a pink cowboy hat with glitter-dusted pink feathers in the hatband. I suggested Magnolia and I ride in the pickup bed this time, but Geoff threw the heavy cushions from the lounge chairs into the pickup bed for better padding for himself and Mac. Mrs. Oldham gave us a big wave from the door of the store. The thought occurred to me that Mac had gotten a lot of friendly information from her—and a cherry sucker too—when he'd gone to pay the RV fee; all I'd gotten was that bony finger pointing to the rent slot.

Which was when it also occurred to me that Betsy—as she'd told Mac to call her—didn't have an eye problem at all. Mac hadn't even realized she was trying to flirt with him with her batting eyelashes.

I'm always finding another reason to love that man. Maybe I shouldn't be so annoyed with Betsy. Mac is a worthy target of some industrious eyelash batting.

The road out to Deadeye hadn't improved overnight, and I didn't see any dust plumes suggesting other travelers were on the road this morning. The metal gate was padlocked when we arrived, but it wouldn't be impossible to crawl through the barbed wire fence. No vehicles in sight. Today I took note of several No Trespassing signs and a road that led on around a low hill beyond the town.

We all got out of the pickup. I took a deep breath of the fresh-scented morning. Sunlight has a special sparkle here on the desert, the sky a special depth of blue, the far mountains a special hint of mystery. An interesting rock formation stood off to the east. Maybe a secret hideaway for desert outlaws long ago? Or, with a little imagination, maybe a castle populated by unicorns and elves. Cactus in various shapes and sizes covered the harsh ground, all prickly, but each one beautiful in its own way. A glow of fuzzy golden cholla, an enigmatic signal in the bent arms of a saguaro, dangerous grace in the long, thorny whips of ocotillo. Even the ever-present creosote bushes had a certain timeless splendor.

Sometimes you have to look for beauty in the Lord's creation, but it's always there, as it was here on this sunlit morning on the desert.

"I really don't think we should wander around inside without someone in charge being here," Geoff said.

From here, all we could see were the back sides of the buildings fronting on the main street of the town, but they were apparently complete buildings, not just fake fronts. Lots of places to hide a dead body, maybe places the deputies had missed. Although this wasn't really an imitation ghost town; it was constructed to look like a populated western town with a sheriff and dance-hall girls. The hidden tunnels Magnolia had earlier suggested as a hiding place for a body seemed unlikely in a movie-setting town.

Magnolia looked disappointed with Geoff's reluctance to rush into Deadeye, but she nodded agreement with his remark and we all piled back in the pickup and followed the road. The flat area on the far side of the hill wasn't a surprise desert oasis, but it was a surprise. An older single-wide mobile home stood at the nearest end of a wide clearing.

Two sleek horses lazed inside a metal corral nearby. The corral connected with an open shed for shelter for the horses, with bales of hay stacked at one end. An old flatbed truck stood beside the shed, and a water tank sat atop a wooden framework behind the mobile.

At the far end of the clearing, several hundred yards away, a rustic wood-rail fence circled a newer double-wide, with an attached double garage. A postage stamp of green lawn grew inside the fence, looking at odds with the dryness everywhere else. TV satellite dishes topped both mobiles, but the double-wide had a second dish I didn't recognize. The double-wide setup was definitely more prosperous looking than the single-wide.

Considering what Betsy Oldham had said about the animosity between the brothers, the long, open space between the mobiles looked as if it might work for a shootout at high noon. There weren't any dead bodies lying there, but halfway between the mobiles a small travel trailer flanked the clearing. The Hamilton Productions SUV from yesterday stood near the single-wide mobile, a tiny blue car by the travel trailer. One of those Smart cars, I thought.

The only movement anywhere was the horses' tails swishing at flies and an occasional stamp of hoof. From here, Deadeye was on the far side of the low hill, no part of it visible.

I was tempted to put a heavy hand on the horn and see if anything happened, but Mac leaned from the pickup bed around the corner of the cab with a better suggestion. "Let's try the travel trailer."

The trailer door opened as we pulled up beside the blue car. A young woman wearing cutoff jeans and a blue sweatshirt, with dark hair in a thick braid reaching almost to her waist, stood in the doorway. We all trooped out of the pickup.

"Hi. Are you looking for someone?" The young woman sounded reasonably friendly, but she took another look at our group presence and added, "There are no public facilities for food or lodging here."

"We talked to Lightning yesterday," Magnolia said. "He was busy with some business associates—" She pointed to the SUV with the Hamilton Productions name on the side. "But he said if we came back today he'd have time to give us a photo and autograph. I have some family information for him too. I think both he and you will find it interesting."

I wasn't so sure about that. Not everyone cares about family relationships separated by a long line of great-grandfathers.

"What kind of information?" She sounded wary.

"Family," Magnolia repeated, her brevity and tone suggesting this was an important and perhaps confidential matter. "You are Lightning's niece, aren't you, his brother's daughter? Mrs. Oldham at the RV park told us you were staying here now. I'm Magnolia Margollin and I'm happy to say we're related." She added a big beam of smile.

The young woman stepped down the single step to the hard ground beside her trailer. She held out a hand to shake, but Magnolia pulled her in for one of her famous—or maybe that's infamous—hugs.

The woman wiggled her shoulders after the enthusiastic hug. I knew the squished feeling.

"I'm glad to meet you. I'm Jenna Langston. Lightning lives down there—" She pointed to the single wide. "And that's my father's place." Another wave, this time at the double-wide. She smiled. "I call this area Deadeye Heights. Give it a little class, you know."

"Such a lovely, peaceful looking place," Magnolia said, although I wasn't so sure of that, considering the found-and-lost dead body.

"Lightning isn't here right now. I saw him head out in the pickup with the guys from the SUV. I think they're probably looking at the terrain that might be useful if they decide to film here. No telling when they'll be back."

"Oh, that's so exciting!" Magnolia said. "Lightning is going to be in a new movie?"

"I don't know any details," Jenna said. "But I'm interested in how you and I are related. I don't know much about my family background."

I thought that was a nice attitude. She could have been suspicious this was some kind of senior-citizen scam game.

"It's rather complicated," Magnolia said. "Perhaps we should save the details for when everyone in the family can be together."

I thought that was a good idea, although the distance between the mobiles and what Betsy Oldham had said about the animosity between the brothers suggested getting them within spitting distance of each other might be like getting a die-hard conservative and a flaming liberal together for tea.

I'd stayed out of the conversation so far, but now I had to ask, "What do you do out here? It seems a bit . . . isolated." And surely boring for a young woman alone.

Jenna turned to me and smiled. A nice smile, and a very pretty young woman with an oval face and big dark eyes. "I'm writing the Great American Novel." She slipped her hands in a downward gesture that dismissed any pretensions of literary grandeur. "More or less."

"This should be a good place for it. Not many distractions. Maybe I can read it when it's published."

The smile turned wry. "Don't hold your breath. I don't think publishers are waiting in line for it."

I eyed the double-wide mobile. "Is your father around?"

"No. I don't know where he is." She also glanced toward the double-wide, and I wondered if his non-presence made him a candidate for the dead body. She didn't seem concerned about his absence, but she didn't know about the dead body yet. "I haven't seen him since I got home last night. I've been in New York with my mother and stepfather. They live up in Scottsdale but Hayden—that's my stepfather—took us on a trip to New York to celebrate my mother's birthday."

"That was nice of him."

"Yes, very nice. He even managed to get tickets to a couple of Broadway shows for all of us."

Stepfather must have some money to pay for that kind of birthday jaunt, but something in Jenna's voice suggested the trip hadn't been any special adventure for her. Which aroused my curiosity, of course. Wouldn't most young women be delighted with a gift trip to New York? Mac says my curiosity can be aroused by a bump in the road, but I'm sure that's an exaggeration. Although you never know what might be buried under a bump in the road . . .

"Was this your first trip to New York?" I asked.

"Oh, no. I lived there for three years." The wrinkle of her nose suggested it was not a fond memory. "I've been here only a few months."

I was even more curious, but under the circumstances I had to prioritize my curiosities. Dead body came first. "Would it be all right if we went back and looked around in Deadeye?"

"It might be better if you wait until Lightning gets back. There's never been any vandalism that I know of, but it's something he worries about." She smiled. "Although you people don't look like serious vandals."

"Actually there's an important reason we'd like to look around," Magnolia said. "We were here a few days ago, and no one was around, and we didn't even know anyone lived back here behind the hill. The gate was open, so I went inside. I found something quite . . . disturbing."

"Disturbing?"

"There was a dead body in the middle of the street."

"A *dead body*?"

Magnolia went on to tell her about calling 911, the deputies' search, and their suggestion that she'd probably mistaken old rags for a body.

"Who could make that kind of mistake?" Jenna scoffed. "There aren't any old rags lying around out there." She paused. "Although one of the windows in the hotel is broken, and there are curtains . . ."

I followed her line of speculation. The wind could have torn curtains from a window and whipped them into a dead-body-sized bundle on the street. But Magnolia said she'd felt a hand on the body. I glanced over and I could see a troubled look on her face. In spite of the hand, I knew she was again having doubts about whether she'd seen an actual body. Perhaps she'd mistaken . . . what? . . . for a hand.

Or maybe it *was* a hand. Maybe someone had wrapped the old curtains around a detached hand . . .

A bundle of old curtains wrapped around a disconnected hand was almost more spooky than an entire dead body. And if that was what had happened, where was the rest of the body?

"Did you tell Lightning about this?" Jenna asked.

"No. It didn't seem appropriate to bring this up in front of his business associates," Magnolia said.

"But you're sure the body was a man?"

Magnolia blinked. The possibility that it might be a *woman* obviously hadn't occurred to her. Or to me. She told Jenna what she'd told me. Heavy, padded jacket. Chinos. Reeboks. No, she hadn't seen the face.

"What about hair?" Jenna asked. "What color was his hair?"

Magnolia shook her head. "I don't know. Maybe he was wearing a hat or cap or something."

"Maybe the jacket had a hood," I suggested.

Jenna was obviously less than convinced, but if Magnolia said there was a body, I was going to believe her.

"We could wait until Lightning gets back to go search for the body, but—" I pulled up a handy phrase from jargon I'd heard somewhere. "Time is of the essence."

"Yes, I suppose that's true," Jenna agreed. She glanced at the double-wide again, and I wondered if her father's absence was taking on some ugly new possibilities for her. "And Lightning and the production company men may be out there all day."

"Perhaps you could come back to Deadeye with us to look around," I suggested.

"Did you notice if the gate was locked? I don't have a key."

"It was locked today, but we could probably crawl through the fence," I said.

Jenna gave Magnolia's generously sized body a doubtful look, but Magnolia drew herself up to her full statuesque majesty and said firmly, "I can do that."

Chapter 4

IVY

And she did.

It took both Geoff and Mac stretching the strands of barbed wire farther apart, and me holding the pink hat, but she made it through the fence with dignity and all body parts intact. Once we were all inside, Jenna took a minute to call someone before we started the search.

"My boyfriend," she said when she stuck the phone in a back pocket of the cutoffs. "He's working now, but I told him what we're doing and he'll come out and help as soon as he can. He's been coming out to feed Lightning's horses while both Lightning and I were gone."

A boyfriend? Maybe life here wasn't as isolated and boring for Jenna as I'd thought. I was immediately curious about how two people managed to meet out here on the desert, especially someone working at home as Jenna did with her writing. The internet, probably. A "Meet Your Mate on the Desert" site? "What does he do?"

"He's an artist and he's very talented, but right now he's painting a house back at Tacna." She smiled. "He says every artist should keep grounded by doing some real painting every once in a while."

I remembered a sign pointing to Tacna on the highway between here and Yuma. No metropolis, but apparently more of a town than Prosperity. I liked Jenna's boyfriend's down-to-earth attitude toward art and painting. No snobbish prima donna here.

Magnolia led us around the corner onto the main street and pointed out where she'd found the body. We gathered around the outline on the ground. Magnolia glanced around and frowned, and I guessed she was again wondering if she'd gotten the outline in the right place. I wondered too. It seemed there should be blood or something within the outline. It was windblown and blurry now but still obviously the shape of a man. With one obvious peculiarity. Jenna pointed it out.

"This was a one-legged man?"

The outline ended at the knee on one leg.

"No. I just ran out of toothpaste," Magnolia said.

Jenna hesitated momentarily, as if she were thinking about remarking on that. But apparently she decided to detour the complexity of a toothpaste-outlined, one-legged, missing body and briskly organized our search. Magnolia and Geoff would take the north side of the main street, Mac and I the south. Jenna would go beyond the main street to search the church and stable.

I thought including a church added a nice touch of authenticity to the town. Even in a rough frontier town, a few people with Christian convictions surely would set up a place of worship. I'd have helped do that if I'd lived back then.

We set out on our assigned tasks. I've stumbled across a few dead bodies, but searching for a lost one was a new experience. A desert wind that had come up in the last half hour blew steadily as we worked our way down the street. A windblown plastic bag tumbled between the buildings. The Elite Barber Shop had a red-and-white striped barber pole outside and an old-fashioned chair and barber tools inside, but nowhere to hide a body. Deadeye Mercantile was outfitted with filled shelves and an old-fashioned cash register. The cabinet underneath the counter, however, held what looked like abandoned pieces of lighting equipment, probably long out-of-date for current filming. The Golden Nugget saloon was complete with a piano, tables, and chairs, and rows of dusty bottles lined the shelf under a mirror behind the bar. We checked every cabinet, even the spaces that didn't look large enough for a body. Mac and I didn't talk about it, but I think the possibility of dismembered body parts occurred to both of us. But we found no hidden body, or, blessedly, no stray body parts, anywhere. We did find a garter with a fancy purple rosette.

Which reminded me of a strange blunder I'd made at our wedding not long ago, when I'd mistakenly worn a gift garter around my neck instead of my leg. Mac's sly smirk as he glanced at me suggested he was also remembering. But his quick peck on my cheek said it was a cherished memory.

The hotel had a lobby with a counter and pigeon holes on a back wall for keys and messages. One room upstairs was authentically furnished for filming purposes. We checked under the bed, of course. Nothing there but aging dust bunnies. The other rooms were empty except for curtains at the windows, apparently to give the hotel an authentic look from the outside. We found the broken window Jenna had mentioned, and only a few shreds remained of the curtain.

A layer of desert dust covered everything, and I could see where the deputies had smudged or rearranged the dust in their search. They hadn't done a magnifying-glass level of inspection, but I doubted they'd missed a dead body.

It took us over two hours to work our way to the end of the street, but Mac and I finished before Magnolia and Geoff, and we went around back of the main street to the church. It looked nicely nostalgic, a weathered log building with a bell in the steeple, like something out of a Christmas card. Although not necessarily authentic. Where would logs have come from if this were an actual desert town built in the early days?

Several steps led up to the front door. Inside, the church had pews with an aisle down the center and a pulpit topped with a large, open Bible up front. Jenna was poking around inside the square pulpit. Mac said he was going to look around outside to see if there was an entrance to a space under the building. Jenna pulled something out of the backside of the pulpit and lifted it up for me to see. A liquor bottle.

"Did pioneers drink vodka?" I asked doubtfully.

"I'd guess this was where the actors or crew stashed their drinking supplies when they were filming one of Lightning's old movies or TV shows." She stuffed the bottle back where she'd found it. "No luck with a body?"

"If someone moved the body, I don't think they hid it here in Deadeye."

Jenna then came up with the same thought that had occurred to me earlier, that perhaps what Magnolia had found wasn't a dead body but an ill or inebriated live person who had then gotten up and walked— or stumbled—off.

"Sounds plausible," I agreed. "Although Deadeye seems an unlikely place for someone to go on a drinking binge. Who would it be? And why here?"

"A transient, I suppose."

"A transient would have to be rather energetic to bother hiking all the way out here to get inebriated." What I was also thinking was that you don't see too many alcohol-guzzling transients wearing chinos and Reeboks. Did Jenna's father wear chinos? Even if she didn't want to think it, her father did seem to be missing.

As if catching those unspoken thoughts, she added, "Dad drinks a little, but just to relax in the evening, not enough to get *drunk*. He's into day-trading on the stock market and that can be quite stressful. I suppose he could have been ill . . ." That thought troubled her enough to crease a worry line across her forehead. "But I can't imagine why he'd have been wandering around out here, especially if he was ill."

A technological epiphany suddenly hit me. "That extra dish on his mobile-home roof—that's a dish for satellite internet! The kind they advertise can get you an internet connection anywhere. It's his link to the stock market."

Jenna nodded. Everyday stuff to her generation, still high-tech voodoo to me. "I wish Mike would get here," she fretted. She slumped into the front pew. "I want to find the body, of course, if there is one, but the idea of actually *finding* it . . ."

Or finding pieces of a body, I echoed silently. Aloud I said, "Mike is your boyfriend?"

She nodded again. "Mike Redstone."

"It's nice you have a boyfriend. I'd think living out here could get lonely and boring otherwise."

"Mike has a trailer parked at a friend's house in Tacna. But even if I didn't have him, living here would still be better than living in an apartment in New York."

Not a fan of the Big Apple, obviously.

"Were you working on the Great American Novel when you lived there?"

"I was getting a nose job. An eyelid lift. Lip enhancement. And a boob job too, of course." She clamped her hands on her hips and thrust her chest up and out.

I avoided inspecting the boob job, but I protested the eyelid lift. "You're too young to need an eyelid lift. And you're very pretty."

"Thank you. But pretty isn't enough in the modeling world. If there were a surgery to make me six inches taller, I'd probably have had that too."

"Why would you want to be taller?" She was a nice height, several inches above my five-foot-ish level. My height—which I used to think of as petite but which seems to be expanding into dumpy—may have hurried me along in this aging-into-invisibility process I've experienced, but I've managed okay with it all these years.

"Height and long legs are *vital* in the modeling world," she said.

"You wanted to be a model?"

"My mother wanted me to be a model. Unfortunately, her big investment in surgery to make me acceptable to modeling-world standards didn't pay off."

A slap of Jenna's hands on bare thighs made a sharp punctuation point to end this discussion. A bit of resentment toward her mother there? Or guilt that she hadn't been able to live up to her mother's expectations? But the mother-daughter relationship was apparently okay now, because she'd been to New York to celebrate Mother's birthday.

"I'm going to check the fence line and see if there are any tracks along there."

I started to follow her outside to go find Mac, but on second thought I went up front and opened the little door on the back side of the pulpit. I grabbed the vodka bottle plus two empty beer cans beside it. A church, even a phony church in a phony frontier town, wasn't the place for them. I didn't have a large enough pocket or my purse along to carry them in, so I marched outside, clutching a vodka bottle in one hand and beer cans in the other.

And immediately ran into a red-haired young man coming toward the church. He stopped short. "Whoa! Looks like I missed a party."

"Do I look like a vodka-and-beer-guzzling party person?" I huffed as a beer can slipped out of my fingers.

He grinned and retrieved the fallen can before the wind could bounce it away. "You look like a woman who conscientiously recycles every can and bottle she finds," he corrected gallantly.

Quick save. I said, "Thank you," and he grinned again.

"Although it looks as if *someone* had a party. Here, let me help you." His big hands managed the bottle and cans much better than mine did. "The people going through the bank said Jenna was around here somewhere."

"She was, but she went to check along the fence line. You must be Mike Redstone, the artist."

"Yes, ma'am. That's me. Artist, house painter, and occasional guitarist in the best little grunge band in the southwest." He tilted his head, red hair churning in the wind. "Or at least the best in this and maybe one adjoining county."

"A man of many talents."

I'm not sure what a grunge band is, but I doubt they play the golden oldies Mac and I enjoy. Although I heard a humorous rapper a while back and was surprised to find I liked him too.

"I understand you're looking for a dead body?" Mike asked.

"Yes. But there's a possibility it was a case of mistaken identity and what my friend thought was a dead body may have been a bundle of rags or an inebriated live person."

"No doubt an easy mistake to make."

Mike sounded as if he wasn't taking this too seriously. Maybe he thought Jenna was pulling a joke on him, that a gang of friends would suddenly jump out waving a scarecrow-type body and yelling "Surprise!"

Mac came out from behind the church. "There is space between the floor of the church and the ground. It's dark under there, but enough light comes through cracks that I could see there wasn't any dead body."

He was covered in cobwebs, his knees and hands gritty from crawling around in the dirt. I brushed him off and made introductions. He and Mike just smiled and nodded at each other rather than trying to shake hands. Mac's hands were grubby with sand and dirt, Mike's hands filled with a vodka bottle and beer cans.

Jenna came running down the street. She and Mike exchanged a hug and she filled him in with more information about the dead body. By then he apparently realized this really was a serious body search, that Jenna hadn't been playing fun and games with him on the phone.

Sounding much more serious now, Mike asked, "Is there any area that hasn't been searched yet?"

"I think we've covered everything pretty thoroughly," Jenna said. "I saw you arrive so I didn't finish walking along the fence line, but it probably doesn't matter."

"I'm sorry I couldn't get here sooner to help."

Mike Redstone didn't look how I'd expect an artist to look. His red hair was thick and curly, his shoulders broad and muscles burly. He looked as if he'd be more at home holding a football or jackhammer than a paintbrush or a guitar. But that was no doubt unfair stereotyping. Big, burly guys can be artistic or musical too. I guessed his age at twenty-four or twenty-five, maybe a year or two older than Jenna.

Magnolia and Geoff joined us as we walked up the hard-packed dirt street. They hadn't found anything either. We paused at the toothpaste outline again. It was even more blurred and ragged now, as if it were turning into something other than human shape. Like those stories about a sinister being who morphs into a werewolf on a moonlit night, this shape appeared to be morphing into a blimp with legs. Well, one leg.

"In spite of what I thought I saw, I guess we can't be certain there ever was a dead body." Magnolia didn't sound *regretful*. She isn't the kind of person who'd want a dead body to show up just to prove she was right. But she did sound uneasy that she might have made such a mistake. The dark cloud of that that *s* word hovered again.

Except I immediately rejected that conclusion. If Magnolia said she'd seen—and touched—a body, I figured she had, even if she was less positive now. Although it wasn't necessarily a *dead* body. I granted that she may have made that much of a mistake. But no senility was involved.

"How about checking your father's house?" I suggested to Jenna. "Just to make sure there's nothing amiss there. You said you hadn't seen him since you got home yesterday."

"I don't think he'd like me rummaging around in his things."

"We won't rummage. We'll just take a peek."

We all crawled through the fence again. Mike's ride was an old Chevy van, color a weathered white, one fender with a Bigfoot-sized dent. He tossed the vodka bottle and beer cans behind the seat, and we made a three-vehicle convoy back to the mobiles. We parked in front of the double-wide. A sprinkler was running on the grass.

"That doesn't mean anything," Jenna said as she opened the gate. "It's on an automatic timer."

The front door wasn't locked when she tried the knob. I thought Jenna seemed a little surprised by that, but she didn't comment. She turned and told everyone to wait outside, but Mike had already stepped inside and I scooted in behind him. Jenna looked a little puzzled when she saw me in there, as if she wondered how I'd gotten inside without her seeing. I just smiled at her. Aging into this state of at least semi-invisibility sometimes has advantages.

"Dad?" Jenna called tentatively. She waited a moment, then repeated the call, louder. "Dad?"

No answer.

Mike said he'd check on the vehicles in the garage and headed for a door on the far side of the kitchen. A key ring dangled from a hook by the garage door.

Nice place. It always surprises me how big and elegant mobile homes are these days. Though I think modular or manufactured home is the preferred term now, and homes this big rarely get moved once they're set up on a foundation, as this one was. The formal, unused-looking living room had a view toward Lightning's place. The dining room looked to the east, where I could see the distant rocks we'd noticed earlier. The table was large enough for a small army of diners, and a hutch held enough dishes in a discreet, gold-rimmed pattern to serve at least that many. There was nothing to indicate they'd never been used, but somehow, I suspected they hadn't. The roomy kitchen held spotless appliances and glass-fronted cabinets.

All of it nice in a colorless, antiseptic way. Who knew there were so many shades of beige?

The family room had been turned into an office with a complete and expensive-looking computer setup, windows blacked out with heavy curtains, walls covered with bookshelves. I got the impression scenic views didn't matter much to Jenna's father. Jenna saw me looking at the filing cabinet standing beyond the computer setup.

"Dad's a real computer expert, but he doesn't trust the 'cloud' everyone uses for storage now. He always keeps a paper backup of anything important." She smiled as if this were a charmingly whimsical trait.

I stepped closer and tried a drawer. The filing cabinet was locked. I'd bet there was some kind of impenetrable password on the computer too.

Dad struck me as not so much whimsical as just a teensy bit paranoid. The kind of guy who'd believe the silver lining in any cloud was actually nuclear radiation disguised.

"There are three bedrooms," Jenna said. "He'll probably be back there if anything is . . . wrong."

She hesitated at the hallway a moment longer, apparently torn between concern about her father and a fear he might suddenly jump out and berate her for snooping, but she finally headed to the master bedroom at the far end of the hall. I followed.

The bed was neatly made, the spread a silky material the same color as the curtains. Beige. No TV. No cell phone on the nightstand. But he no doubt carried that with him. Am I the only person in the world who forgets to carry a cell phone at all times? This room did have some unusual wall decorations.

"Dad's collection of paper money," Jenna said as I inspected the framed collections of money on the walls. The bills were between two sections of glass, so both sides could be examined. Confederate bills, old paper bills in denominations of less than a dollar. I'd never known fifty-cent bills once existed. Two framed collections of two-dollar bills. Some silver certificates and a dozen obvious counterfeits, including both a million-dollar bill and a three-dollar bill.

Money seemed a suitable collection for a man who apparently devoted much of his life to it.

I checked the medicine cabinet in the bathroom. No opioids or any prescriptions suggesting some exotic ailment that made him fall into a dead-body swoon at times. Just aspirin and laxatives and a generic sleeping pill. However, an interesting calendar hung on the wall. It had check marks on most dates, sometimes two on one date, and *x* marks on others. I studied it, puzzled. Some enigmatic code about activities—maybe when he used illicit drugs?—related to his disappearance or even death?

His closet was precisely organized, pants at one end, shirts at the other, plus what seemed a rather large section of heavy jackets. I remembered Magnolia saying the body had been wearing a heavy jacket. Two suits, both charcoal, in a separate section by themselves. I took a closer look at the pants section. A couple pairs of little-worn jeans; all the others were chinos. Tan. Beige. I didn't remind Jenna that Magnolia said the body had been wearing tan chinos.

Shoes were neatly organized in a wooden shoe rack. Mostly loafer-type slip-ons. No cowboy boots. One pair of hiking boots with no wear, as if he'd contemplated hiking on the desert but had never actually done so. No Reeboks. But there wouldn't be, if he'd been wearing them.

Jenna took a peek into the other two bedrooms, which, peering around her, I saw held mostly shelves lined with boxes. "This was my room when I stayed here, but it looks as if Dad got rid of my bed."

The boxes were all exactly alike, and each one carried a label pasted in exactly the same position. There was a lone recliner in each bedroom/storage room. Apparently, Dad liked to peruse his records in comfort. Each room also had a stepstool for easy access to the higher shelves. "Your father—what's his name?"

"Warren."

"He's a very . . . well-organized and tidy man."

"Maybe that's what made him such a sharp accountant. He keeps every detail organized and rarely throws anything away. It was also one of the traits my mother says used to drive her crazy. They divorced when I was fourteen. She says he was a picky fussbudget, that he did things like reorganizing her perfume bottles so they were in alphabetical order. And she shuddered at the way he kept a calendar record of his bowel movements."

So, that was a quick explanation of the mysterious markings on the calendar in the bathroom. Not exactly a hot clue to his disappearance. I felt a little embarrassed that I'd studied the calendar so closely.

"I noticed he had several heavy jackets in his closet. I wonder why he needs so many here in southern Arizona."

"Dad is always cold." Another wry smile. "Mom said it's because he has such a cold, cold heart that it affects every part of his body."

"I take it their relationship isn't exactly friendly?"

"That's putting it mildly."

"Does he have any enemies?"

"You mean someone who might have *killed* him? Oh, I don't think so. He hardly knew anyone around here. I don't know anything about his relationships back when he was working, but I don't think he kept in touch with anyone."

"He's retired?"

"He was the head accountant at the company that produced Lightning's movies and TV shows. Craigmont Productions. But he's so busy with day-trading on the stock market that I wouldn't call him *retired*. He was active in the stock market even when he was working at Craigmont, and then he made a real killing on one of those IPO stock market things after he left the company."

45

Jenna sounded as if she wasn't much more familiar with the stock market than I am, although I do know what an IPO is. Initial Public Offering. Although I have no idea how you make "a killing" on one.

"Did he come here to live as soon as he and your mother were divorced?"

"Oh, no. He stayed on at Craigmont for quite a while. Craigmont had some real blockbuster movies and TV shows after they got out of westerns. The thriller *The Killer from Beyond* was one of their biggest. Maybe you saw it?"

I had to shake my head no. My real life has had more killers than usual for one little old lady, and I don't need any more of them on a movie screen.

"But Craigmont went bankrupt a couple years ago. Dad got out before that. I suppose, as head accountant, he saw it coming."

"Did he move out here to be near his brother?"

She laughed and shook her head. "Unfortunately, no. Dad and Lightning make those Hatfield and McCoy feuding hillbillies look like friendly neighbors. I think he just wanted to get out of the LA rat race."

We were back in the living room by then, and I was looking at a painting of an Italian scene—in beige-y tones—when Mike came in from the garage.

"The SUV is there, but the Jeep isn't," he reported. "I looked all around out back too, around the pump house and toolshed, and everything looks okay, all locked up."

"He probably went somewhere in the Jeep, then. He goes down to Algodones once in a while. It's over in Mexico. Have you been there?" she asked me. "It's an awesome shopping experience, and lots of people go there for dental work."

"Does your father stay overnight when he goes there?" I asked.

"I don't remember him doing that. Though he has gone up to Las Vegas a time or two and stays for a weekend there. He's talked about doing some traveling too. I think he has a bucket list. Exotic places like

Machu Picchu and the pyramids and Madagascar." Her expression brightened. "The Jeep may be sitting in the long-term parking area at the Yuma airport while he's off exploring some exotic place."

"Would he just take off and leave without saying anything to you?"

Jenna tilted her head and looked off into space before she nodded. "He might. I mean, I didn't ask him if I could go to New York with Mom and Hayden, and he didn't tell me beforehand the last time he went up to Vegas."

"You live separate lives."

She nodded. "We've never really been close since the divorce. He thought my dropping out of college and 'running off to New York' was a bad idea. And he was right, of course. I should never have let my mother push me into it. I didn't have much contact with him while I was living there."

"But you were close enough that you came here to live when you left New York."

Her light laugh was wry. "The biggest reason I came here was that my mother was really upset when I gave up on modeling. I didn't want to hang around Scottsdale and listen to her nag me on a daily basis. Dad offered to help me financially if I wanted to concentrate on my writing."

Ah. What's that old line? *Follow the money.* "He wanted you to live here?"

"I think he had in mind that he'd provide the money and I'd live *somewhere* while I wrote, and he was rather shocked when I showed up here and said I'd like to live with him for a while. That lasted about a month. Then he said he thought we'd both be happier if I had a place of my own and bought the travel trailer for me."

By that time I was standing in front of another painting, this one also a beige-y Italian scene. Mike came over to look at the painting with me.

"As an artist, what do you think?" I asked.

"It's a little . . . outside my taste. Although I'm sure Warren paid a bundle for it."

The tone of his comment suggested there was no great fondness between himself and Warren. From what little I knew of Warren so far, I suspected he'd prefer a daughter's boyfriend with an occupation more substantial than art or playing in a grunge band.

I noted a space on the wall where it appeared another painting had once hung but was now missing. Maybe Warren had tired of beige?

"What do you paint?" I asked. "Landscapes? People?"

"I like to look at whatever I'm painting from a new perspective. Paint in a way that brings out the *essence* of a person or place, not just what you see on the surface. And *color.*" He sounded almost fierce about his painting. *Color* was certainly at odds with Jenna's father's dedication to beige. I wondered if I'd been mistaken about Mike. At the moment he did sound like something of a prima donna. With what sounded like exasperation, he added, "But what I *sell* are roadrunners."

"Roadrunners?"

"Roadrunners. You know, those birds you see running all over the desert around here? I paint them running and standing and pecking at snakes. I paint them in sunlight and moonlight and thunderstorms. Big roadrunners. Little roadrunners. Middle-sized roadrunners."

"People are wild about his roadrunners," Jenna put in. "They're in several gift shops in Phoenix and Yuma, and they sell out quickly. I have a couple in my trailer if you'd like to see them."

I didn't say it out loud, but I admitted to myself that I'd probably rather have a roadrunner than something painted from a "new perspective." Whatever that meant.

"Have you studied art and painting?" I asked.

"I wanted to study art in college, but my father thought I should major in business administration. He wanted me to go into banking with him." Mike shrugged. "Doesn't matter. My father passed away and I ran out of money and dropped out after my sophomore year.

I've taken a couple of art classes since then, but I mostly paint things as I see them."

I expressed my sympathy for the loss of his father.

We took a final look around. I glanced at the names on the wine bottles in the tilted rack in the dining room. Sangiovese. Solaia. Bianco Trebez. Barolo. I assumed Warren's choice in wines said something about him, but I didn't know what, since I'd never heard of any of these wines. Or maybe that in itself said something about him. A wine snob. Perhaps an art snob too. Maybe the man should get himself a six-pack of 7UP and a nice roadrunner painting.

No dirty dishes in the kitchen sink, of course, and when I opened the dishwasher I saw that it was also empty. A rack held a set of upmarket steak knives with carved teak handles.

"Mike said something about a pump house. There's a well?"

"Dad spent a fortune having one drilled. I think they had to drill into that Center of the Earth territory Jules Verne wrote about, but he does have plenty of water."

"Lightning also has a well?"

"Yes, but it's not much good. Sometimes in the summer it goes dry and he has to have water hauled in and stored in the tank."

Sharing the water with Lightning would have been the brotherly thing to do, but Warren apparently hadn't done that, even though it was Lightning's property. I was developing something of a distaste for Warren Langston.

The contents of the refrigerator were clean and neatly organized; no moldy leftovers here. Fruit and vegetables in their proper bins, eggs in their little egg-shaped receptacles, bottles of Perrier water in a neat row.

I started to peer into the kitchen cupboards, but as I looked at the orderly contents, I felt a sudden and unexpectedly urgent need to get out of here. If Warren Langston came home, he'd be furious to find strange people—and I suspected he'd include Jenna and boyfriend in that category when it came to snoopers—in his house. No point in fueling any more family hostilities than were already present around Deadeye.

I headed for the door. Jenna and Mike followed.

Chapter 5

MAC

I spotted a dust cloud and the pickup at Lightning's place just after Ivy zipped out of Jenna's father's house. Three men got out of the pickup. Two of them shook hands with Lightning and then got in the SUV, apparently the conclusion of whatever discussions they were having about using Deadeye as a movie or TV site. Successful? I couldn't tell.

"No sign of Jenna's father, but everything looked normal in there," was all Ivy said about their tour inside. "His name is Warren. He drinks wines I've never heard of and likes beige."

What Ivy notices about people is not necessarily what most people notice. What she notices can often be more informative than what other people see, but a preference for beige and unusual wines didn't strike me as particularly helpful.

"What about vehicles?" I asked.

Jenna, who'd followed Ivy outside, answered. "His SUV is in the garage, but the Jeep isn't. Although even when he's home he usually leaves it parked outside."

She glanced around as if hoping to spot the Jeep tucked away somewhere nearby, but the bare dust was short on tucking places. She looked more troubled than before they went inside. I guessed that unpleasant possibilities about her father were skittering around in her head now.

Lightning had to see us parked here at his brother's place. I expected him to come this way, eager to connect with his fans from yesterday, but he headed for the corral instead. We could have walked, but we drove to the corral instead. Jenna left her car at her father's place and rode in Mike's van.

Lightning was snipping open a bale of hay when we arrived. One of the sleek horses reached a nose over the divider to bump his shoulder affectionately. That horse was sorrel colored with a blaze face, the other buckskin with a dark mane. The black horse, Thunder, from Lightning's heyday in TV and movies, was no doubt long dead. I was surprised there wasn't a dog or two. Lightning struck me as a doggy kind of guy. He greeted us more enthusiastically than I expected.

"Hey, good to see you folks again! I'll go in and get those pictures I promised you soon as I get these starvin' nags fed." He gave us each a strong cowboy handshake. "I didn't want to come down and interrupt your visit with Warren."

"Actually, Dad isn't there," Jenna said. "We were looking for him. I haven't seen him since I got back yesterday."

"That right? I just got back yesterday myself. Been over in LA talkin' to a couple of outfits interested in using Deadeye for some upcoming productions and then been chasin' around with those fellers who came to check it out. But, come to think of it, I didn't see any lights on in Warren's place last night, neither. You think somethin's wrong?"

I wondered if Lightning had always talked with this folksy drawl or if he'd acquired it for his cowboy roles. Or if he just put it on for temporary use with "fans" such as us.

"Maybe Magnolia should tell you about what she found that has us all a little concerned," Ivy said.

Lightning gave Magnolia his full attention. "You found something? Yes indeedy, young lady, tell us all about it."

Uh-oh. If there's one thing Ivy hates, it's that "young lady" term, and she no doubt feels just as strongly when it's directed at a friend the same age. Ivy and Magnolia are both sharp, attractive, youthful-in-spirit women . . . Ivy, especially, although I may be a bit prejudiced about that because I love her . . . but *young* they are not.

I felt her bristle beside me, but she managed to keep silent, and Magnolia told Lightning about the events of the last few days. He interrupted only once.

"I seen that funny-lookin' outline in the dirt. I figured it was just some prankster got in there havin' fun. Sometimes I think I oughta build me a ten-foot-high chain-link fence around the whole place. Not that I'd fence *you* out, young lady," he added magnanimously to Magnolia, "but you know, keep them troublemaker types out."

Magnolia continued with the tale of our search for a body and finding nothing. "But with Jenna's father missing—"

"He isn't *missing*," Jenna protested. "He just hasn't been home for a couple of days."

"And, of course, I may have been mistaken about what I found," Magnolia said. "It may not have been a dead body at all."

"I got a couple of deputy friends in the sheriff's department. Maybe I'll see if I can find out anything from them."

I couldn't tell, from the rather offhand way he made the statement, if he really intended to do it or not.

With considerably more enthusiasm, he said, "You know, long time ago, *Frontier Lawman* had a situation kinda like that. Feller found what he thought was a body, but when I investigated I found it was some kind of effigy thing stolen from an old Indian graveyard." This must have been a scriptwriter's imagination, but Lightning spoke as if he had actually investigated a real situation. "But, you know, some strange things happen over there in Deadeye. Once I found moccasin footprints there in the dust at the telegraph office, couldn't tell where they come from or where they went. They was just *there*, like the person in 'em dropped out of the sky and left the same way. And there's noises too. I've heard music and laughter coming from the saloon, like people was really whooping it up in there."

And I wondered if maybe Lightning hadn't had a few too many solitary drinks out there in Deadeye himself. Maybe that was his vodka bottle in the pulpit. Or maybe he was just trying to distract us with some tall-tale *non sequiturs* here. Distract us from what? At this point, he didn't seem overly concerned about his brother.

I went back over the time line. Magnolia found—and lost—the body a day before we arrived. Jenna and Lightning both got home yesterday.

Or was one of them not telling the truth about when he or she got home? Had Warren Langston been here all the time the two of them were gone? Had anyone else been here? How long had that body—if it was a body Magnolia found—been lying there in the street?

I glanced over at Ivy. I could practically see some of these same questions scrolling through her mind.

I managed some answers to those questions—although my answers were more like questions too. Had Jenna come home earlier than she was saying, done something dastardly to her father, then hid his body when Magnolia and Geoff showed up in their motorhome? Terrible thing to think, a daughter doing bodily harm to her father, but it's been done. But, no motive there. At least none we knew of.

Or had Lightning come home earlier than he said, before Jenna's return, had a shootout with his brother, left, and returned later with the representatives from the movie production company? Plenty of motive there, if the antagonism between the brothers was as deep as Mrs. Oldham had said. Was Warren planning to block Lightning's plans with the movie production company?

Then I gave myself a kick in my mental behind. Just because Ivy seems to have this peculiar affinity for getting involved in murder cases didn't mean *this* was a murder. Although that left the question about the body Magnolia had found out in Deadeye. If it was a body. Then I realized that while my mind was meandering, the conversation had taken another turn.

". . . under the assay and telegraph building," Lightning was saying. "Of course, it was mostly caved in, even back then, and probably more so now."

"What was caved in?" I asked.

Ivy gave me an exasperated look. I think she was trying to raise one eyebrow—she keeps working on that—but she hasn't gotten the hang of it yet and instead gets this sweet, ambling-caterpillar look with the eyebrows.

"Lightning was telling us there were a couple of old buildings here before Deadeye was built," Ivy said, "and there was a caved-in old mine tunnel underneath what is now the telegraph building."

"Are you thinking the body could be hidden down there?"

"Couldn't be." Lightning shook his head. "There's still a trapdoor going through the floor of the old building to get into the mine shaft, but it's covered with old carpet now. Nobody but me even knows it's there."

Could he be sure of that? I glanced at Jenna. She was squinting at the far horizon as if using super-vision to look for a lizard on a cactus out there somewhere. Did that mean she knew about the trapdoor and the tunnel but wasn't about to let on that she knew?

I looked back at Lightning. It sounded as if he didn't want anyone prowling around under his telegraph office floor, and I could tell that immediately aroused Ivy's curiosity. Uh-oh. Ivy's aroused curiosity is a formidable force. Think bulldozer, avalanche, tsunami.

Now, however, all she said was, "I hope your meeting with the movie production people went well?"

"You betcha it did." Lightning nodded vigorously. "It's time for the good ol' western to make a comeback, and these folks are gonna make it happen."

"You'll be in it?" Ivy said.

"I'll probably have more like a consultant role, thought I might have one of those . . . what do you call 'em? . . . cameo parts," Lightning said. "I'm not as agile with the ridin' as I usta be. But I can be sure they get things right. It'll be a while before they get anything going, but if you're still around, maybe I can get you in as extras." He gave Magnolia an appraisal and nodded approvingly. "They've got a good script in mind, and you'd do fine as the madam running things upstairs in the saloon."

Magnolia gave a muffled gasp, and I couldn't tell if she was appalled or just startled by that assessment. Whatever it was, she hastily asked about the pictures and autographs.

Lightning went back to the mobile home to get them, and we petted and scratched the friendly horses. Ivy, ever curious, of course, asked Jenna if Lightning had a wife.

"Not now. He's been married a couple of times—maybe even three—but he says a wife is more trouble than a whole herd of horses."

Lightning returned a few minutes later with photos of himself and horse Thunder for each of us. He was at least twenty years younger in the photos, quite a handsome guy. His mustache had enlarged since then. The photos were signed with an oversized autograph, the zigzag of a lightning bolt punctuating the center of his name. Magnolia got out her cell phone and had Geoff take a couple of photos of her with Lightning. Lightning didn't mention anything about wanting photos himself.

After the photos, Magnolia said, "Oh, I almost forgot." She tapped her throat in a jittery, how-could-I forget-when-it's-the-very-reason-we-came gesture, but I suspected being seen as a madam in an over-the-saloon bordello might be enough to play tricks with her mental focus. "You and your brother and I, and Jenna too, of course, we're all related!"

"That so?" Lightning said. He sounded a little less friendly, as if he suspected this was a lead-in to one relative hitting up another for money.

"Magnolia has done a lot of research into the genealogy of her family," Ivy said. She isn't into genealogy herself, but she always supports Magnolia's involvement in it, and she sounded protective now. "She found a connection between her family and the Langston family going way back through some great-grandfathers."

"That so," Lightning repeated.

Magnolia launched into a long explanation that left me edging back toward the horses. Geoff edged that way too. He always supports Magnolia's ardor for genealogy, never a word of complaint about running all over the country to find people on her many-branched family tree, but I think he has a limited interest in hearing the details. Again.

"What do you think?" I asked him as we leaned against the corral fence. "About the dead body, I mean."

"Much as I'd rather she hadn't, I think Mag really found a dead body," Geoff said. Ivy says Geoff is the only person in the world, including herself and all those people in the family tree, who can get away with shortening Magnolia's name to Mag. "But, since the deputies searched and couldn't find one, and we did the same, I don't know that there's anything we can do about it." Pause. "Unless Ivy . . ."

Oh yes. Unless Ivy had other ideas. Tracking-down-a-killer ideas. Ivy does that.

We wandered back to the group when Magnolia was concluding the family relationship story. Lightning and Jenna both thanked her, although I noticed neither had been taking notes. We all thanked Lightning for his hospitality and photos, and he shook hands with each of us. Jenna was still standing there, and Ivy said, "If there's anything else we can do to help—?"

"I want to say, 'I'm sure everything is fine,'" Jenna said. "But . . ." Her voice trailed off uncertainly, and she looked back at the double-wide mobile again.

"Why don't you go to the Yuma airport and see if your father's Jeep is parked there," Ivy suggested.

Jenna brightened. "Yes. Great idea! We'll do that."

"Although he might have flown out of the Phoenix airport. Or even LA," Mike said.

"We can at least look at Yuma first."

IVY

We all showered after we got back to the motorhomes and then had a late, light lunch. I tucked our autographed photos in a drawer. The meeting with Lightning had been friendly enough, but he hadn't said anything about keeping in touch or meeting other family members, and I thought Magnolia was a little disappointed.

We sat under Magnolia and Geoff's motorhome awning and discussed what we were going to do next. We looked at a Baja map and decided that San Felipe, about a hundred and fifty miles south of the border, looked like a good destination. Magnolia didn't have any more relatives to chase down at the moment, and Geoff suggested they go down there too.

Magnolia immediately said, "I'd rather stay around Yuma for a while."

Geoff looked surprised. "But before you said—"

"I really *want* to stay in Yuma."

"Well, okay."

Geoff is a great guy, but sometimes a woman has insights that a man misses. Magnolia had one here. A honeymoon is a twosome event, not a foursome. She looked at me and gave me a conspiratorial wink, and I winked back.

So we talked a little more and decided we'd all go over to Algodones tomorrow. From there Mac and I would continue on down into Baja for our honeymoon, and Magnolia and Geoff would return to Yuma.

Plans change.

Chapter 6

IVY

I heard a patter of raindrops on the motorhome roof in the night, along with the sound of coyotes yipping somewhere in the distance, but by morning the sky was cloudless again. We wanted to restock the refrigerator before we went down to Baja, so I was cleaning out the shelves and drawers when Jenna's little blue car pulled up alongside the motorhome. I went out to meet her, surprised to see her here.

"Ivy, I'm so glad I caught you before you left. I found something." She reached in her pocket and pulled it out. Her hand shook a little as she showed it to me. A cell phone.

"Your father's?"

She nodded. "I didn't get all the way around the fence yesterday when we were searching so I decided to go back out there this morning. I found the phone around on the back side of Deadeye, a few feet from the fence."

Mac had been checking on some equipment in the storage compartment under the motorhome, and when he came around we all three looked at the cell phone as if it might announce its reason for being in such a troubling place. The phone wasn't the most expensive model on the market, but it was in a class well above what either Mac or I use.

"Dad wouldn't have any reason to be walking out there," Jenna said.

"So you think—?" I hesitated to state aloud what instantly came to my mind, but Jenna herself voiced exactly what I was thinking.

"I don't want to think *anything*, but I have to wonder if somebody carried his—" She swallowed hard, as if she didn't want to say the word. "Carried his body back there and threw it over the fence and the phone fell out of his pocket."

"But there isn't a body there now."

"And then, whoever it was, crawled through the fence and moved it somewhere else."

"Have you talked to Lightning about this?" Mac asked.

She looked around guiltily, as if he might be hiding nearby, listening. "No, I came here. Dad and Lightning have some . . . issues. And I . . . well, I have to wonder . . ." Another big swallow.

She wasn't openly accusing Lightning of anything, but her thoughts were obvious: if someone had killed her father and carried his body off, that someone could very well be Lightning. I wondered what their "issues" were.

"How about the sheriff's office?" I asked. "Have you talked to them?"

"No. Yesterday, after you left, Mike and I drove into Yuma and checked on the long-term vehicle storage area at the airport. They had no record of Dad ever arranging to leave the Jeep there. But, as Mike said, if he decided to do some traveling, he could have flown out of some other airport and left the Jeep wherever that was." She paused. "But I'm also thinking, if he was ill . . . or something . . . and collapsed on the street out in Deadeye, that when he got up he was, you know, disoriented and confused. He could have wandered to the fence and crawled through."

"And dropped his cell phone."

Jenna nodded. "And now he's lost, wandering out there on the desert."

She looked at me as if hoping I'd agree with that possibility. I'd like to, but lost on the desert sounded only a little less likely than that he'd been snatched by aliens and was now in a galaxy far, far away. But getting disoriented and lost on the desert *was* a minuscule possibility, so it probably should be checked out.

"Perhaps you should file a missing person report," Mac suggested. "They might send out a search team with dogs."

"You could also tell them about the possibility he's traveling. They surely have the resources to check with other airports," I said. "Have you told Mike about finding the phone?"

"He's still house painting today. I tried to call him, but he didn't answer."

Mac asked the obvious question. "Have you looked on the phone to see what calls your father recently made or received? Maybe that would reveal something."

Jenna nodded. "That was the first thing I did. The last call he made was several days ago. It was to a tire store in Yuma, and the last one he received was from them. He'd cleared the call log before that."

"Was clearing the call log something he did frequently?" I asked.

Jenna lifted her hands helplessly. "I have no idea."

So maybe clearing the log this time was just some minor action to keep his phone from being cluttered with meaningless information. Or had he done it because he didn't want a record of certain calls on the phone? Actually, I was surprised that Warren didn't have the phone protected with a password that would keep Jenna or anyone else out of it.

She brightened. "Hey, I didn't think of it until just now, but calling a tire store probably means he was getting the Jeep ready for a trip somewhere. New tires or something."

"You could call them and ask if he brought the Jeep in and had tires installed," Mac suggested. "Maybe he mentioned to them where he was going. You know, just an idle chitchat sort of thing."

Jenna nodded. "Yes, I'll do that." She smiled a bit ruefully, as she often did when talking about her father. "Although Dad isn't much of a chitchat kind of person. Look, I'm sorry I bothered you guys. It's just that I kind of panicked when I found the phone. But I'm sure he'll have some logical explanation when he gets home." Another pause. "Although I may not ask him. Sometimes he gets annoyed if I ask about things that are . . . none of my business."

Probably none of *my* business, but I'd say this father and daughter needed better communication skills. The thought also occurred to me that the law authorities could probably obtain a record of the calls, even if Warren had deleted them.

"Why don't you call the tire store right now?" I suggested.

She did.

They tried to be helpful and took the time to look into their records, but Warren Langston hadn't had any new tires installed or any other work done in their shop. Whoever Jenna talked to didn't know anything about the calls made to or from Warren's phone to their store recently. They didn't keep a record of all the calls the store received, and they had no record of him as a previous customer.

Jenna's face drooped. She obviously felt let down by this dead end to what might have been a helpful clue to her father's whereabouts.

I glanced at Mac. I could tell from the way he was looking at me that he suspected what I was about to say. Another delay in our honeymoon plans. But, being Mac, he didn't raise a fuss about the delay. Instead, he cleared his throat and made the suggestion himself.

"How about if we come back out to Deadeye and help you look more thoroughly along the fence line? Perhaps look farther out from the fence itself."

It's good to be married to a man who thinks like you do. They say married people eventually start to look alike too. I gave him a quick glance. Mac is a good-looking guy, with a good-humored quirk to his mouth and an attractive . . . okay, it's more than that. Let's say it like it is. He has a sexy sparkle in his eyes! Yes, I could live with our growing to look alike. Without the beard and mustache, of course. But I'm getting off the subject here.

"I'd appreciate the help," Jenna said. "I'm really beginning to get worried about Dad. Maybe we can find something else he dropped or tracks to show where he wandered off."

I reminded her about making a missing person report.

Jenna looked a little embarrassed. "I'll wait another day or two for that. If Dad comes home and he's just been, you know, away on a trip or something, he'll really be disturbed if I've reported him missing and have everyone trying to find him. He's a very private person."

"Does your father have a girlfriend he might visit for a few days or take a trip with?" Mac asked.

"I don't think so." Jenna's shoulders lifted in a helpless gesture. "But I don't *know*. We don't, you know, talk about things like that."
**

Magnolia and Geoff aren't usually hiking people, but Magnolia came up with a pair of many-pocketed cargo pants I didn't know she owned, plus some sturdy walking shoes and her walking stick. The walking stick had belonged to a relative who'd supposedly climbed in the Himalayas with it, and Magnolia looked ready to tackle the Himalayas herself. Jenna went on ahead and we all headed for Deadeye after making sure Koop was comfortable for the day. This day we took BoBandy along. Dogs have good noses. Maybe he'd pick up on something.

I drove the pickup again, with Magnolia riding shotgun and Mac and Geoff riding in back, and parked beside Jenna's car at the gate into Deadeye. Either we were getting accustomed to eating dust, or last night's rain had settled the dust somewhat because I didn't feel nearly as gritty as when we'd made the trip before. After the sprinkle of rain, the desert air smelled fresh washed, maybe even newly created.

Jenna took charge again and split us into two groups. Mac, Geoff, and Magnolia would follow the fence to the left of the gate. Jenna and I would go to the right, and we'd all meet on the far side of the town. Mac scowled at being separated from me, but he didn't say anything so neither did I. BoBandy chased back and forth between our little search parties and finally decided to go with Mac.

Actually I was rather pleased with the arrangement. It would give me a chance for a conversation with Jenna that wouldn't be possible if there were more than the two of us.

Although I soon realized conversation wasn't going to be all that easy because she also separated us for the fence-line search. No doubt a more efficient way of searching than walking together but not conducive to carrying on a conversation. She walked about ten feet from the fence line and put me another ten feet farther out. The distances varied, of course, because we had to circle around cactus and rocks and creosote bushes. Sometimes we were within two or three feet of each other, sometimes twenty feet apart.

"Watch out for rattlesnakes," she called over to me once.

"I'm already doing that. Are there any other creatures to watch out for?"

"I've heard about scorpions, but I've never actually seen one. I think they usually hide under rocks. I don't think they jump out and attack."

Good. I'd really want to be with Mac if there was an imminent scorpion attack. Cholla cactus is sometimes called "jumping cactus" because it almost does seem to jump out and grab you. I've read that air movement caused by your body when you pass by the cactus is actually what makes it seem to jump, but by the time a third clump of the needle-sharp stuff grabbed onto my sleeve, I was ready to go with the theory of deliberate jumping.

We moved at a slow pace, zigzagging to cover as much ground as possible, stopping now and then to get rid of the clumps of cholla caught in our clothing. Jenna said the best way to do it was with a comb, but neither of us had one.

I kept my gaze glued to the ground, but on this hard, gritty earth, I suspected a whole herd of inebriated or ill men could have wandered around without leaving visible tracks. I picked up a couple of pretty rocks, and I spotted a roadrunner making good time on a run through the cactus. Also lizards running around doing whatever lizards do, and various birds darting and swooping overhead. But I saw no sign Warren Langston or any other two-legged creature had been out here within the last century, and I didn't spot any ominous sign of vultures circling overhead.

I wanted to get Jenna to stop so I could talk to her for a minute, and I was tempted to make up some appropriate reason. I could say I was tired. After all, I am a Little Old Lady, and LOLs get tired. Or my knees hurt. But we weren't actually walking fast enough to be tiring, and my knees are in pretty good shape. So it would have to be a fib. My inevitable aversion to untruths kept me from doing that, so I was actually grateful when I felt something digging into my heel.

"Hey, I've got a rock or something in my shoe. Can we stop a minute while I get it out?"

"Sure. C'mon over here. There's a good rock to sit on."

She brushed grit off the flat rock. I sat down, untied my shoe, and, hoping there weren't any scorpions around that didn't know scorpions weren't supposed to leap out and attack your toes, I eased into what I wanted to talk about.

"You mentioned your father and Lightning have some 'issues.' Does that make living there between them uncomfortable?"

"My trailer is kind of a neutral zone. I don't think Dad and Lightning have ever been inside each other's homes. They sometimes use me to pass messages back and forth instead of actually talking to each other. Which, to tell the truth, does get kind of uncomfortable sometimes."

"No friendly family get-togethers, then. No potlucks or barbecues."

"I've gone horseback riding with Lightning a few times. I went over to Algodones with Dad a couple of times. But nothing with both of them. That's kind of sad, isn't it? A family living so close together but avoiding even speaking to each other."

"It's too bad Lightning and your father have run into difficulties in their family relationship now that they're living so close together."

"Actually, their—to use a rather melodramatic term—bad blood goes back a long time. Dad was head accountant at Craigmont, as I think I told you, and Lightning's show was cancelled after Dad's figures showed westerns, and Lightning's show in particular, were turning into money losers. The cancellation of Lightning's show pretty much ended his career, and Lightning blamed Dad for that. But that was Dad's job, of course." Her tone went mildly defensive. "And the company did much better after they got rid of the westerns."

"Although they did eventually go bankrupt."

"Well, that's true. But I think they tried to expand into . . . I don't know. Something else. Maybe foreign films or something. Bad investments of some kind."

"It was nice of Lightning to let your father come here to live, don't you think? With all that 'bad blood' between them."

"It isn't just Lightning's property. Dad and he are joint owners. They bought the property together and had the town built back when it looked as if owning a western setting for movies and TV would be a good investment."

"I see." And what I saw was that Lightning probably resented rather than welcomed his brother moving in. I found the tiny rock caught in my sock and brushed it off.

"Although, since Dad has been here they've had various other disagreements."

"Oh?"

"The well Dad had drilled, for one thing. Lightning said it was 'criminal' to tap into what was down there so deep. And then Dad wanted to asphalt the area around the houses to keep the dust down, and Lightning wouldn't go for that. He said asphalt would make it like a city out here. Lightning does some target practicing out back of his trailer, and Dad doesn't like the noise."

Lightning could go farther out on the desert to target practice, so I had to wonder if he did it close to home just to annoy his brother.

"But it isn't like some big range war," Jenna said. "They aren't out gunning for each other. Mostly they just stay out of each other's way."

"They agree on using Deadeye as a site for a new movie or TV show?"

"Dad isn't enthusiastic about it. He figures the place will be overrun with people. Trailers for cast and crew to live in, people to feed them, lookie-loos too. But I think Lightning needs the money having a movie made here would bring in."

Jenna's father didn't need money. He had his day-trading and the big money he'd made on the stock IPO. Not very brotherly of him to keep Lightning from income he needed.

"It's a sore point between them. Dad likes his privacy."

I guessed privacy was the big reason her father hadn't used some of his money to fix that bad road into Deadeye. He didn't want to make it easy for anyone to come out this way.

But Lightning was going ahead with plans to use Deadeye as a movie or TV site. Was that disagreement enough to turn into murder? I wouldn't think so, but murder has happened over foolishly small things.

I slipped my shoe back on.

We spotted Mac, Geoff, and Magnolia coming up the far side of the fence line and met them a few minutes later. BoBandy was making forays into the desert that took him twice as far as the people were walking. Jenna couldn't remember exactly where she'd found the cell phone, and we didn't find any helpful lost-man tracks to follow into the desert.

I looked behind us. I couldn't even see our own tracks on the hard ground, although I supposed someone more experienced at tracking might be able to spot something. I gave BoBandy a hopeful glance. Dogs with their super-sensitive noses are better than any human at tracking. But BoBandy's interest apparently centered on lizards, maybe scorpions, and at the moment he was energetically digging under a creosote bush. A few seconds later a lizard scurried out and ran.

So much for BoBandy's tracking abilities.

Walking back through the streets of Deadeye was a shorter route than following the fence line around to our vehicles. Mac and Geoff helped Magnolia through the fence and then held the wires apart for Jenna and me. Jenna waved them off.

"I'm going to walk back to the trailer." Jenna made a circular gesture around the end of the low hill that stood between Deadeye and the mobiles. "I'll get my car later."

I didn't know her reasoning for doing this, but I promptly said, "I'll come with you." BoBandy opted to join us. I think he feels obligated to give Mac and me equal time.

Jenna headed off through the creosote bushes and cactus, and I followed. The mobile homes weren't visible until we rounded the end of the hill. A couple of times I spotted small indentations or scuffs in the earth that might have been part of a footprint. Or might not.

And then BoBandy unexpectedly proved he could find more than a lizard.

Chapter 7

IVY

He started digging directly in front of me. I jumped back to escape the volley of flying dirt.

I didn't know what he was digging for, but what came with the flying dirt was a scrap of paper. I grabbed it eagerly and found it was a faded receipt for a purchase from Walmart. Was that what made him dig? I doubted it, but whether he dug on purpose because he had sleuthing ambitions or dug purely for the joy of digging, this find might be something important.

Jenna was fifteen or twenty feet ahead of me, long braid swinging briskly with her stride. Yeah, I was lagging behind. The LOL legs were getting tired. "Jenna," I called, "BoBandy just dug up something."

She turned and trotted back to me. BoBandy was still digging.

It was a cash receipt, not a credit card payment. I couldn't make out what it was for or the exact amount, only that the figure ended in .98. I handed it to Jenna and she studied it, tilting it to sunlight and then shading it with her hand as she tried to make out what the faded printing said.

Although the name of the product and the full price were no longer visible, I took the receipt to mean that somebody had carried her father's body through here and the receipt dropped out of his pocket, just as the cell phone had done.

Jenna interpreted it differently. "Dad *was* walking out here, then! He was digging in his pocket looking for his phone, and this receipt fell out!"

I knew she didn't want to come to a stark realization her father was dead. I also didn't want to prove he was dead, but this struck me as an overly optimistic interpretation.

"I wonder where he is now, then."

"Just where we thought before. Gone on a trip somewhere." She paused and studied the far horizon. "Unless he did get disoriented and is lost out there somewhere." Then in another one-eighty-degree modification in possibilities, she added, "Although this could be anyone's receipt, couldn't it? Maybe those movie production men walked around out here."

"How does your father usually pay for purchases?"

"I'm sure he *has* some credit cards, but he prefers cash. He usually carries quite a lot of money in his wallet." She sounded as if she made the admission reluctantly.

Jenna not wanting to admit her father was dead was understandable. Daughterly love. But part of my mind shouted out the old line that says *Everyone's a suspect.* Accompanied by the ugly thought that maybe Jenna already knew he was dead because she had something to do with his death and this was an elaborate act. New York model turned writer turned actress to hide a deadly secret.

But she couldn't have done it. She was back in New York when her father was killed. At least that's what she claimed . . .

Get off it, Mrs. Mac, I told myself firmly. *We don't know the body Magnolia found, if it was a dead body, was Warren Langston. And even if it was, it could have been a natural death. Or there are any number of people other than Jenna who may have killed him. Lightning, for one.*

I didn't like that possibility any better than thinking Jenna may have done it. Lightning was a likeable guy.

The trouble, however, is that a murderer is who he is, not whom we'd prefer him—or her—to be. I didn't have any preferences for a murderer in this situation anyway, except maybe a generic SODDI. Which translates to Some Other Dude Done It. Yes, Some Other Dude was definitely preferable to either Jenna or Lightning as a killer.

Actually, Jenna's father, the loner with hidden psychotic tendencies, sounded more like a potential killer than anyone else. But that didn't work; Warren was the one who was dead.

But if he wasn't dead, if he'd killed someone, could he have gone into hiding?

With a jaunty my-work-is-done-here wave of tail, BoBandy gave up on digging, and we trekked on back to the mobile homes. I don't think Jenna even intended to mention the receipt to Mac, Geoff, and Magnolia when we met, but I suggested we show them what we'd found, and Jenna pulled it out of her pocket.

They each inspected it, but as Geoff pointed out, the faded receipt may have been out there for a few days or a few weeks, maybe even a few months. Magnolia, who has better eyes, or maybe better glasses, than the rest of us, did discern that the total price had been $15.98. Which was not exactly clue-of-the-year helpful.

Jenna took back the receipt. "I'll keep it. Just in case." Then, to me, "Would you like to come to the trailer and see a couple of Mike's roadrunner paintings?"

Jenna hadn't invited the whole gang, but everyone trooped along behind us. I'm not the only curious one in this group. Jenna opened the trailer door and we all squeezed inside. She had a full desktop computer and a small printer set up on the little dinette-type table. Scraps of paper with handwritten notes on them were scattered everywhere.

"I don't have internet here," she said. "But that's okay. Not having an internet connection keeps me from getting sidetracked. But I can use Dad's computer if I desperately need to get on the internet."

She smiled as if to acknowledge that getting on the internet wasn't ever a "desperate" need, although I had to agree that it sometimes felt as if it were. Strange, isn't it, how something we lived most of our lives without can now seem like a necessity?

Dirty dishes filled the sink. An empty yogurt carton and a half-filled cup of cold coffee stood by the computer. I know some computer users keep everything on the computer and barely use paper, but Jenna had a wastepaper basket half filled with crumpled pages.

She gave the crumpled pages a rueful glance. "The Great American Novel in progress."

There wasn't much wall space for displaying anything in the compact trailer, but she'd managed to hang two small roadrunner paintings on the cabinet doors over the dinette. They probably weren't great art, but I liked them. Mike had caught the *essence* of roadrunner in them, a slightly quizzical expression, a comic touch that caught their humorous aspect without making caricatures of the long-tailed, scrawny-legged creatures. He'd included footprints behind one bird, the well-known X shape which makes it almost impossible to tell which way the bird is going. He'd signed the paintings with the single name "Redstone."

"Mike sells most of his paintings through gift shops, but I'm sure you can get one direct from him, if you're interested."

My compatriots decided to exit the trailer, perhaps thinking this was going to turn into a sales pitch for her boyfriend's paintings, but I was really quite charmed by the roadrunners. I had to ask, of course, "How expensive are they?" Our budget for art is, well, nonexistent.

"I'm sure Mike can come up with a price that works for you. Would you like to see something else he did? It's kind of big, and I haven't had it framed yet because I don't have any place to hang it."

She went to a storage space that ran across the front of the trailer above the sofa and pulled out a rolled canvas. She spread it on the sofa to show me, all bright slashes and cubicles of color. A hunk of dark hair here, red lips in a box there; a luminous eye, a leg starting below the lips, a hand off by itself. A second eye on the big toe of another leg flung upward.

"What is it?" I asked doubtfully.

Jenna laughed. "Don't you recognize it? It's me!"

This body-parts puzzle was how Mike saw Jenna? *Creepy*. Rather too much like an ax-murderer portrait of a dismembered victim.

But then I tilted my head and looked further. Deeper. I stepped back and tilted my head the other way. I blinked. Twice. Squinted. And then, yes, as Mike had done with the more realistic roadrunners, he'd somehow caught the *essence* of Jenna in this disjointed painting. Her dark hair, her mouth, her nicely shaped legs, the expressive . . . if disjointed . . . eyes. And there was a definite Jenna-type exuberance in that leg flung upward.

The painting was intriguing, but I could see why customers probably weren't lining up to buy.

"Want him to do a portrait of you?" she asked with a playful quirk of eyebrow.

And find myself depicted with my nose in my belly button? My toes sticking out of my ears? "You might ask him about my buying a roadrunner."

Jenna laughed again, apparently appreciating what she took as my tact in not expressing an opinion of the painting of herself. "I'll do that."

She took a moment to study the painting, which I'm sure she'd done before, and then rolled it to fit back in the storage space. I couldn't tell if she was thinking that she loved the odd portrait or if she loved the man in spite of a weird streak. "I showed it to my mother a while back. She said she thought it expressed an 'awesome talent.'" Jenna smiled. "But, knowing Mom, that doesn't necessarily mean she liked it."

"Have she and Mike met?"

"No." Jenna's lips quirked. "I'm not sure, but I think he may be avoiding the meet-the-mother event."

"Does she come here often?"

"Oh, no. But she and Hayden called when they were on their way to San Diego not long after I got my own trailer. Dad had gone into Yuma that day, so I told them to come on out. It's the only time Hayden has been here, but Mom has been here a couple more times. Though Hayden may not know that."

"He doesn't like her visiting you?"

"Mom thinks Hayden is afraid Dad might lure her back to him."

"Is that a realistic fear?"

"Mom living out here on the desert is about as likely as one of the local roadrunners renting a New York apartment."

"Do your mother and her husband travel a lot?"

"No, but Hayden used to be the golf pro at a country club in San Diego and they were headed there for a tournament the day they stopped by here. He's a golf pro in Scottsdale now, a very successful one. People line up to take lessons from him. They live in a community built around the golf course."

Definitely a more ritzy lifestyle than here in Deadeye Heights. My ever-curious—and ever-suspicious—mind immediately tossed out a thought. Had mother and husband Hayden any reason to want Jenna's father dead?

Although we didn't know for certain that Warren Langston, or anyone else, was actually dead.

"Did you meet Mike through his painting?"

"In a way." She told me how Mike had come out to Deadeye after hearing there were some old buildings out here and thinking they might be good background scenery for roadrunner paintings. With the gate padlocked and the No Trespassing signs plastered around Deadeye, he'd followed the road on back to the mobiles, looking for someone to ask about getting inside.

"I was taking a break from writing, so I took him over to Dad—Lightning wasn't here—and introduced them and got a key to the gate. From there on we just kind of . . . clicked." She smiled.

"He seems like a nice guy," I said. Although a question—hopefully irrelevant—occurred to me. Did that disjointed painting show chop-'em-up killer tendencies?

"He is a nice guy. Will you and Mac be heading out now?"

"We're planning on going down to San Felipe." I didn't mention that we were still trying to have that honeymoon. I think Jenna, like most people, assumed we'd been married for years rather than being newlyweds.

"Hey, I wonder if Dad went to San Felipe? I've heard it's a great place, with a beautiful beach. I think the road is good that far down, but it gets pretty rough farther south on the Sea of Cortez side of Baja."

"I kind of hate to leave with everything so . . . unfinished here. Your dad missing and all. We might stay around until next week," I added, although that wasn't something Mac and I had discussed. "We usually go to church on Sunday, wherever we are. Is there a church around here somewhere?"

"I don't know. There might be one in Tacna. I can ask Mike."

"If we can find one, would you like to go with us?"

She looked startled, as if church were a totally foreign concept. "I guess I could. I haven't been for a long time, but I went to Sunday school when I was a kid. How about if I check with Mike and then call you?"

"Great! See if Mike wants to come along."

"Well, uh, okay."

I'm not one for nagging or dragging anyone to church, but I certainly don't miss an opportunity to give an encouraging nudge. And a prayer or two. I gave her my cell phone number.

Jenna called that evening and said Mike had seen a little church in Wellton, which was on the far side of Tacna. He'd checked, and the service started at ten o'clock on Sunday. We arranged a time for her to come by the RV park so she could lead the way to Mike's trailer. He was coming too, which I think surprised Jenna even more than it did me.

**

Jenna seemed in good spirits when she came by on Sunday morning, although she didn't know any more about her father's whereabouts than before. The four of us, in Geoff's Subaru, followed her into Tacna. Jenna led us to Mike's tiny trailer, he jumped in with Jenna, and he apparently gave her instructions on finding the church in Wellton.

The church was a nondescript, flat stucco building that gave no clue what it had been before it was converted to a house of worship, but inside a cross made of pieces of the wooden skeleton of a cholla cactus gave an earthy, desert touch that was very appealing. The service was presented by a young, energetic pastor who even managed to inject a bit of humor as he spoke about Job's troubles and how Job had dealt with them. I wished it had been Communion day. It had been a while since we'd shared that special time with the Lord.

Jenna and Mike were noncommittal when they came outside after the service ended, and then Mike surprised us by suggesting we all go over to his trailer for barbecued burgers. No doubt considering what looked to be Mike's "starving artist" financial status, Mac quickly said we'd bring the hamburger and meet them there.

By the time we went to a store and arrived at Mike's trailer with the meat and buns, Mike had charcoal briquettes turning whitish in the barbecue. Jenna had set condiments, a green salad, a bowl of potato chips, and a pitcher of lemonade on the backyard picnic table. Mike's friends, who lived in the house behind which his trailer was parked, apparently weren't home today. Mike barbecued hamburgers to a just-right stage of doneness and seasoning, and the lemonade was a just-right blend of tart and sweet. I asked Mike about buying one of his roadrunner paintings.

"Jenna showed me the two she has, and I really like them."

"I've been thinking I might try an abstract of a roadrunner," Mike mused.

A picture with a head sprouting out of tailfeathers? A snake devouring it instead of the other way around?

"Umm . . ."

Mike laughed good-naturedly. "Jenna showed you my painting of her."

"Umm . . ."

"I don't have anything on hand. I took a load of paintings up to Phoenix a week ago, and I've been house painting since then. But if you're going to be here for a few days, I can have something for you."

"We're planning to go down to San Felipe," Mac said, "but if the painting isn't done by the time we leave we can come by here after we're back in Arizona."

I had to smile. Mac was determined to have that honeymoon. Though I noticed he wasn't calling it a honeymoon now, as if using the specific term might jinx the whole project.

Mike and I settled on an agreeable price for the painting, and we were sitting there feeling well-fed and relaxed when a woman came around the end of the trailer.

The woman stopped short and Mike jumped up.

"Mom!"

The woman looked as surprised to see all of us as Mike obviously was to see her. "I'm sorry. I didn't realize you had company."

Both Geoff's and Jenna's vehicles were parked beyond the garage, where she apparently hadn't seen them.

"I didn't know you planned to stop by," Mike said.

"Barbecuing burgers was kind of a last-minute thing," I put in. "But we were about to leave—"

"No, no," the woman said hastily. "I'm just passing through. Mothers shouldn't arrive without forewarning." She gave Jenna a quick smile.

Mike introduced us. The mother's name was Leanna. I was surprised to realize she and Jenna had apparently never met, although I thought she must have at least heard of Jenna. They hugged, but I could see them surreptitiously sizing each other up.

Leanna looked fiftyish, with short, brown hair which I assumed meant Mike's curly red hair came from his father's side of the family. She wore skinny white jeans, a red tank top, and red sandals. Gold hoops hung from her ears, and several bracelets jangled on her left arm. Altogether, a nicely festive look on an attractive woman. Except half-moons of shadow darkened the skin under her eyes, and her figure was a bit too thin. Although maybe that was an unfair thought, brought on by the fact that I'm now having to fight a weight gain, something I'd never had to do in my younger years.

I remembered Mike saying his father had passed away and he hadn't money enough to continue college. Perhaps life hadn't been easy for Leanna since her husband's death.

"You live here in Tacna?" I asked.

"No, I have a trailer too, but I'm over in San Diego. I'm just headed home after visiting some friends in Lake Havasu. But if I'm interrupting—"

"Oh, no!" Jenna said quickly. "I'm so glad to have a chance to meet you." She pushed the lawn chair she'd been sitting in toward the older woman.

Leanna said, "A pleasure for me too," but she didn't sit down.

The conversation seemed oddly stalled, and Mike, as if he were trying to fill a blank spot, said, "We were just sitting here talking about something that happened over at Deadeye. Magnolia"—he motioned toward Magnolia—"found something in the street over there. It may have been a dead body."

"Really. How strange." She shot her son a look that I couldn't quite interpret. Concern? Annoyance? Almost as if she'd like to give him a small-boy scolding. Then she gave what struck me as a nervous laugh. "But you don't know who it was?"

"We don't even know for certain it was a body. I may have been mistaken," Magnolia said.

Another oddly stilted silence, and Mike offered a bit of irrelevant information to fill it. "Mom is a hair stylist at a beauty salon over in San Diego." He was still standing and Leanna hadn't taken the chair Jenna had pushed toward her.

"Well, maybe I am," Leanna said. "The shop is closed because of plumbing problems. That's why I've had a few days off. Except the landlord is being a real jerk about fixing anything, so Maxine may just close the salon permanently."

"You could move over here," Mike suggested.

I gave him a glance. Did he really want Mom living nearby or was this just a polite gesture? Or maybe he knew what her answer would be.

"Thanks, hon, but I don't think so. San Diego is home."

He didn't argue. "Sit down and I'll fix you a burger," he urged. "I have some of that jalapeno cheese you like."

I still couldn't tell what kind of answer he'd have preferred to his comment about her moving here. He didn't strike me as a mama's-boy type of guy, but the caring way he guided her to the chair showed his concern for her. She really was too thin. Her sharp collarbone jutted above her tank top, and the jangly bracelets looked ready to fall off her thin arm.

"Thanks, but I'm kind of beat—"

"You're not going to try to drive on home tonight." Mike's voice held a hint of alarm, but it was more statement than question. I could tell he wasn't going to let her do it.

"I'll get a room at Sandy's Inn. I think I'll just run on over there now and take a nap."

She looked more than tired. She looked as if she needed to sleep for a week. I wished I could do something to help.

"I'll come over later, okay?" Mike said.

She nodded, told Jenna again that she was glad to meet her, made some polite murmurings to the rest of us, and disappeared around the end of the trailer.

There was another awkward silence after she'd left, although I was uncertain why. The meeting, although it was a bit awkward, hadn't been unpleasant.

Then Mike said, "I think it would do Mom good to get out of San Diego, but I don't think she'll ever leave there. That's where Dad's buried."

Mike's concern for his mother was obvious. Mac reached over and squeezed my hand. We both knew how hard it is to move on after losing a loved one, how you feel guilty for even trying to move on. But we'd both come to see that moving on didn't mean abandoning the love we'd felt for those spouses in the past; we'd just made room for the new love for each other. The Lord wisely made love expandable.

Mike slapped his hands on his thighs. "Hey, anyone for ice cream for dessert?"

With protestations that we were too full of the great hamburgers to eat any more, the four of us said our thank-yous and goodbyes. Jenna apparently didn't intend to leave just yet.

We headed back to Prosperity. Mac and BoBandy and I took another walk out into the old subdivision. We found an old hole that went down about seven or eight feet. BoBandy barked enthusiastically as he looked down into it, paws scratching as if he'd like to dig it a little deeper. Bo has a fairly large imagination when it comes to things to bark at. But the old hole made me think of that mine shaft and tunnel that were supposed to be under one of the buildings in Deadeye. I wished we'd had a chance to at least peek into it.

I was surprised when, just before dark, Jenna's little blue car pulled in beside the motorhome and she came to the door. She looked surprisingly happy.

"I thought you might like to see this. I get my mail in a post office box there in Tacna. Mike usually brings it out to me, but I went over and picked it up myself today." She handed me a postcard.

Chapter 8

MAC

I was looking over Ivy's shoulder when Jenna handed her a postcard. On one side the picture showed city buildings and a spectacular fountain, with a banner proclaiming Welcome to Fabulous Las Vegas! The other side had a hand-printed message: "Hi! I'm taking a few days off. If the blackjack tables keep paying off big $$$ I'll be here a while! Love, Dad."

"So I can stop worrying," Jenna said. "He's okay."

"That's good to know," Ivy agreed. "He sounds as if he's having fun. Your dad likes to gamble?"

She laughed. "Personally, I think stock market day-trading is a constant gamble, but I'm glad he's taking a little vacation and enjoying himself." She took the postcard back and studied it for a moment. "I'd think about going up and joining him, but he doesn't say where he's staying."

She was silent for a moment, and I wondered if she was thinking, as I was, that Dad hadn't told her where he was staying because he didn't want to encourage company. Perhaps a girlfriend Jenna hadn't met was with him? Although Jenna and her father didn't strike me as enjoying the type of father-daughter relationship that included taking off on impulsive jaunts together, even if there wasn't a girlfriend. Of course, if he was already dead, and Jenna knew that, as Ivy and I have discussed, this could just be another staged distraction.

"Your father prefers printing to handwriting?" I asked. Even though I had immediate reservations about the authenticity of this postcard, I was reluctant to undermine Jenna's apparent relief at receiving it. I wondered what Ivy was thinking.

"Dad always prints. So do I."

I wondered if the wording sounded like her father, and I also wondered about the postmark, but before I could check it out, Jenna stuffed the postcard in her pocket.

"This does leave us wondering what your friend Magnolia saw there on the street in Deadeye, of course," Jenna said, but she didn't wait for a response. She breezed on by this question as if whatever Magnolia had found was of minor importance now. "I'll stop and tell Lightning that Dad's okay too. It's been so great meeting you people! If you come this way again, be sure to come out and see us."

She gave Ivy an exuberant hug, the reassuring postcard apparently lifting her spirits considerably. Or more expert acting.

"We'll be back after we go down to San Felipe. I have to pick up my roadrunner painting," Ivy reminded her. "But I've been thinking, if we come back out to Deadeye tomorrow morning, could we take a look under that telegraph building? We're really intrigued by the idea of an old mine tunnel under there."

This was news to me. I took a quick peek inside my mental workings. Any old-mine-tunnel intrigue lurking in there? No, not a speck. All I saw was an already-too-long-delayed honeymoon.

Did this mean Ivy's intuition suggested that the body Magnolia had found was hidden in that old tunnel? Ivy sometimes has great intuitions. Although sometimes her intuition makes a fortune cookie look like rocket science. That's probably one of the many reasons I love Ivy: she isn't always right . . . and she's always cheerfully ready to admit when she's wrong. I have to work on that for myself. Sometimes I'm a little grumpy about admitting I'm wrong.

"We might uncover something of real importance to local history," Ivy said.

That was possible. Okay, if Ivy really wanted to take a look, and apparently she did, I was willing. Maybe I could get a magazine article out of it.

"I'd like to do it," Jenna said. "I didn't even know there was a tunnel under Deadeye until Lightning mentioned it. But I can't do it tomorrow. Mike has to work on his house painting job, so I suggested I take his mother to Dateland for lunch and one of their awesome date milkshakes. I'd like a chance to get to know her better. How about the next morning?"

Ivy looked at me. Another delay in the honeymoon. But wasn't there some old saying about *the longer the wait, the sweeter the reward?*

"We can do that," I said.

Ivy and Jenna arranged that we'd meet at Deadeye day after tomorrow about nine. After Jenna left we went over to see if Geoff and Magnolia wanted to go mine-exploring with us that day. On the way over I asked Ivy what she thought about the postcard.

"I wondered about a couple of things," she said. "But I managed to answer my questions myself. Kind of."

"Such as?"

"Why didn't he do something more personal than send a postcard? Call her or send a text message? But then I realized a postcard, rather than something more personal, is probably her father's rather detached style."

"So you're comfortable with the postcard?"

"Well . . . I thought it sounded, oh, a little *gushy* for what we know of him." She gave me a glance. "Do you have some doubts? You asked about the handwriting."

"Jenna answered that with her comment that her dad always prints."

"You thought that was a good answer?"

"More or less. I wondered about the postmark too. But by the time I thought about that, Jenna had already put the card away."

"I checked the postmark," Ivy said.

That didn't surprise me. I gave her shoulders a squeeze. "Great minds think alike," I said.

Or maybe that should be *Happily married couples think alike.* Because we seemed to be thinking more alike all the time.

"It was definitely sent from Vegas," Ivy said, "but I couldn't make out the postmark date."

IVY

Without mentioning our mutual doubts, we told Magnolia and Geoff about Jenna's postcard from her father and discussed going out to Deadeye to look into the old mine tunnel. Magnolia wasn't particularly interested in underground exploration, and by now she was also leaning closer to the idea that she'd mistaken something for a body rather than finding an actual dead body.

"I'll just leave the dead-body-finding to you."

But the fact was, she'd found *something* there on the street in Deadeye. Where was it now? Who had bothered to remove it? And why?

"Why don't Mac and I go have a look in the tunnel, and we'll tell you if we find anything interesting?"

"I'll take photos too," Mac said.

So that evening we watched another old Lightning movie and the next morning, with nothing better to do, we decided it was a good day to do a washing. Mac went to ask Betsy Oldham where we might find a laundromat, and she offered to let us use her washer and dryer.

I had the feeling that if I'd gone to ask, I'd have gotten that bony finger pointing down the road. "How was her eye problem?" I asked.

"I didn't notice it today, but now she seems to have something wrong with her hair or scalp. She kept tossing her head around and tucking her hair behind her ears. I'm wondering if she has some kind of scalp problem."

Head tossing and hair tucking? Sounded more like flirty gestures than a scalp problem to me. But Mac apparently didn't have a clue because, although he sounded guilty even thinking such a thought, he said, "Maybe hair lice?"

I doubted speculation about hair lice was the reaction Betsy was going for. In any case, if she thought she and Mac were going to have a cozy tête-à-tête while washing and drying clothes together, she was mistaken. I went along. With two loads of washing and a rather prickly attitude.

Betsy, however, apparently figuring out that eye batting and hair tossing were wasted effort with a spouse as firmly attached as I was, turned out to be quite interesting, even fun. She told us about the woman who'd tried to worm her way into a fairly wealthy local rancher's affection, only to have him die and leave everything to his favorite mule. And the Eastern newcomers who arrived announcing they were going to live off the land and left declaring rather sourly that unless you liked eating cactus, there was no way to live off the land in Arizona.

I asked Betsy about that big hole we'd found when we were walking out in Prosperity, and she said some years ago somebody got the dumb idea (her words) that there might be gold out there. So for a while, dozens of people came to try prospecting with everything from picks and shovels to a foil-and-wire contraption a would-be prospector wore on his head.

"Looked like something from outer space, he did. Good thing we didn't have a thunderstorm or he'd probably have 'lectrocuted himself," Betsy declared. "All those people must of dug a dozen big ol' holes out there and a whole bunch of littler ones. I could of told 'em they was wasting their time. They'd of had better luck staying home and digging for gold in their cat's litter box."

"What about Deadeye?" Mac asked. "Ever heard anything about an old mine over there?"

"No, never heard that. But you could ask Lightning. I'm sure he's explored every inch of the place." She giggled. "He was one of those hopeful wackos prospecting out in Prosperity."

We didn't tell her we were going to see the Deadeye mine tomorrow or about the maybe-dead-body out there, but I worked in questions about Warren Langston and Jenna. Betsy knew about Jenna being a model in New York, and she surprised me by also knowing something about Jenna's mother.

"She was a model too, did you know? She tells people she quit when she got married because she believed a mother belonged at home with her kids. Actually, even though she's tall and skinny, she just never made it big as a model, and Lightning says she latched onto his brother like she was grabbin' a lifejacket. Maybe that's why she pushed Jenna so hard to be a model. The vicarious thing, you know."

I felt a little guilty, because I wouldn't have guessed Betsy had ever even heard the word *vicarious*, let alone knew how to use it in a conversation. But it was a plausible explanation about why the mother had pushed Jenna so hard, even to all those surgical alterations. She hadn't been a big-name model herself, so she was determined to live the successful model's life vicariously through Jenna.

"You know Jenna's mother?"

"Nah. Lightning is really fond of Jenna, but he says her mother's a stuck-up witch—" Betsy gave me a sly wink. "Except he spelled it with a *b*. Living on a golf course and going to fancy spas and knowing snooty society people and all." She leaned closer, as if we were in a little conspiracy together. "Lightning likes to talk, you know. He comes over and drinks my coffee and eats my cinnamon rolls and tells me all kinds of stuff. He's a worse gossip than an old lady in a knitting circle."

"What about Jenna's mother's current husband? Hayden, I think his name is."

"You'd think a woman would know enough to pick somebody different the second time around, but Lightning says Hayden is practically a clone of Warren. A real fussbudget. The kind of guy who wouldn't pick his nose without disinfecting his finger first."

The crude comment startled me, but I managed to discard the image it presented. We already knew Lightning liked to talk. I wondered if *vicarious* and *clone* came from him. Though the information about Jenna's mother's current husband surprised me. Did it say anything about his capacity for murder? Probably not. It also didn't say anything about a possible motive. But it might say something about his ability to tidy up afterward.

**

The following morning, Mac and I headed out to Deadeye. Magnolia and Geoff had decided to try Dateland for lunch and date milkshakes. We were equipped with a short-handled shovel, two heavy-duty flashlights, and extra batteries. Mac's camera dangled from a strap around his neck.

I was surprised to find both Jenna and Lightning waiting when we reached the gate. Lightning carried a big, lantern-type flashlight. "Jenna told me you want to look in that old mine tunnel under the telegraph building so I thought I'd come along and see if I could be of some assistance."

"That's nice of you," Mac said. "We appreciate the help."

Lightning's help was nice, but this "helpfulness" opened a new and uneasy thought in my mind. Could Lightning and Jenna have worked together in some murderous plot involving Warren Langston? I glanced back and forth between them. I could see motive there. Jenna would undoubtedly inherit that big "killing" her father had made with the IPO in the stock market. Lightning could probably acquire full ownership of all the property they owned here together; it might even be a survivor type joint ownership.

Was Lightning here to make sure we *didn't* find anything down there? But surely he wouldn't have mentioned the tunnel to begin with if he'd hidden something there.

"Have you been in the tunnel before?" Mac asked.

"It's been a long time. I found it when we were first building Deadeye, so I had to have a look-see, of course." Lightning unlocked and opened the gate as he talked. "It was caved in even then, and it's probably worse now. We did use it in an episode of *Frontier Lawman*. This bank robber hid down there, but I rousted him out."

Lightning headed around the corner and down the street to the telegraph building. Faint traces of Magnolia's toothpaste outline remained, although the shape looked a little ghostly now. Along the way, I asked Jenna how her lunch with Mike's mother had turned out.

"We didn't get to go after all. The plumbing at the beauty salon where she works in San Diego got fixed, so she went on home."

"Maybe she'll come back for another visit and you can take her then."

"I hope so." She hesitated. "But I'm afraid the truth is that she just didn't want to spend time with me."

Was Mama worried about this attractive young woman taking her son away from her? Not an admirable attitude, but I knew it could happen.

Lightning opened the door to the telegraph office. Mac and I hadn't been in there the day we were searching for a dead body; it was on Magnolia and Geoff's side of the street.

One side of the room held a long counter and the telegraph equipment, just a small machine with brass knobs and a finger-sized pad on the end of a metal lever for tapping out messages. The corner end of the counter held big books and assay equipment, including scales and beakers and test tubes. Glittery rocks, too, as if they were awaiting testing. Lightning said he didn't know anything about the mine's origins or if anything valuable had ever come out of it.

Mac helped Lightning roll back the threadbare flowered rug, and there it was, the outline of a trapdoor cut into the floorboards. There wasn't a handle, which suggested a body-hider would have had difficulty getting the trapdoor open quickly enough to stuff a body down there. Mac said he might have something in the pickup that they could use as a pry-bar, but Lightning rummaged around in a cabinet and came up with an old piece of metal sharpened at one end.

Hmm. If someone knew where that was, as Lightning apparently did, he could have opened the trapdoor quickly after grabbing the body off the street.

Although that would also mean, if Lightning was willing to open the trapdoor now, he'd moved the body from the tunnel.

He stuck the short length of metal in the crack in the floorboards, and the trapdoor came up with a squeak and squawk when he pried on it. An old-mummy scent of ancient air and dry earth wafted out.

Mac aimed his flashlight into the mine shaft, and we all leaned over to look. A rickety ladder leaned against the wall, crumbled dirt around the bottom of it. The hole wasn't deep, not more than a dozen feet. A narrow tunnel braced with aged wooden beams led off to one side. No mummies or dead bodies visible, but the beams slanted at a dangerously iffy angle. Definitely not something that would meet the approval of a building code inspector.

"The bank robber was hiding about ten feet into that side tunnel," Lightning said. "It was a dangerous move, but I went right down there after him."

Lightning again spoke as if this were an actual event, as if he'd heroically gone into the tunnel after the bad guy. Did he confuse a half-hour TV script with real life? Had he done that out there on the street, confused real life with an old script, and killed someone?

Then Mac said, "Must have been difficult filming down in there."

If Lightning was having trouble keeping fact and fiction straight, that jerked him back to reality. He straightened up. "Well, most of the actual filming was done out back where they set up a scene that looked like the tunnel but could accommodate the cameras and lighting."

His jump back to reality relieved me, although it didn't fully cancel my uneasiness that he may have killed someone. Maybe even his brother, because I also wasn't convinced that postcard meant Warren was still alive.

The uneasiness returned when Lightning suddenly clapped his hands. "Okay, folks, lights, camera, action! You or the young lady going down first?" He stepped back and swooped a hand toward the hole.

"Young lady" immediately ignited my kick-'em-in-the-shins urge, but I let that go with a more important thought. Mac goes down there. I follow him. If Lightning and Jenna were conspirators in some murderous scheme, they could slam the trapdoor on us, roll the rug back over the trapdoor, and there we'd be. Trapped. Never to be heard of again in this century.

My mind didn't stop to consider *why* they'd do that. Or how they'd explain our disappearance. Magnolia and Geoff knew where we were going today. But my mind just clamped onto one thought, like BoBandy with a bone. *Don't go down there.*

Mac turned and put a foot on the top rung of the ladder. I grabbed his arm. "Maybe we've . . . uh . . . seen enough."

"I want to get some photos from inside the tunnel. I'm thinking I might get a travel magazine article out of this."

I gave him a glare. Stubborn man. Didn't he see the danger? Sometimes we *didn't* think alike.

"Publicity?" Lightning sounded interested but Jenna immediately squelched the article idea.

"We don't want some bunch of nosy gold hunters snooping around here."

Did she say that because she knew her father wouldn't like tourists stomping around? Or because she and Lightning had some nefarious conspiracy going and didn't want nosy lookie-loos around? Or because she'd done something on her own that Lightning didn't know about?

Whatever the reason, Lightning now said, "Yeah, I didn't think of that. Come to think of it, maybe you'd better not go down there at all."

So instead of steadying Mac so he could start climbing down the ladder, Lightning yanked him upward. "You go down there and get hurt and first thing happens, you're suing me for a million bucks. That's what everybody does these days. Get a finger scratched or a toe bruised and *Boom*! Lawsuit."

"We're not going to sue you," Mac protested.

"I'll go down and if it looks safe, you can come down." Lightning grabbed his own flashlight and started down the ladder.

My suspicious thought: Lightning goes down alone, tells us it doesn't look safe enough for anyone else, and leaves the body hidden there undisturbed. Did that mean Jenna had put it there and he didn't realize that until now? Was he trying to protect her? Or had he hidden the body down there himself and since moved it, but he was now concerned there might be some giveaway evidence remaining?

Never let it be said that I'm at a loss for a parade of suspicious thoughts even if they're at odds with each other. I also felt as if I were trying to follow a roadrunner's X-shaped tracks, unable to tell which direction my various suspicions were leading.

However, Mac waited only until Lightning ducked into that side tunnel and then, flashlight in hand, went down the ladder himself. Jenna jumped into the downward parade. I wanted to follow, but I decided I'd better stay here on the surface in case of calamity down there.

Light from the flashlights flickered in the opening of the side tunnel. Voices drifted upward, although I couldn't make out their words. Several times a brighter light flared, probably the flash on Mac's camera. A thump when someone apparently hit one of the supporting timbers. I tensed, waiting for a rumble of impending doom as the tunnel totally collapsed. But what came was Jenna's laughter, then Mac's.

Laughter?

I felt mildly indignant. They hadn't discovered a dead body or anything else creepy or scary; they were just down there having a good time. Without me.

I aimed my flashlight into the hole. I was just about to climb down the ladder myself when Jenna squeezed out of the side tunnel. Mac showed up right behind her. Dirt smeared his left cheek. They climbed up the ladder and Lightning followed.

"So?" I brushed the dirt off Mac's cheek, perhaps a bit more vigorously than necessary.

"Looks just about the same as when I went after the bank robber down there years ago," Lightning said. "Tunnel blocked with rubble from a collapse that might be a hundred years old."

"No body or anything Magnolia might have mistaken for a body," Mac agreed.

"Did you get anything useful for a magazine article?" I asked Mac. "It sounded as if you were all having a good time."

"Nothing useful for a magazine article. We were just laughing at a big pile of beer cans and old potato chips sacks, along with a sign saying Buried Treasure Here and an arrow pointing straight down."

"Some of the crew must've been partying down there when I didn't know about it." Lightning sounded mildly annoyed.

He closed the trapdoor. Mac covered it with the carpet, and that ended our mine exploration. We again said our goodbyes and drove back to the motorhome. I felt let down. I'd had this definite . . . what? hunch? intuition? . . . that something important was hidden down there. But apparently I might as well, as Betsy had suggested about the gold prospectors, have looked in Koop's litter box instead.

Back at the motorhome, BoBandy and one-eyed Koop were glad to see us. I knew they must be getting tired of being left home alone, but they don't hold grudges.

Magnolia and Geoff weren't back from their lunch yet. Mac downloaded his photos onto the laptop, and I studied the results. A beer-can mountain. Rubble. Crumbling tunnel walls. Although Jenna looked as pretty and perky as ever. Since we didn't know any history of the mine, I suggested to Mac that he might do a "mystery tunnel" type article, but he reminded me that Lightning and Jenna didn't want any publicity that might draw nosy tourists or amateur prospectors with foil lids on their heads.

Magnolia and Geoff came home with enthusiastic praise for date milkshakes, and we decided we'd go try one after we took BoBandy for a run.

Except this time Bo turned up something more important than a faded receipt.

Chapter 9

MAC

We took time for a quick lunch and then put on our hiking shoes and headed out to the old metal arch on the border of Prosperity. BoBandy chased lizards and barked at that old hole we'd found before. I stopped a couple of times to sniff the desert-scented air. Cactus and creosote bush, dry dirt and sunshine. Not the kind of perfume you'd find in a bottle at some expensive boutique, but a rather heady perfume nevertheless. *Nice touch, Lord!*

We went farther this time, heading for an interesting rock formation in the distance. Four-wheeler tire tracks cut deep in places, the tracks swirled where the driver had popped a wheelie or two.

I didn't pay much attention when BoBandy started barking again. He's great about not barking in the motorhome, but get him out running loose like this and he finds anything from a bird's nest in a cactus to a pile of old tin cans bark-worthy.

His barking at this other hole was persistent enough that I finally went over to see why. I expected to find him interested in anything from a sardine can to a tattered plastic sack, but what I saw was a humped oblong of rocks and dirt at the bottom of a wide hole.

I felt a sudden chill that was at odds with the sweat I'd worked up on our hike.

Of course, it was probably nothing. Weathering. Erosion.

But these rocks had a definite piled-up-by-human-hands look, and there were small pits in the sides of the large hole that showed where the rocks had been removed. I rejected the thought that instantly came to me about what might be buried under that body-sized mound of rocks. It could be the burial of a beloved St. Bernard. Disposal of a transmission.

But something was sticking out the far edge of the pile, a pale tan something.

Ivy was looking for rocks some distance away. I called her over. I didn't have to point out the pile of rocks and dirt or the something sticking out of them. She spotted them herself. And a moment later, before I could even suggest I might climb down into the hole, she was slipping and sliding down into it. BoBandy slipped and slid right behind her. Ivy touched the pale tan thing sticking out of the pile.

"It looks like the corner of a blanket," she said, and I slipped and slid into the hole too. It was shallower than the other holes we'd seen. Easier to get into and out of. Especially if you were carrying a body . . .

It occurred to me that we might be destroying evidence left by whoever had been in the hole before us. "Maybe we should call the sheriff's office or 911 before we touch anything more."

She stopped in mid-toss of a rock, a stricken look on her face.

"But then, if we call and they find someone just disposed of a pile of trash or an old mattress or two, they might not be too happy with us," I added.

Rationalization works. We dug.

It took us several minutes to toss aside enough rocks to uncover a blanket-wrapped something. Without ever touching the blanket itself, we both knew what was wrapped within it. The blanket-bundle had a giveaway size and shape.

Body.

A surprisingly neatly wrapped body. Buried under all the rocks, scavengers hadn't yet gotten to it, and the edges of the blanket, except for the corner that had showed on the surface, were carefully tucked in and held with a red cord and a neat, bow-tied knot.

IVY

Mac boosted me up so I could drape a handkerchief over the arm of a saguaro to mark the area. It's easy to lose track of a particular spot on the desert, which is probably how "lost mines" get lost. It's also difficult to describe a location on the desert, so Mac had told the woman on our cell-phone call to 911 that we'd meet the deputies at the Prosperity arch and show them the way. We hiked back there to wait.

"It looks as if whoever used the blanket to wrap something was a neat and tidy person," Mac said as we sat on a rock under the arch.

"And cared about what he, or she, was wrapping," I agreed.

We contemplated that thought for a few minutes until Mac finally said, "Warren Langston was a neat and tidy person."

Right. But Warren was the person who was missing. If that was him in the blanket, he certainly couldn't have wrapped himself up.

Jenna's mother's current husband, Hayden, was also neat and tidy. But would he and Jenna's mother have cared enough to wrap the body so carefully and fasten the blanket with a bow-tied knot?

I suspected that Jenna, if she were involved, would care enough to do it that way.

Would Lightning, if he'd killed his brother? Brother killing brother was as old as Cain killing Abel back in Biblical days. Had Cain felt remorseful afterward and buried his brother with an early-times version of a nice blanket and a bow-tied knot?

Was the body-wrapper the same person who had sent that diversionary postcard from Las Vegas? The body could have lain out here for weeks or months if we hadn't accidentally stumbled on it. Was that what the body-burier hoped for—months before it was found?

"Someone had to use a vehicle to bring the body out here," Mac pointed out. "But I didn't notice if there were tire tracks near the hole. Did you?"

I shook my head. Warren Langston's Jeep was missing. Had it been used to bring the body to the hole? If so, where was it now?

It took almost an hour for two deputies to arrive. We rode in their SUV to guide them over the rough ground to the handkerchief-marked spot. BoBandy sprawled on my lap.

From that point on, law enforcement took over. More deputies and official-looking cars, a couple of them highway patrol, and various other people arrived. Yellow crime scene tape went up, although it seemed rather insignificant enclosing a tiny square in the vast, empty space of the desert. I saw someone making casts of nearby tire tracks.

We were questioned briefly and then told we should wait back at the motorhome, that someone would come to interview us more extensively later. We didn't tell the deputy at that first brief questioning that we suspected the body was Warren Langston, but we did mention the found-and-lost body over at Deadeye. The deputy said they'd also talk to Magnolia later. He offered to drive us back to the motorhome, but we chose to walk.

We didn't talk much. Finding a dead body tends to have a subduing effect. Even BoBandy seemed restrained now. He didn't even bark at a rabbit that ran by and practically dared to be chased.

I went over and told Magnolia what we'd found and that an officer would be by to talk to her later about what she'd found at Deadeye. Then we sat in the motorhome and waited, and I did a lot of wondering.

I wondered if the body would be unwrapped there in the hole or transported somewhere else to be unwrapped. I wondered if there would be any identification on it. I wondered if one of the numerous vehicles we saw going out to the site belonged to the medical examiner.

I wondered if identification of the body was going to be a terrible shock for Jenna or if the shock would be that the body had been discovered so soon, that she was hoping it might not be found for weeks or months.

I wondered if Lightning had anything to do with the death. I wondered if Jenna's mother and stepfather were involved.

I wondered, rather hopefully, if the body was someone unknown to any of us, the killer just as unknown.

I wondered why that curiosity gene didn't take a hike and let me think thoughts on less murderous subjects. Like how to make a date milkshake. Or how much fun a honeymoon in San Felipe was going to be. But thoughts about the body and a possible killer stuck as if superglued to my brain.

Several hours passed before a sheriff's department vehicle parked beside the motorhome. Two officers got out. One officer went to Magnolia and Geoff's motorhome; the other came to our door. He set up a small machine to record the interview before asking questions.

This interview wasn't exactly soothing, but it was less disturbing than some I've had in the past when I seemed to be more suspect than helpful observer. Although there's something about talking to a law officer that makes you feel guilty even if you haven't done anything. His questions went all the way back to the original phone call from Magnolia that had brought us here to Prosperity and our search for the missing body in Deadeye. He asked us to come into the office the following day and sign statements. Before he left, he also said they couldn't require us to remain in the area, but they'd appreciate it if we would stay in case more questions arose.

Magnolia and Geoff came over and we rehashed everything. They'd had the same request to stick around, and their interview was also recorded. I eventually fixed a hamburger casserole for dinner. Just as we finished eating, Betsy Oldham showed up and said an officer had also questioned her. We rehashed it all again, although with her we didn't include our suspicions about anyone.

Betsy's fertile imagination suggested it was probably a drug cartel or Mafia killing, or maybe a government conspiracy to conceal the body of an alien found in a crashed spaceship.

Okay, I'd settle for that.

MAC

Going along with the officer's request, the next morning we drove in to sign our statements, then came home and hung around the motorhome. It wasn't good traveling weather anyway. The wind blew hard enough to rattle the walls of the motorhome. Although, blessedly, there were no trees nearby to send branches hurtling through the roof, as a wind had done to us on the northern California coast.

I spent the afternoon working on a freelance article from some research I'd done on the redwoods in that northern California area— no rush because it wasn't an editor-assigned article with a deadline. Ivy read a mystery on her e-book reader. She and Magnolia got together and tried a new recipe for a dish called Pasta and Pickles. They both decided it was not a keeper. Geoff and I silently agreed. Even the best cooks occasionally come up with a loser.

We wondered about the body, but no one seemed inclined to supply us with any information. An officer did come and talk to Magnolia again but not us. On the following day, the wind let up and just before noon Jenna's familiar little blue car pulled up beside the motorhome. Ivy opened the door as Jenna got out of her car.

"I thought I'd come by and let you know—" Jenna broke off, her lips compressed. She studied the piece of carpet we always spread out below the steps, but I could see she'd been crying. It was a long moment before she could continue.

"Come by and let you know about my dad. It was his body you found out here somewhere." She grabbed hold of the door to steady herself. "I just went in to Yuma and identified him."

Which apparently meant there had been no wallet with driver's license or other identification on the body. Did that mean this may have been a simple robbery by a stranger rather than a planned murder with a personal motive? Jenna had said her father tended to carry quite a lot of cash on him.

"He looked . . . strange. Kind of . . . discolored. But maybe it was just that I-I've never seen a dead person before."

I wanted to ask, *Strange how?* Were there gunshots or knife wounds visible? Some other indications of how he'd died? But I didn't want to put Jenna through any more misery, and I could tell Ivy didn't want to, either, because she just reached out and hugged Jenna.

"Oh, sweetie, I'm so sorry. Would you like to come in and sit down for a bit? You look so tired."

Tired. Bedraggled. Beaten down. Grief stricken. Lost. I felt a little guilty about my earlier suspicions of her. This was not a young woman who had anything to do with her father's death. She probably shouldn't even be driving.

She straightened her sagging shoulders. "Thanks, but I should get back to the trailer. One of the deputies said they'd be out soon to look at Dad's place."

Look at. Which I was sure meant, in more blunt words, *search.* I wondered if they needed a search warrant for a dead person's residence or if it was just a standard step in an investigation.

"My mother is on her way here too. I called her right after I talked to Mike. He said I should." She glanced at her watch. "She might already be at the trailer because that was a couple hours ago."

She did not sound enthusiastic about the mother's visit, and I momentarily wondered why the woman was coming. It didn't seem likely she was all that broken up over an ex-husband's death.

"That's good of her," Ivy said. "You need family support at a time such as this."

Of course, that was the reason, I realized after Ivy pointed it out. Family support. Mother coming to offer her daughter help and comfort. Not for any of the number of ulterior reasons that had instantly shot suspicious darts into my mind.

"She says she wants to help," Jenna said.

"Is her husband coming too?" I asked.

"No," Jenna said, "but she said he could be here in a few hours if we need him."

"Have you told Lightning about your dad yet?"

"He's over in LA meeting with that production company again. I tried to call him but he didn't answer his phone, and I didn't want to just leave him a voice mail. He and Dad had their differences, but I'm sure this is going to hit him pretty hard." As a kind of afterthought, she added, "I'm supposed to feed the horses while he's gone." She sounded vague about that, as if at the moment she wasn't sure what horses were or how to feed them.

"What about Mike?" Ivy asked.

"He's coming over as soon as he can."

I was curious about whether she knew any more about how her father had died. Asking when she was so upset seemed insensitive, so I didn't do that, but on her own she came up with a different bit of information.

"They found his Jeep. It was parked at a mechanic's shop in Yuma. His wallet and almost two thousand dollars were in it. The shop owner assumed someone had left the Jeep for repair and would be in to make arrangements about it, so it wasn't immediately reported as abandoned."

Which meant what? The wallet and money in it were stronger indication that this was not a robbery that had expanded into murder.

Had Warren left the Jeep there, or had someone dumped it in an effort to further delay or confuse the situation?

"We're so sorry about all this. We know what a loss it is for you." Ivy didn't make some generalized offer to help, as most people would. She came up with something specific. "How about if we follow you out to Deadeye? We'll feed the horses and take care of anything else that needs doing until your mother or Mike gets there."

Jenna visibly tried to pull herself together, lifting her chin determinedly. "I can do it," she said. It didn't work. She blinked and pulled a tissue out of her pocket to wipe her eyes and managed to smile wanly.

"Or maybe not. Yes, I'd appreciate it if you'd come with me."

Chapter 10

IVY

We followed Jenna to her trailer. I noted that someone had been out to Deadeye and put yellow crime scene tape across the gate. Which must mean the authorities were giving credence to the idea that Warren Langston's dead body buried out on the desert was the same dead body Magnolia had found on the street in Deadeye.

Jenna just sat there in her car for a few moments, as if unable to muster the energy to get out. Mac opened the car door and offered his arm for help. She grabbed onto him as if she were drowning, and he helped her up the step to the trailer.

She was fumbling with her key at the trailer door when a silver sedan whipped around our pickup and parked beside Jenna's car. As usual, I'm no good at car identification, but I could see the Mercedes name on the rear of the vehicle. A tall, slim woman with dark hair that qualified as a romance-heroine's lush mane slid out of the car.

"Mom!" Jenna sounded as if she was trying to inject enthusiasm into her voice. "I didn't expect you so soon."

"I came as fast as I could. I didn't want you trying to cope with this all alone."

Mom may not have managed big success as a model, but she emanated an enviable energy and was certainly a striking woman. Her skinny-legged jeans fit the way skinny-legged jeans are supposed to fit, and her legs looked long and lean enough to kick the moon. Her tunic was a bold design of geometric shapes, and her black boots were sleek and high-heeled.

Not exactly a mourning outfit.

Mom gave us a curious look, and Jenna managed an introduction, including that we were friends who'd done much to help her. Mom's name was Sable. I wondered if she'd always had the name or if she'd adopted it as a brand when she was a model to fit that tumble of lush, dark hair. *Snarky, Ivy,* I chastised myself. And why? I didn't even know the woman. No need to be having snarky thoughts about her. At least not yet.

She thanked us profusely for helping her daughter and then added to Jenna, "There are things that need to be done, and I'm here to help." She put an arm around her daughter's shoulders and gave me a dismissive look that plainly said, *I'm here now. She doesn't need you anymore.*

"What things?" Jenna sounded totally blank.

I didn't expect Sable to elaborate right there, but she instantly got down to the nitty-gritty. "There's the will, of course. We need to find that right away. And you need to keep on top of the stock market account. We need to make arrangements about burial too."

She hasn't gotten inside Jenna's trailer yet, hasn't even been here five minutes or offered a word of comfort, but she's already churning up a whirlwind about a will and getting her ex-husband planted in the ground. Did she think she might be in the will, even though she and Jenna's father were long divorced?

"Won't his lawyer have all that?" Jenna asked.

"Possibly. Do you even know the lawyer's name?" Sable answered the question herself. "I doubt it, given how secretive Warren was." She glanced toward Warren's double-wide. "But maybe we can find it in his office. We really should go over there immediately. Do you have any idea how soon a death certificate will be available?"

Jenna looked horrified at the mention of a death certificate, and I was appalled too. Mother Sable seemed to have a rather high-powered help agenda in mind. Yes, Jenna would need a death certificate. Numerous copies of it, I'd guess, remembering long ago when my husband Harley died. But surely her mother could be a little more sensitive than rushing Jenna into all this right now.

"You have a key to his house, don't you?" Sable asked.

"The deputy said someone would be out soon to look around. I don't think we should be prowling around and touching things in there before they get here."

"They're going to *search* the house?" Sable threw up her hands in horror. She sounded as appalled as if a herd of vandals was en route. "Jenna, you can't let them do that! What you need is a lawyer. *Now*, before—"

"Mom, I don't *care* about any of that right now. Let them search!" A blaze of anger sparked on Jenna's tired face. "I know you didn't care about him anymore, but I do!"

Sable drew herself up even taller. "Sweetie, you don't need to get all huffy with *me*. I know how devastating this is for you—your father not only dead, but *murdered*. I'm just trying to *help*."

"I know, but . . ."

"Warren may have left instructions in or with his will about what he wanted in the way of final arrangements. Which is another reason we should go over to his place right away before—"

Jenna's anger at her mother blazed again. "Mom, all I'm interested in right now is finding out who killed him."

"Oh, sweetie, of course that's the most important thing. We'll do everything possible to find out who did this." Sable squeezed her arm around Jenna's shoulders again, but it was only a semi-retreat from her main agenda. "But we have to be practical. You don't know what the authorities may haul off, and if the will is in something they take, it may not be available for *months*."

I didn't know if that was true or not, but it certainly made plain where Sable's priorities lay. It seemed unlikely to me that she stood to gain from the will, but I tried to give her the benefit of the doubt. She was probably just hyped-up in an over-eagerness to help her daughter.

I didn't want to abandon Jenna, but I also didn't think we should get in the middle of a family skirmish. So I said, "We'll run over and feed the horses now, okay? We'll be back in a few minutes."

MAC

The horses gave us welcoming whinnies and trotted across the big corral to meet us. I opened a bale of hay, the scent fresh and sweet, and Ivy scooped grain into the feed buckets. The water tank was full, an automatic valve apparently keeping it that way.

That's all there was to the task of "feeding the horses," not exactly a monumental undertaking, but we hung around for another fifteen minutes, picking up droppings in the corral and socializing with the horses. Ivy scratched one on the shoulder, and we both laughed as the big buckskin stretched out his neck and wiggled his upper lip in horsey delight. But our delay was mostly to give Jenna and her mother a little time to smooth out their differences.

The smoothing, however, apparently resulted in a victory for Sable, because when we got back to Jenna's trailer, Sable and Jenna were just entering Warren's front door. I wondered if it was still unlocked or if Jenna had produced a key.

"Should we go over and help?" Ivy asked.

"I don't know what we could do to help. The computer is surely where Jenna will have to look for information, and we aren't exactly computer experts."

Ivy gave me an exasperated glance. "You're going to make me admit that I'm just curious, aren't you? That I'm wondering why Jenna's mother is so gung ho to snoop around in her ex-husband's affairs."

"She says she wants to help."

"I think it's more than that."

I sometimes worry about Ivy's curiosity getting her into trouble—and it has—but I gave this a moment's thought and couldn't see any danger here. I made a grand gesture toward Warren's double-wide. "Then, by all means, let's check it out."

We walked the short distance, and Ivy made the formal gesture of knocking rather than just barging in. Sable opened the door.

"You're leaving now? It's been good meeting you, and thanks so much for helping Jenna in this tragic time—"

"We thought perhaps we could be of some help here," Ivy said.

"Thanks, but we just need to collect a little information from the computer, and Jenna is quite familiar with using her father's computer so—"

"No, I am not familiar with his computer!" Jenna came to the door of the office, still clutching the wireless mouse to the computer. "I told you, all I can get into is my e-mail and an internet connection for research for my book, and that is *exactly* all I can do. Dad has everything else password protected, and I have no idea what the password is. I hardly ever even used this computer."

I couldn't tell if she was upset that she couldn't get into most of the computer's contents or if the upset came from her mother pushing her into doing this.

"That's so unfair of him," Sable complained. She looked at us again. "Shutting his own daughter out of information she should have access to. Information she *needs* to have access to. But that's the way he always was. Secretive as a government spy."

"Umm," Ivy said. Her favorite non-comment.

Sable turned back to her daughter. "But we'll manage, sweetie. There's still the filing cabinet."

"It's locked."

Now I was certain Jenna sounded mildly triumphant, as if she felt a definite satisfaction in finding that her father had outmaneuvered Sable again.

Sable gave a ladylike roll of eyes. "That is so like Warren. When we divorced, I even had to hire a private investigator to locate all his—all *our*, actually—assets."

Jenna looked as if she was about to make some caustic remark, but instead she abruptly burst into tears. "I feel like a-a *vulture* trying to snoop around in everything. Dad is dead! I don't want to do this!" Tears didn't streak her makeup because she wasn't wearing any, but she grabbed a tissue and stalked down the hallway to the bathroom. Perhaps to make facial repairs. Or maybe just to get away from Mom.

IVY

"Oh, poor Jennie. Maybe I am rushing her," Sable said. "But I'm so worried."

"It's a worrisome situation," I agreed.

"But there's more than you know. Her father was murdered, and I'm worried that Jennie may also be in danger."

That thought hadn't even occurred to me. "Why would she be in danger?"

"Well . . ." Sable looked around furtively, as if some listening figure might be lurking behind the drapes. "Maybe I shouldn't say anything . . ."

A statement that often suggests a certain eagerness *to* say something. Possibly even that it would take unexpected vocal paralysis to keep it from being said.

"The thing is, from what Jenna says, what he's let her *think,* Warren has done very well with his day-trading. But I can't believe that. He was never all that clever with the stock market when we were married.

I've long suspected his story about day-trading was really to cover up the real source of income."

"Even in this time of low interest rates, he surely had income coming from all he made on the IPO offering," I said.

"Hayden has always thought there was something fishy about that too."

"I'm not sure what you're getting at."

"Blackmail! That's what I'm getting at. *Blackmail.*"

"You think someone was blackmailing Warren?"

"No, of course not." This time her eye roll put me in my place.

Then it got through to me, and I was taken aback by this unexpected accusation. "You mean you think Warren was blackmailing someone?"

She nodded forcefully. "Yes! And whoever it was got tired of paying off and killed him."

"That's what you thought Jenna might find on the computer? Information about a person he was blackmailing? How much he was receiving?"

"Warren was an absolute fanatic about keeping records of everything."

Remembering that calendar record in the bathroom, I could agree with that.

"That's why he had everything on the computer protected with a password," Sable added. "So Jenna couldn't see any of it."

Mac and I exchanged a quick glance. Did this mean there was a line missing on our list of suspects, a killer who was totally outside our radar?

Mac had been silent, but now he said, "I think this is something you should tell the deputies or detectives about immediately."

"Yes, I suppose so, but I hate to disillusion Jenna about her father."

Not disillusioning Jenna about her father's possible involvement in blackmail sounded semi-noble, but Jenna would obviously have found out about it if the computer search Sable had demanded had been successful.

Sable broke off as Jenna came back down the hall, her face scrubbed and her hairline damp. I don't know if she intended to go back to work on the computer or tell her mother to just forget this snooping, but a knock on the door startled us all.

Jenna pulled herself together and opened the door. Two uniformed officers stood there and two more were getting out of a second vehicle. Obviously not a social call. One of the officers handed her an official-looking paper and announced that they were here to do a search of the premises and would leave a list of all items removed when they were done. Sable stepped up as if she were about to do an over-my-dead-body objection, but Jenna stuck out an arm and blocked her. Personally, I figured that searching the double-wide for any possible clues to Warren's killer was a good thing.

Were they working on a theory that Warren had been killed here and then buried in that hole out on the desert? But if that were true, why would the killer have done a stopover with the body on the street out in Deadeye?

Sable gave her daughter an *I-told-you-so* look and muttered something about never finding out anything now. But we all exited like good citizens and went over to watch from Jenna's trailer.

Sable was right about one thing. She and Jenna weren't going to be snooping in Warren's computer or file cabinet anymore, even if they could find a password or keys. Within minutes, the deputies hauled both computer and file cabinet out to one of the SUVs and then, after another hour of searching, drove away. If they took anything else with them, it wasn't something large enough for us to see. I remembered they were required to leave a list showing whatever they'd taken. We were all inside Jenna's little trailer by then. Sable, although her nose wrinkled with distaste at her daughter's choice in coffee, had made instant coffee for everyone.

I could tell Mac thought it was time to leave, but I wanted to know more about this blackmail suspicion of Sable's. I was trying to figure out how to talk to her again alone, and, unexpectedly, the opportunity arose. Mike's van drove in only a couple of minutes after the official vehicles drove away. Jenna gave a little cry and ran out to meet him.

Chapter 11

IVY

"I don't believe you've met Mike, have you?" I said to Sable as we watched him jump out of the van and wrap Jenna in a hug.

"No, but I've seen his paintings. Have you seen the one he did of Jenna? Awesome! I'm sure he'll be of much help to her during this terrible time." In spite of her enthusiastic words, Sable's eyebrows scrunched in a frown, and I suspected Mike was not really up to her standards for a prospective son-in-law. She'd probably have an even dimmer view of him if she saw the tiny trailer in which he lived. I wondered how Warren had felt about him.

"Almost certainly someone from his days back at Craigmont. As head of the accounting department, he had access to personal information about a lot of people. Company people, of course, but also stars in some of their movies. He told me once how much a certain star's breast augmentation had cost. He was the kind of man who probably had a file somewhere labeled Dirty Secrets of the Rich and Famous."

Warren blackmailing some wealthy movie celebrity? On a practical basis, I wouldn't think blackmail would be a time-consuming endeavor, and from what Jenna had said, Warren had spent considerable time on the computer. Which sounded more like day-trading than blackmail to me. Even so, the investigators should know about this, and I repeated Mac's earlier statement to her about telling them.

"I know. I'll probably have to do it." Big sigh. "But the worst part will be telling Jenna. As I said before, I hate to disillusion her about her father. Although it's always disturbed me that he helped her waste all this time in her life on writing a *book*. When she was a girl, I bought her a diary and she never wrote a word in it."

Which obviously meant Sable had sneaked into the diary to see what her daughter had to say. Smart Jenna, not writing anything in it.

"Will you be staying for a while?" I asked.

"I was supposed to be with my husband at an important fundraising dinner tomorrow evening, but helping Jenna is more important, of course. I'll be here as long as she needs me."

Sable's tunic was a bit colorful to qualify as sackcloth, but her virtuous tone suggested full martyr status.

Jenna brought Mike in and introduced him to her mother. Sable made a gushy show of being so glad to finally meet him. I asked Mike about his mother. He said she claimed she was fine.

"But I have some doubts. She's had some serious bouts of depression ever since Dad died, but she doesn't want to worry me."

I gave Sable a surreptitious glance. She made a little murmur of sympathy, but another scrunch of eyebrows said to me this put Mike even farther down on any prospective-son-in-law list; her daughter didn't need a depressed mother-in-law in addition to the financial limitations of an artist/housepainter husband. I strongly suspected she'd try to persuade Jenna to move away from Deadeye Heights as soon as possible.

**

We felt rather at loose ends driving back to the motorhome. We could leave on our honeymoon now. The law enforcement people might prefer we stay around, but we didn't have to. Jenna didn't really need our help; her mother and Mike were both there for her. But . . .

"I don't feel very honeymoon-ish," I admitted.

Mac didn't ask what brought that on. "No rush," he said. Then he voiced what I was already thinking. "If neither Sable nor Jenna tells the authorities about the possibility of Warren being killed by someone he was blackmailing, we should probably do it."

I nodded. "But I'm reluctant to say anything unless there's more proof than Jenna's mother's suspicions. Although if there *is* a blackmailee-turned-killer, there may be reason to be concerned about Jenna's safety. He might think Jenna knows whatever her father knew, or at least has access to the information."

"Right."

There was not a lot to do around Prosperity. Magnolia and Geoff had said they were driving up to take a look around Gila Bend, and their car wasn't at the motorhome. We decided on another hike out through Prosperity, which BoBandy greeted with enthusiastic approval, of course.

I couldn't see any vehicles out where we'd found Warren's body, and when we reached the hole, we saw that the yellow crime scene tape had been removed. There had been so much activity from people and vehicles around the hole that tracks of all kinds scarred the hard earth now. It looked as if there had been a convention of do-si-do-ing square dancers. We stood at the edge of the hole, the edges now crumbled, and looked down at where the body had been. The peaceful silence and the dry desert scents were at odds with what we'd found here.

"This isn't a place a killer would stumble on by accident," I said.

Mac nodded. "The killer would have to know about it beforehand. The corner of the blanket showing above the rocks suggests the body was buried at night. If it were in daylight, the person doing the burying would surely have noticed it."

"A really hard place to find at night."

We contemplated that until Mac finally said what I was also thinking. "Lightning has lived around here for years. He knows the area. He was also out here looking for gold, according to Mrs. Oldham. Maybe he even dug this hole back then."

Would the person being blackmailed, if there was someone being blackmailed, know the area as well as Lightning did, well enough to use this as a burying site? Was it possible Lightning was the person Warren had been blackmailing? Doubtful. From all we've seen, Lightning didn't have that kind of money.

BoBandy started barking at something over beyond a cluster of cholla cactus. Mac and I looked at each other, thinking the worst. Another body. . .

No. This was more standard BoBandy. He was barking at an empty beer bottle. The bottle was not a clue, however. It had been out here long enough that the label was almost weathered away. I picked it up anyway, doing my one-piece-at-a-time effort to help clean up the planet. The Lord gave it to us clean, and I figured we should make an effort to keep it that way.

We went back to the motorhome, and I took Koop for a shorter stroll around the RV park. We still had never met anyone living here. Had the deputies talked to any of the unseen residents to find out if they'd seen or heard anything? Magnolia and Geoff came over when they got home. By now we'd had enough Lightning westerns to last for a while, and that evening we watched an old Steve Martin comedy on DVD. Next day Mac and I decided to go in to Dateland and try their date milkshakes, which proved well worth the trip. By late afternoon we were again feeling restless, and Mac came up with the idea that we should check on the horses, that maybe Jenna would forget to feed them.

A rather anemic reason for a trip out there, but it worked for me.

Neither Jenna's little car nor her mother's Mercedes was present when we arrived. No pickup at Lightning's mobile; no official vehicles at Warren's double-wide. Deadeye Heights seemed abandoned until a horse whinnied at us. Jenna hadn't forgotten the horses; hay still spilled out of the feeders. We gave them a little scratching and attention and were just about to leave when Jenna's little blue çar pulled up beside our pickup. I walked over to the car as she rolled down the window.

"Thanks for checking on the horses again. I appreciate it. We were halfway to the highway this morning before I remembered I was supposed to feed them and turned around to come back and do it." She made an effort to sound perky, but grief and weariness dragged her pretty face down.

I looked around, wondering where her mother was.

"Mom went home. I convinced her there was nothing more she could do here."

"Does she want you to move up to Scottsdale as soon as possible?"

"How'd you guess?" Jenna smiled wryly. "We drove into Yuma . . . her car, of course, because she won't ride in mine . . . and made arrangements to have Dad cremated when his body is released, no services. Did you know they did an *autopsy* on him?" She shuddered.

"I think they usually do that in . . . your father's type of death."

We still didn't know exactly how Warren had died, except there seemed no doubt that it was murder, but I didn't want to upset her further by asking for details.

She swallowed and added, "The deputies left a filled-out form after they finished searching Dad's place. They didn't take anything other than the computer and file cabinet."

Apparently the calendar in the bathroom didn't interest them, although I didn't mention that to Jenna.

"After Mom left, I drove back to Tacna to see Mike. I appreciate Mom coming, but I didn't want her to stay any longer. Mom has so much *drive,* she wears me out. But then, after she was gone . . ."

Drive translated to *push,* I suspected. Even so, with Sable gone, I could see that Deadeye Heights must have felt empty as a graveyard for Jenna. And with certain unpleasant similarities.

"But Mike was just leaving to go over to San Diego. His mother fell in the laundry room at her RV park."

"A serious fall?"

"She hit her head on the concrete floor. Not life-threatening, but she's in the hospital."

"Give him our hopes for a quick recovery, will you?"

"I'll do that. When Mom and I were in Yuma, we also learned that it will probably be several days, maybe even a couple of weeks, before an official death certificate is issued. Mom wanted me to try to hurry them up on that, and we got in a big argument because I wouldn't do it."

Why was Sable in such a rush for a death certificate? Apparently Jenna had also wondered.

"I guess it's kind of a . . . you know . . . closure thing for her."

I wasn't convinced, but I nodded. "Did you talk to the sheriff's department while you were in town?"

"You're asking if Mom told them about Dad being a blackmailer. That his victim might have killed him."

So, Mom did reveal her blackmailing suspicions to Jenna. So much for not disillusioning her about her father.

"I told her I didn't think we needed to do that. If he was blackmailing someone, I'm sure there'll be a record of payments on his computer. He was like that, a record of everything. Their experts will get past that password protection and find it, if it's there." Another wry smile. "Given how picky Dad was as an accountant, he probably even reported payments from a blackmailer on his tax returns."

I wondered how you report blackmail on a tax return. Probably there were creative accounting words to cover it. Privacy enhancement protection? Information security shield?

"But you don't really think there was any blackmail," I guessed.

Sigh. "I don't know. I don't like to think it, but . . ." She let the thought trail off. "But Mom is right, of course, about my needing the will. And the name of Dad's lawyer. I wish he'd shared that much with me."

"You know, I was thinking . . ." I hesitated, not wanting to push her the way her mother did but wanting to help. "Have you considered all those boxes in the storage rooms at your dad's place? The original will wouldn't be there, I'm sure, but there might be a copy. And possibly correspondence with his lawyer that would at least give you his name."

"That's true! I was so mad at Mom wanting to snoop around in Dad's records. I just didn't think it was any of her business. He never quizzed me about *her*. But there are things I do need to find." She looked along the bare stretch of hard dirt to Warren's double-wide. "And if he *was* blackmailing someone . . ."

"I'll be glad to help," I offered.

Okay, the curiosity gene was like a racehorse in the starting gate, eager to run, but I really did want to help Jenna if I could.

"I'd appreciate that." She looked at the sun setting in a dark bank of clouds off to the west. Her shoulders sagged. "But not right now. It's too late, and I'm beat. Tomorrow?"

"What about your being alone out here tonight?"

"I've been here alone before. And Lightning called earlier today to say he'll be getting home late tonight."

"That's good."

"I don't know why he bothered to call." She sounded fretful now, almost annoyed with Lightning. "It isn't as if we keep track of each other's comings and goings."

"Did you tell him about your dad?" Although my wary thought was that only the finding of the body might be news to Lightning; he may already have personal knowledge about his brother's death and where the body was buried under those rocks. Was the phone call to Jenna basically to find out what kind of situation he might be walking into when he got home?

"I didn't intend to tell him until I could do it in person, but he asked if I knew anything more about what your friend found over in Deadeye. So I told him."

"How did he take it?"

"I'm not sure. I mean, he said all the right things. He even kind of choked up. He said he'd do anything he could to help find out who did it. But . . ."

"But?" I repeated.

"Lightning is an actor."

**

I was back the next morning, a bright and sunny day. It might even be bikini weather, if I were a bikini sort of person. But, since I'm just me, I was wearing old denim shorts and a T-shirt with "My Invisible LOL" printed across the front, a red heart on each side of the words.

The T-shirt was a custom-made gift from Mac gently teasing me about the feeling I've had for some time that I've aged into invisibility. So often people just don't seem to *see* me. The message might be confusing if the LOL is interpreted as Laughing Out Loud, from the usual internet usage, but it actually stood for Little Old Lady. Which all together made a claim that I was Mac's invisible little old lady. Which I was proud to be.

Mac and I had talked it over and decided he couldn't be of any help prowling through Warren's boxes today, so I'd come alone. He and Geoff were planning to dig into the inner workings of the generator on Geoff's motorhome. Geoff thought it wasn't running quite right.

Lightning's pickup was parked by his mobile, but I didn't see him around anywhere. Warren's door was unlocked when Jenna and I reached his double-wide, and she said that she hadn't been locking it because she didn't have a key to get back in. "Which says something about Dad's and my relationship, I suppose," she added.

"Did you have a key when you lived with him?"

"No. I asked him about it a couple of times, but he kept 'forgetting' to have one made for me."

Yes, that said something about Warren's relationship with his daughter and the man himself. Maybe dear old Dad *was* the kind of person to have hidden secrets about blackmailing someone.

We went inside. The room felt cool, almost chilly, in spite of the warmth outside. I wished I'd worn something other than shorts. Jenna left the door open to let some of the outside warmth in.

We went first to the office and looked to see if anything that might hold records had been left behind by the search team. Warren's desk and well-filled bookcases were still there. We looked through the desk drawers, but they held only neatly organized office supplies. Doesn't everyone have a messy junk drawer holding some loose change, a stray mint, and a key that fits no known lock? Not Warren.

Something could, of course, be hidden in the pages of one of the many books on the shelves, but the thought of pulling out each book and flipping through it was rather like trying to dig through an anthill to find one specific ant.

We went to the bedroom that had briefly been Jenna's room and which now held shelves lined with boxes, more boxes piled on the floor. The boxes were exactly alike, as if Warren bought them by the truckload. The room had a strangely morgue-like feeling.

"It's rather . . . intimidating, isn't it?" Jenna said.

"The boxes all seem to be labeled. Maybe that will help." The labels were also exactly alike, a uniform 2 x 3 inches, wording in the same computer font on each label.

I read labels as we circled the room slowly. I knew it was probably too much to hope for that we'd find a helpful *Will* label, and we didn't. Neither was there a *Dirty Secrets of the Rich and Famous* box. I did expect an orderly arrangement to the boxes, given the orderly sort of man Warren seemed to be, but if there was some overall plan, I couldn't discern it.

What we found was a whole row of boxes labeled *Miscellaneous Receipts,* each box with a year to date it. I peeked into one from a dozen years ago, long before Warren came to Deadeye. Grocery receipts from Safeway (oranges, oatmeal, broccoli), drugstore receipts from Walgreens (antacids, laxative, shaving cream), underwear from some outlet store I'd never heard of. The receipt indicated Warren wore boxer shorts, a fact I really didn't need to know. Apparently he hadn't yet made the big bucks on the IPO, because these expenses looked fairly frugal. One showed a return of three grapefruit for a cash refund.

What the man should have done was read a few books on how to downsize your clutter. Or better yet, he should have lit an enormous bonfire.

We finally decided to start with the top shelf on the left and just work our way through the boxes. Jenna said that if her father actually had any records here about blackmail that he may have purposely mislabeled the box.

She took the first box, labeled *Property – California.* She had to stand on a stepstool to drag it down. I took the second box, labeled *Property – Arizona.* Inside my box I found records on getting the double-wide set up here. There were the big expenses: cost of the manufactured home itself, payment for extending the electric line, drilling the well. But also $4.79 for duct tape and $1.19 for screws to put up a hook in the garage.

I also found confirmation in this box of something Jenna had said earlier: Warren and Lightning had originally bought the property together. And the ownership was set up with right of survivor.

Lightning definitely had something to gain by Warren's death.

I moved on to *Single Socks.* Not a record of socks but a box of actual socks without mates. *Keys.* A lightweight box that rattled. Inside, four keys that Warren apparently couldn't identify. Although I had to admire that low number. Over the years I've collected enough unknown keys to sink a rowboat.

After digging through everything from records of dates coyotes had wandered onto the property and a box of recipes marked *Bad recipes*, D*o not use,* I finally came to something that looked more worthwhile, a box labeled *Divorce*. In it was a record of expenses and details of various meetings and correspondence with a lawyer, Roger Neville. Was he still Warren's lawyer? I set aside a page with his name and phone number on it.

Then I found something more disturbing. Before the divorce, Warren had hired a private detective to investigate his wife's activities, obviously with a suspicion of infidelity. I perched on the arm of the lone easy chair to read further.

With a wary glance at Jenna, not certain she should see this, I skimmed through the reports. Sable went on a weekend trip to Tijuana without Warren. Another trip to Lake Tahoe. She went out to lunch frequently, often to rather expensive restaurants. She shopped as if it were a full-time job.

However, the report on the Tijuana and Tahoe trips showed them to be just girlfriends having fun; no males involved. The lunches were merely solo or girlfriend excursions; she ate salads at expensive restaurants with them, but she occasionally slipped and indulged in a burrito at Taco Bell or a peanut butter parfait at Dairy Queen. Her shopping excursions were dedicated to shoes, handbags, and makeup, not excuses for meeting some man.

By the time I finished the reports, I was rather shocked at how much money Sable must have spent that she concealed from Warren, but also a little annoyed that Warren had snooped into his wife's innocent activities, obviously with the idea of finding something to use as leverage in the divorce.

Warren had larger secrets. These appeared in reports from a different private investigator, the one Sable had used, revealing the assets he'd concealed from her. I wondered how Warren had managed to acquire reports from *her* investigator, reports that showed he'd concealed everything from bank accounts to property ownership from her. A man of devious means and, altogether, a picture of an unhappy marriage loaded with secrets and suspicion. Had he also used a private investigator to collect incriminating information on people whom he then blackmailed?

At the bottom of the box were the actual divorce papers and property settlement. I hesitated. Reading the details of their sneaky maneuverings was beginning to feel almost voyeuristic. Yet a need to be thorough in our search . . . plus maybe an over-the-cliff shove from that mutant curiosity gene . . . made me read the divorce papers too.

On page four I found the reason Sable was so eager to obtain a death certificate.

And an excellent motive for murder.

Chapter 12

IVY

I was so wrapped up in this startling discovery that I jumped when Jenna spoke.

"Mom was wrong about Dad." She was sitting cross-legged on the floor with files scattered all around her, and she sounded triumphant, almost gleeful. "He was making good money, *great money*, with his day-trading. I've just been through three boxes of stock market records and there are six more to go. He didn't need to blackmail anyone for money."

I knew that must be a relief for her, although I wasn't totally convinced. Blackmailing could still be a profitable sideline, especially for a man who didn't seem to have much going in his life other than making money.

She looked up and saw me clutching the divorce papers. "Have you found something?"

I hesitated. Was there any point in her seeing these papers that revealed various less-than-admirable activities of both parents? The divorce papers also showed a powerful motive for her mother to kill Warren, but Sable couldn't have done it. Apparently recognizing that I'd found something more significant than mateless socks, Jenna jumped up and grabbed the papers before I could decide whether or not to show her what I'd found. She came to page four with an admirable reading speed. She gave a little gasp.

"This says her alimony would end if she remarried, which it must have, a long time ago. But Dad was required to keep a life insurance policy in force no matter what, with Mom as beneficiary." She looked up at me, eyes wide in shock. "Mom gets two million dollars of insurance money now that he's dead! That's why she's so anxious to get a death certificate!"

Jenna obviously made an immediate money-murder connection, but she shook her head in instant denial. "I know there were hard feelings when they divorced, and Mom never had anything good to say about Dad. But she never would have *killed* him, no matter how much money was involved!"

I privately suspected Sable may well have wanted her ex-husband dead so she could get at that insurance money, but what Jenna was saying, that she couldn't have killed him, was true. Although not for the generic Mom's-not-a-killer reason Jenna was thinking. It was the timing.

"Magnolia found the body over in Deadeye before you got home. You and your mother were both in New York when your dad was killed."

Jenna swallowed. Her gaze played uncomfortably over the scattered stock market reports she'd been studying. "Actually, that isn't quite . . . right. I stayed in New York four days after Mom and Hayden flew home. I'd managed to set up appointments with several literary agents so I changed my ticket without telling Mom until the last minute so she wouldn't have a chance to change her ticket too. I didn't want her to stay and do something that might sabotage my appointments. Mom is . . . not enthusiastic about my writing."

Not enthusiastic. A nice euphemism, considering that Sable had said Jenna was wasting her time trying to write a book. Although Jenna's use of "sabotage" now was fairly blunt.

A wry tilt of Jenna's head. "Not that my scheming did me any good. The agents all turned me down."

"Was your mother upset that you didn't come home when she did?"

"Actually, she took it better than I expected."

Maybe with good reason. Jenna's change of plans may have opened an unexpected window of opportunity for Sable. Knowing Jenna would be away for several days, she could have rushed down here after she got back to Scottsdale, killed Warren, and scurried home again.

A time line that apparently became as obvious to Jenna as it was to me, along with something I didn't know. "Mom knew Lightning wouldn't be here either. I'd mentioned his going over to LA to talk about a new movie production in Deadeye. She knew Dad was here alone." She said it with a kind of dread in her voice. A road sign to murder.

I couldn't think of anything but my ever ready, "Umm."

"Two million dollars. Two *million*." Jenna breathed the words as if they were an evil incantation. "Mom has . . . expensive tastes, but she's never had that kind of money."

"But Warren's body was removed from the street over in Deadeye and hidden very quickly in the short time Magnolia went back to the motorhome parked at the gate. Your mother didn't know enough about the town to do that, did she? Then it was moved again, over to Prosperity. Surely she didn't know the area well enough to do *that*. And somehow I doubt she could have done all that carrying and moving alone."

"Mom's in good shape. She works out at a gym twice a week, and she has a couple of fancy machines at home that both she and Hayden work out on. She ran a half marathon last year. And Dad wasn't a big man like Lightning. He didn't weigh much more than Mom."

So Mom had the muscle and strength to carry her not-big ex-husband around like a sack of onions. And she definitely had the motive. Jenna's earlier declaration that her mother couldn't have killed Warren was rapidly evaporating.

"But there's still the matter of her being totally unfamiliar with Deadeye and Prosperity," I pointed out. "And the Jeep was found in another location entirely."

"Maybe she didn't hide the body herself. Maybe she hired someone who knows the area. Maybe she even hired someone to kill him."

Most of us don't have a hired killer on speed dial. Although there was another possibility. "Would her husband help?"

Jenna tilted her head thoughtfully. "Hayden? Maybe. But I doubt it. Hayden isn't really *wimpy*. He's in pretty good shape, actually, but he'd rather use charm than muscle to accomplish anything. I once heard someone say that he could 'charm the socks off a giraffe.' Whatever that means. I'm not sure if it was a compliment or a complaint. I think a lot of the women golfers find him *quite* charming."

"Oh?" I hesitated. "You think—?" I left the question open-ended.

"Well, I have to admit I've wondered," Jenna said. "But Mom's never seemed concerned. Actually, I've always figured he'd make a great con man. But not a *murderer*. The sight of blood makes him go weak in the knees. I remember when I was cutting up a cantaloupe in the kitchen one time, I cut my hand really bad. I was bleeding all over the counter and floor, and he accidentally stepped in a puddle of blood and practically fainted."

"Umm."

"Then one time our yard maintenance man was using the Weed-Eater and a rock flew up and cut his head. When Hayden saw all the blood, he just keeled over and hit his own head. And then when he saw his own blood, he really had a meltdown. He needed an ambulance more than the guy did." She shook her head. "I can't imagine him doing something *messy*. He gets a little greenish just getting a steak that's too rare. When I was a teenager and still living with them, I was sometimes tempted to stick a piece of raw liver in front of him just to see what would happen."

We still didn't know how Warren had been killed, but I was pretty sure he hadn't been charmed to death. There must have been blood, though we hadn't seen any within that toothpaste outline Magnolia had drawn. But people sometimes do things we could never envision them capable of doing. Who'd envision me, an invisible LOL, getting involved with dead bodies and murders? But it seems to keep happening.

"Although I can see him helping hide the body," Jenna admitted reluctantly. "At least if it wasn't all bloody."

"The authorities still haven't told you how your father was killed?"

"No. And all I could see was his face when I identified him." She handed the divorce papers back as if she suddenly found them distasteful. "Let's just keep looking for a copy of the will."

She didn't mention blackmail again, and I could see she faced some tough possibilities here. Her father as a blackmailer. Her mother as a killer. Maybe both?

I was undecided as well. Sable struck me as a bit shallow and self-centered, but that didn't make her a killer.

Warren seemed so detail oriented that he may well have accumulated incriminating information he could use for blackmail. But that didn't make him a blackmailer.

It also occurred to me that Sable could have invented the blackmail story out of thin air to divert attention away from her own guilt. I remembered the basics of narrowing down suspects in a murder. MOM. Motive. Opportunity. Means. Sable had the Motive: two million dollars' worth of motive. The Opportunity: several days in which she could have come down here and killed Warren while Jenna was in New York and Lightning was in LA. Means: I couldn't think of any means by which she could have done it, at least in part because we didn't know how Warren was killed. A gun seemed the most likely possibility.

"Is anyone in your family familiar with guns?"

"There was a series of awful murders in Scottsdale a few years ago and Mom got all worried, so she and Hayden both took lessons at a local shooting range. Although Hayden quit about halfway through. But I don't know that Mom ever actually bought a gun."

But Jenna also didn't know that her mother *hadn't* bought a gun.

By the end of the day we'd finished with the boxes in that room. Warren must never have thrown anything away. We'd found records of lottery tickets he'd bought from years back and what he'd won and lost. A box labeled *Puzzles* that I thought might contain mysterious unknowns about various people—maybe for blackmail purposes—was instead exactly what the label said: puzzles. Two 1,000-piece puzzles, one that was all ocean and must have been mind-boggling to put together. Had Warren ever done it? Well, yes, he had. Under the tumbled pieces was a photo of the completed puzzle with a completion date.

There was a box with an old electric toothbrush and a manual for using it. I was surprised and touched to find a box containing a single lock of rough hair and an old dog collar that Warren had identified as coming from a dog he'd owned when he was a boy, a dog named Lucky. Not a sentimental gesture I'd have expected of him. Another box was all photos. Not family pictures but autographed publicity photos, some of them actors I vaguely remembered from old movies. Were any of them—maybe even all of them—victims of his blackmail?

And yes, we'd also found boxes of old calendars. I knew what those check marks on them meant. Although there was another set of calendars, these marked with various letters of the alphabet. I decided I'd just as soon not know what they might be a record of.

"Are you up to tackling the boxes in the other room tomorrow?" Jenna asked. "I don't want to impose on you."

"No imposition, but tomorrow is Sunday. We'll go to church. Perhaps you'd like to come with us again? And then we can come back to the boxes in the afternoon or on Monday."

"I think Mike is still over in San Diego with his mother. But he might get back tonight."

She didn't give me a chance to point out that she could come to church without him.

MAC

Geoff and Magnolia drove their car, and Ivy and I took our pickup to church this time. They planned to go on into Yuma after the service so Geoff could get a part for his motorhome generator, but we didn't have any reason to go. I didn't really expect Jenna and Mike to show up at church again, but they hurried in several minutes after the service started and sat behind us. It was another good sermon, this one making an unexpected connection between Job's suffering and Jesus's death on the cross. At least unexpected to me, a rather new Christian who is often surprised by the many cross-connections in the Bible that reinforce each other.

Mike looked thoughtful when they followed us out to the pickup. I decided giving him a Bible of his own would be a good idea. We had a couple of extras back at the motorhome. But I wouldn't ask him if he wanted one. I'd just give it to him.

"Can we take you somewhere for lunch?" I asked them.

"Mike just got his bike back from the friend who borrowed it to ride down to Baja. We like chasing around off-road and we're going to do that this afternoon. Bike as in motorcycle," Jenna added.

I suppose we look like people who might be confused by the terminology and interpret *bike* as *bicycle*. Actually, we have bicycle-bikes and have talked about also getting a motorcycle, even looked at a couple of smaller Honda 250s. An uneasy thought occurred to me.

Someone who rode around off-road might be familiar with the Prosperity area. Such a person might even know it well enough to find their way around out there at night. Could that mean Mike helped Jenna hide the body out there in the desert? But Jenna was in New York when Warren was killed. Or was she?

"You do a lot of off-roading?" I asked.

"It's not really an off-road bike," Mike said. "We just use it that way occasionally."

He didn't say it in an unfriendly way, but it struck me as an end-of-conversation kind of statement.

"I'll see you tomorrow morning, then," Ivy said to Jenna. "Maybe we can get through that second roomful of boxes."

"Actually, I've decided to do something else tomorrow." Jenna glanced at Mike. "I'm going into Yuma and demand to know more than they're telling me. I think I'm *entitled* to know more." She sounded determined.

I assumed Mike knew about this plan, but from his dismayed look, he was obviously surprised. "Are you sure that's a good idea? It might just, you know, antagonize them."

Was he really saying, *Don't rock the boat or they might start suspecting you?*

I'd mostly crossed Jenna off any list of suspects. And yet . . .

Jenna ignored Mike's concerns. "If you have time, we could continue the morning after that," she said to Ivy. "Or maybe I should just thank you for all the help you've already given me. I know I've been imposing on you."

"I could work on the boxes by myself tomorrow," Ivy offered.

"Really? You'd do that?"

"If you don't mind my going through your father's things when you're not there."

"Mind? Ivy, you've been a life saver. If you want to do it, I'll—I'll pick up a date milkshake for you on my way home."

A bribe that made Ivy smile.

We went back to the motorhome, took BoBandy and Koop out for a walk, and then had lunch. Geoff and Magnolia weren't back yet. The day was pleasant and after sitting around for a while, perhaps with the earlier reference to bikes/bicycles on my mind, I said, "We could get out the bikes and go for a ride."

Ivy jumped on that idea, and we unloaded the bicycles from the carrier on the rear end of the motorhome. We didn't want to get out on the highway with bicycles, so we took the not-quite-a-road going back into Prosperity. It was more beaten down with all the recent traffic from law-enforcement vehicles but still rough and bumpy for bicycle riding, with sand patches that were like trying to pedal through molasses.

By the time we got back to the motorhome, Ivy rubbed her tired bottom and said, "Maybe we *should* get an off-road motorcycle."

IVY

Without any preliminary notification, a different man showed up to question us the following morning, this one a young detective in plain clothes instead of a deputy in uniform. He asked basically the same questions we'd been asked before, although this time there were new questions that included Jenna's mother. It made me suspect they'd found something on the computer about her and the insurance, although the detective gave no specific indication of that, of course. Mac asked if there was any reason for us to remain here longer, and we got the same answer as before. They couldn't legally *require* that we stay, but they'd appreciate it if we would.

"You ever been on a honeymoon?" Mac inquired grumpily when the detective was at the door leaving.

The young detective looked wary of the unlikely question, but he answered politely enough. "No, I haven't. But I'd like to someday."

"Me too," Mac muttered.

Mac had decided to accompany me to help search in Warren's boxes today, but a few minutes before we were ready to leave, Betsy showed up at our door. She had a doctor's appointment in Yuma, but her car wouldn't start. Could we take her to the appointment? I told her I was already occupied this morning. She looked at Mac as if she'd just picked the right numbers in a lottery and he was the grand prize.

"Perhaps you could take me? I'll be happy to give you a couple of night's free rent here at the RV park in exchange."

Mac looked at me. Mac is a helpful kind of guy, always willing to lend a hand, but he obviously viewed this as akin to a hike across the desert barefoot. But he swallowed a sigh and said, "I'll take you. Free rent won't be necessary."

I trust Mac. He's as dependable as gravity. "You can drop me off at Deadeye and take Betsy on to her appointment," I told him.

"Yeah, I guess so," Mac muttered.

I smiled at him. *Serves you right for being such an attractive old fox.*

**

Jenna's car was gone when we arrived, and so was Lightning's pickup. Mac dropped me off with a goodbye kiss at the gate to Warren's yard. After he and Betsy were gone, the inevitable cloud of dust following them, I was surprised to find I felt uneasy being here alone. After locking the door, I headed immediately for the unexplored room of boxes and started with the first box on the top shelf. Blessedly, there weren't nearly as many boxes in this room. That first box was, surprisingly, taped shut, which none of the boxes in the other room had been. I thought that might indicate something important inside. I got out the little pocketknife I always carry in my purse and sliced through the tape.

Important? Well, perhaps importance is, like beauty, in the eye of the beholder. Because what was in the box were old movie scripts. Movies I'd never heard of. Which didn't necessarily mean anything, of course, since three movies a year is about my limit. Or were they scripts of movies that had never been made, possibly with some potential value? I set the box aside to show Jenna.

The uneasiness increased as the morning wore on. I kept hearing odd noises. Scratchy noises . . . as if someone were doing something at the doors or windows? A thief snooping around? A killer trying to get inside? Hiding behind drapes, I cautiously peered out several windows.

I didn't see anything unusual. Nothing moved.

Which didn't mean I was safe here. The thief/killer could be skulking so close to the wall that I couldn't see him. I'd strongly consider leaving, except that without a car, I couldn't. Maybe I should call Mac? I wished I'd brought BoBandy along. Maybe Koop too.

I waited until the sounds finally stopped before going back to work.

I went through a box of old appliance manuals for everything from a toaster and a blender to a black-and-white TV. A box with records about books purchased from some book club to which Warren had once belonged, complete with a copy of a blistering letter about a book charged for but never received. Warren obviously didn't depend on charm to get *his* way. Two boxes held old federal and state income tax returns. These looked interesting. Would Warren actually have reported money received from someone he was blackmailing? But I stopped before digging into them. This was very personal information that I hesitated to explore. I set them aside to show Jenna and went on to a box labeled *Feet*, which held details, complete with photographs, of a foot fungus problem he'd had some years ago.

The noises began again. I listened to them for a couple of minutes and then marched into the kitchen. Enough of this. I wasn't going to cower in here like a scared heroine in a romance novel and let a stalker corner me. I poked around in the kitchen and found an oversized knife. Without taking time to speculate on what Warren may have used it for, I brandished it in a few experimental swipes and jabs. But after barely missing my knee, I finally decided I didn't want to wind up with the knife stuck somewhere in my anatomy and settled for a potato masher. I didn't let myself think that it might be rather difficult to mash an intruder into surrender.

I had to go through the garage to get out where the noises were coming from. I cautiously cracked the garage door on the back side open.

And there was my dangerous stalker pecking at the door.

A roadrunner.

He . . . she? . . . gave me an *it's-about-time* cock of head, and I made another unexpected realization about Warren. Unlikely as it seemed, he must have been feeding this desert creature. I went back inside, found a package of hamburger in the freezer compartment of the refrigerator, zapped it in the microwave to thaw it, and took a marble-sized lump out to my noise maker.

The roadrunner wound up eating half a dozen more lumps of raw hamburger. I took several photos with my phone, laughed at myself for being paranoid about strange noises, and thought about that old saying revised to apply here. *Give a roadrunner a hunk of hamburger and you feed him for a day. And from then on he'll pester you regularly.*

After I went back to work, I was tempted to start skipping some of the boxes with unlikely sounding labels, but Jenna had suggested her father might deliberately mislabel a box to conceal the true contents. So far the labels had all been bluntly accurate, but I resolutely opened every box. I finally came to the last box just as I heard more noises outside. This box was labeled *Gambling System* and contained exactly that: pages and pages of numbers on some gambling system on blackjack that he'd worked out with mathematical precision. Along with the conclusion that the system was eventually doomed to failure.

Good ol' Warren, keeping detailed records of his failures as well as his successes. Which said to me that if he'd been blackmailing anyone, there would definitely be records somewhere. But apparently not here.

I tried to ignore the noises the roadrunner was making now. But then a louder clunk made me wonder if the persistent bird might do some actual damage with all that pecking. As I went through the kitchen I grabbed a kitchen towel with which to flap at him and then yanked the back door open.

Not a pecking roadrunner.

Chapter 13

IVY

Lightning and I stared at each other.

"What are you doing?" I asked.

He held a tape measure in one hand, a carpenter's pencil in the other. Not exactly deadly weapons, but probably more effective than my dish towel. Even if I flapped it really hard. I took a step back just in case.

"Hey, I didn't mean to disturb you! I didn't know anyone was here."

Obviously.

"Did you want to get inside the house?"

"No. I just wanted to get in the pump house. I'm thinking maybe I could run the water on down to my trailer. But the pump house is padlocked. I thought maybe Warren kept a key around here . . . somewhere." Then, as if deciding to switch tactics and operate on the old adage that offense is the best defense, he said, "What are *you* doing here?" Except, with an apparent attempt at joviality, he added, "Young lady."

Someday I really am going to kick someone in the shins for using that term, but I managed to keep my foot on the ground again this time. The Lord boomed a stern reminder out of my conscience: *Kicking shins won't keep you out of heaven, but do you really want to have it on your résumé for the Lord?*

"I'm helping Jenna get things straightened out," I said with a deliberate lack of precision. I heard a car around front. "That must be her now. You should talk to her about the water."

Although on second thought, I realized that probably wasn't necessary. With Warren dead, Lightning would own all of Deadeye and the surrounding land now. He could do whatever he wanted with the water. So why was he sneaking around when he thought no one was here? I wasn't convinced he wasn't trying to get inside.

I shut the door, locked it, and went back through the house to let Jenna in through the front door that I'd locked.

She opened the gate just as Lightning came around the side of the house.

"Howdy there!" he said as if his being here was an everyday event, although Jenna had once said he'd never even been inside Warren's house. "Everything going okay?"

"Not exactly. But I'm doing the best I can."

"Lightning was checking on the water system," I offered, then made a sneaky addition. "He said."

Jenna didn't seem interested. In fact, in old-fashioned terms, she looked rather "peak-ed." Kind of pale and droopy eyed. Bad news in Yuma?

"I think Tony might have the beginning of a crack in his left front hoof," she said to Lightning. "You might want to have your horseshoer look at it."

"I'll do that."

Lightning gave her a little wave and strolled off toward his own place. Jenna didn't seem to give his presence a second thought but I did. Although I was distracted when she handed me a straw and a tall cup with a plastic bubble for a lid.

A date milkshake! "Thank you!" I inserted the straw and took an eager gulp.

"Find anything in the boxes?" she asked.

I led her into the storage room and told her what was in the boxes I'd set aside. She dismissed the movie scripts as irrelevant but peeked at the income tax records.

"I'll tackle these sometime, but not right now."

"You look as if you don't feel too well."

"Actually, I feel terrible. Mom says I'm probably allergic to the dust or something here because I'm always getting sniffles and itchy eyes. But it feels like something more than that this time." She plopped into the lone chair in the room.

"How did things go in Yuma?"

"Everyone was very pleasant, very nice, very sympathetic, very encouraging." Her sour tone stomped on the congenial words. "But I still don't know anything. Not how Dad was killed or if they have any suspects or how the investigation is progressing. Or if it is progressing."

"I think you can demand a copy of the autopsy report," I said.

"Maybe I should. But I don't want to see lurid photos or read details about Dad's internal organs and his brain and what they weighed and all that." She shuddered. "I think they may be withholding details because there may be some clue to who did it and how it was done. Is that possible? Or am I just getting . . . I don't know . . . paranoid or something?" She got up from the chair and stared out the window.

I know law enforcement does occasionally withhold information from the public, but I had to wonder if the reason they weren't telling Jenna much was because she was still on their persons-of-interest list. Maybe high on it. Was she thinking that too?

"I don't know if they were able to get into the computer, but I think they want to talk to Mom. They asked for her current address. Maybe they found something in the computer about her getting all that insurance money."

"Nothing about blackmail?"

"Not that they shared with me. How come you're here without the pickup?"

"Mac dropped me off. He was taking Betsy Oldham to a doctor's appointment."

Jenna unexpectedly smiled. "Good ol' Betsy. I like her, but Dad would drive all the way into Yuma rather than buy something at her little store. He said the couple of times he went in there she asked all kinds of nosy questions and practically talked him to death." She gave a choked gasp at the awful reality of the common phrase she'd accidentally used. Her father hadn't been "talked to death," but he'd certainly been done to death somehow.

"Have you tried to contact that lawyer, the one who handled the divorce?"

"Not yet. I need to do that. Maybe I should also call Mom and warn her someone from the sheriff's department is probably coming to question her."

I'd rather the detectives hit her by surprise, before she had a chance to manipulate her story, but I didn't say that. I heard a vehicle pull up outside. "Looks as if Mac is here." I was reluctant to leave when she obviously didn't feel well. "Is there anything I can do to help before I go?"

"No. I'll be fine. I do so appreciate all the help you've already given me."

"Will you call me if you need anything?"

She dodged the question. "Mike should be here soon. We're going to move my computer over here and connect it with Dad's satellite system so I can get on the internet."

"Maybe you should wait until another day to do that."

142

"Maybe I will. I really do feel like I've been dragged through a keyhole."

Mike's old van pulled up as I stepped out the door and headed toward our pickup. I stopped to say hi and ask about his mother again.

"I think I've persuaded her to come stay over here for a while. She needs time to recuperate from her fall in the laundry room," he said.

But I was barely listening. My gaze riveted on the little ornaments dangling from the rearview mirror inside the van. I didn't remember seeing them before. Mike noticed where I was looking.

He touched one of the two little roadrunners made with yarn and beads, and they both danced merrily. He smiled. "A clerk at one of the gift shops that sells my paintings makes them. She says my roadrunners inspired her, and she's created a little side business for herself making and selling them in the gift shop. She gave me these two the last time I was in Phoenix."

"They're very cute and clever." But I wasn't really looking at the little yarn roadrunners. I was looking at the cord draped over the mirror that held them together.

A red cord.

Mike? I gave him a dismayed look. I'd never even considered Mike as a possibility in Warren's death. There was no reason to suspect Mike. Unless . . .

No, no, no! I chided myself even as the thought barreled through my mind: if Warren was opposed to Mike's relationship with Jenna, and they got into an angry altercation about it—

You're jumping to conclusions. Like a grasshopper on steroids. You don't know anything about how Warren felt about Mike. And disliking each other surely wasn't enough for murder.

It was also just a piece of red cord. It didn't necessarily match the cord that was tied around the blanket wrapped around Warren's body. I'd barely seen that cord. This might be a totally different kind of red cord. Maybe the woman who made the little roadrunners had tied them together herself.

I hopefully asked that question. "The woman makes them to use as decorations to hang on a rearview mirror?"

"No, the gift shop just sells them as little souvenirs of Arizona. I tied them together myself so I could use them this way." Mike gave one of the little roadrunners another tap to send it spinning and dancing. I guess I was still staring, wondering if there was a whole spool of red cord stashed back there in the van, because he finally said, "Is something wrong?"

"No. No! I was just . . . admiring the roadrunners." And I did admire them. They were cleverly crafted little souvenirs. I hastily changed the subject. "Jenna isn't feeling well."

"She didn't tell me that."

"Maybe you could persuade her to see a doctor or at least take it easy for a day or two."

"I'll do that."

I hastily scooted around the van and jumped in the cab of our pickup with Mac and Betsy. That scrunched Betsy up against Mac, but I was too rattled by what I'd just seen to care. I was anxious to tell Mac about this, but I didn't want to do it with Betsy listening. I managed to instead ask if her appointment with the doctor went okay.

"I get these odd little spots on my skin every once in a while, and they did a biopsy on this one." She fingered a small, round bandage on the back of her neck. "Too much sun, you know. Skin cancer. I've had it several times. I hope you're using sunscreen. I never did."

I assured her I regularly used sunscreen with a high SPF rating, and she chattered on about other people she'd known with skin cancer problems. That subject morphed into a one-sided conversation about a woman with an ingrown-toenail problem and another with hemorrhoids.

"Of course sunlight didn't have anything to do with either of those," she assured me.

MAC

When we got to her little store, Betsy thanked me effusively for taking her to the doctor, including a friendly squeeze of my leg. I was a little startled. Certainly not something I was expecting. I'm beginning to think that woman may have designs on me.

I immediately scoffed at that thought. Ivy sometimes calls me a "silver fox," but her opinion is probably biased. I'm just blessed that she has designs on me.

Betsy said she'd put a battery charger on her car and that should take care of the non-starting problem. I probably should have offered to do it for her, but at the moment I was a little wary of Betsy and her roving hand. I drove on to our motorhome. As soon as we were inside, I asked Ivy what she was so eager to tell me. I know Ivy, and I could tell there was something.

She told me about seeing the red cord in Mike's van and that it looked like the same cord we'd seen tied around Warren's body. "I don't want to think Mike had anything to do with Warren's death. I like Mike. But . . ."

"What possible motive would he have?"

"Maybe Warren didn't approve of his relationship with Jenna."

Possible. "But killing him seems like a rather extreme reaction, don't you think?" I liked Mike too. I liked his concern for his mother and his hard work ethic. I liked how he seemed really interested in the message at church on Sunday and the way he treated Jenna with such care and respect. "Mike strikes me as the kind of guy who, if his girlfriend's father didn't like him, would just work harder to win his approval."

"But what if there was something, you know, really *unpleasant* in Mike's past, something he didn't want Jenna to know?"

"Such as?"

"Something foolish or maybe even criminal, maybe something from back when he was in college. Kids do some dumb things in college, you know. Or maybe something even worse. A prison record. Or maybe he did something and didn't get caught, and somehow Warren found out about it and threatened to tell her."

A kind of moneyless blackmail? "Too bad we don't have internet service here. We could see what we could find out about him."

"Yes! The internet knows all. There's probably some place in Yuma where we can do it. You know, one of those cybercafé kind of places."

**

So here we were the following morning, not at a cybercafé but at the local library, which generously allowed even non-cardholders like us to use their public computers. We squeezed around one that wasn't in use, and after a bit of fumbling with the unfamiliar machine, I got Mike's name into the search line.

It's no doubt true that the internet knows all. In fact, sometimes it knows too much and still can't tell you what you want to know. We got a website for a Mike Redstone landscape service in Pennsylvania. An obituary in Alabama. A birth announcement in Texas. Several Mike Redstones existed on Facebook, none of whom was the one we wanted. We finally found a lone mention of the right Mike Redstone, along with a photo of one of his roadrunner paintings, on a Phoenix gift shop site. It was no more informative than a boy telling you what happened in school today. *Nuthin'*.

IVY

I was disappointed that we didn't find anything helpful about Mike on the internet. It was almost as if he had no past at all. But then I decided I was looking at things backward. Not finding anything was *good* news. It meant there wasn't something troublesome hidden in his past. Although we weren't exactly experts at this, and someone more knowledgeable than we are could search much deeper and possibly find something. I wondered if Jenna had ever looked him up. Is that something young people routinely do about each other these days?

As long as we were in Yuma, we decided to visit the Yuma Territorial Prison, now a state historic park. We wandered through the museum and cell block, including the chilling "dark cell" for punishing the worst of criminals with isolation, and climbed to the guard tower. Afterward we ate great enchiladas and tacos at a Mexican restaurant named the Red Bull, with, appropriately, a pawing, snorting red bull painted out front. It was a fun day, and I almost forgot about murder and the troubling possibilities about the identity of the killer.

Almost.

By the time we got back to the motorhome about midafternoon, I was still concerned about Jenna and the way she'd looked and felt yesterday. With a flash of inspiration, I started a big pot of soup with a package of chicken thighs from the freezer. Chicken soup isn't a cure-all for everything, but it's a good start.

**

Jenna's car was at her trailer when I carried the soup in two Mason jars to the door. She called to us to come in, and Mac opened the door. She was propped up in bed with a couple of pillows, hair tangled, eyes bleary. Her computer still sat on the dinette table.

"I look worse than I feel," she said. I doubted that.

"We brought you some chicken soup. Can I heat some for you now?"

"Oh, that would be wonderful! I had some tea, but I haven't eaten all day. It just felt like more trouble than it was worth."

I rummaged in the tiny kitchen for a pan and then poured one of the jars of soup into it. I put the other jar in the refrigerator.

Mac perched on the chair in front of the computer. "We thought Mike might be here taking care of you."

"He wanted to, but he was supposed to start a new painting job today and I didn't want him to miss that. He'll be over later."

I kept seeing those two little roadrunners tied together with red cord dangling from the rearview mirror in Mike's van. But my thoughts also drifted back to Mom as a possible killer, and, as if my thinking conjured her up, Jenna's cell phone beside her on the bed made a peculiar noise.

Jenna smiled. "Grunge music." She looked at the little screen, and then with a perkiness that sounded as phony as an e-mail from Nigeria wanting to share millions of dollars with you, she said, "Hi, Mom."

I couldn't hear all of both sides of the conversation, but Sable's voice was so loud and angry that I couldn't miss some of her words. Especially when Jenna held the phone away from her ear, wincing at the shrill blast of her mother's voice.

Sable didn't ask if Jenna was okay or if there was any news about Warren's case. She just jumped into unhappy news of her own. Two men from the sheriff's department in Yuma had come up to question her. They'd left just a few minutes ago. "Thank goodness they didn't arrive with siren screaming and lights flashing. They weren't even wearing uniforms, and I made them show identification, of course. But Tammy Morrison across the street was watching like a hawk. Who knows what kind of rumors she'll spread?"

Without uniforms, they were detectives then, rather than deputies. Did that mean anything?

"They wanted to know *everything*. It was like an *invasion*. I'm a nervous wreck."

"I don't think it's anything to be upset about, Mom. It's just part of their investigation," Jenna soothed. Then a long pause from Jenna while Sable yelled something more. I caught enough to tell that she was talking about the insurance policy on which she was beneficiary.

"And you say they didn't ask if there was such a policy?" Jenna asked. "They already knew about it?"

"Yes!"

"Mom, I think you're overreacting. Just because they already knew about it doesn't mean they think you killed him."

Maybe not. But I'd guess it certainly aroused their suspicions. The information must have come off the computer. I wondered if they'd also found anything about a blackmailing scheme.

Apparently Sable thought she had to explain existence of the policy to Jenna. She went on and on with the details, including an extensive list of Warren's shortcomings as a husband. Sable's tirade made it plain that not even two million dollars of insurance money was enough to repay for all she'd endured. Her claim of not wanting to "disillusion" Jenna about her father had apparently fallen by the wayside because this list included everything from his penny-pinching stinginess and fanatic workaholism to a possible infidelity. Jenna's reaction was a roll of eyes.

The conversation finally narrowed down to a firm statement from Jenna. "No, Mom, I do *not* think you should come down here now and complain to the sheriff's department about invasion of your privacy." Pause as Sable ranted some more. "No, Mom, I do not think you need to hire a lawyer. Unless they do arrest you, of course."

Jenna ended the conversation with that, a bit of snark in her tone almost suggesting she wouldn't mind if they did arrest Sable. Although I knew that wasn't true; Jenna was just feeling frustrated and impatient at the moment. I dished up the hot soup.

"Sorry about that." Jenna grimaced as she took the bowl of soup. "Mom can get really wound up."

I glanced at Mac. Should we pretend not to have heard anything on the phone call? I decided that was pointless. With the smallness of the trailer and the bullhorn loudness of Sable's words, we'd have needed concrete ear plugs not to hear. "She sounded upset," I said in as neutral a tone as I could manage.

Jenna snorted a laugh at my understatement. "Upset? She's ready to go into orbit. And she's going to come down here again. I just know she is."

While we waited for Mike to arrive, we made small talk with Jenna about Mike's mother's accident over in San Diego. I managed to sneak in a subtle question about the relationship between Mike and Jenna's father. Mac gave me a sharp look when I asked it, so maybe I wasn't as subtle as I gave myself credit for, but Jenna didn't take offense.

"They weren't big buddies," she admitted. "Dad asked me once how long Mike intended to play around with this 'artist stuff' instead of getting a real job."

How would Mike have reacted if Warren had used a term even more derogatory than "artist stuff" in a direct conversation? Along with some dramatic "Stay away from my daughter" mandate.

Jenna smiled wryly. "But then, Dad wasn't exactly a big-buddy kind of guy."

Given Warren's general standoffish attitude, maybe he was lucky to have even that hungry roadrunner as a friend.

A rumble outside announced Mike's arrival in his old van, and we said our goodbyes to Jenna.

"Hey, I'm glad I ran into you guys," Mike said when we met him outside. "I'm going to run over to San Diego and get my mother, and I'm hoping you'll keep an eye on Jenna while I'm gone. She still wasn't feeling good when I talked to her earlier. I'll leave tomorrow and be back the next day."

"Sure," Mac said. I wondered if his easy cooperation meant he'd given up on the honeymoon. "Will your mother be staying with you?"

"No, I'll pull her trailer over here. There's an RV park in Tacna where she can stay."

"Jenna seems to be feeling a little better," I said. "We brought her some chicken soup."

"Hey, thanks! Chicken soup was always Mom's cure-all when I was a kid. And I have your roadrunner finished. I didn't bring it along today, but I'll get it to you as soon as I get Mom over here."

"Thanks. I'm looking forward to it."

When we passed the van on our way to the pickup, I gave Mac a little nudge to look at the decoration hanging from the rearview mirror. Then I looked closer myself.

"It's gone!"

Chapter 14

IVY

The two yarn roadrunners were still there. But not the red cord. Now they were connected by a short strip of shiny red ribbon.

"He's changed them!" I said with a gasp worthy of a romance-novel heroine. "The red cord is gone."

Mac, bless his heart, didn't suggest perhaps I hadn't actually seen what I thought I'd seen before, that maybe the red ribbon had been there all along. Although the thought occurred to me.

"Did he realize you'd noticed it?" he asked instead.

"He knew I noticed the little roadrunners. We talked about them."

Did this mean that after Mike and I talked he realized I may have seen that same red cord wrapped about Warren's body? Why else would he have exchanged the cord for a ribbon? I looked closer. The ribbon and the cord weren't really close in appearance, but they were both red. Similar enough that if I said anything, Mike could act surprised and say I'd made a mistake, that the little roadrunners had always been tied with a red ribbon.

But they hadn't been. In spite of that first moment of doubt, I was sure of it. Was a spool of red cord still tucked away in the van somewhere? Maybe, after Mike went inside the trailer, we could sneak in through the rear doors in the van and look for it.

No, dumb idea. Mike would have gotten rid of whatever was left of the red cord after he realized I recognized it, no doubt censuring himself for carelessly using the same red cord for both projects. A toss in a trash can somewhere, or maybe even a ceremonial burning out on the desert. And what could we say if he caught us rummaging around in the van? *We were looking for our pickup and must have made a wrong turn* wouldn't cut it.

Did I still like Mike as much as I thought I did?

We went back to the motorhome and ate leftover chicken soup and toasted cheese sandwiches for supper. Later we went over to Geoff and Magnolia's motorhome and watched an old Hallmark movie on DVD. We took both BoBandy and Koop for a walk and had a dish of Chocolate Ribbons ice cream when we got back to the motorhome.

A good movie and a pleasant walk, but I couldn't get my mind off the van and the disappearing red cord. Had Mike hauled Warren's body in the van? There might still be traces of fiber from that tan blanket Warren was wrapped in. Should I mention the strange situation about the red cord to Jenna?

She'd be devastated if it turned out that Mike was her father's killer, and the possibility that Mike killed Warren turned the ice cream into rumbling lumps in my stomach. And yet, if he'd actually done it, we couldn't just ignore the incriminating red cord as if it were a minor mistake on a roadrunner painting.

Next morning Betsy came over and said she was still having trouble with her car, and would Mac come take a look at it? Mac, no doubt to Betsy's dismay, enlisted Geoff's help, and they all trooped off together. I cleaned Koop's litter box, and then Magnolia and I had a cup of tea and some pecan cookies she'd made. After lunch, Mac got out our maps and we discussed whether we might go down the Pacific side of Baja instead of the Sea of Cortez side on our honeymoon.

Until finally he, apparently as restless as I was, said, "We said we'd keep an eye on Jenna. Maybe we should go over and check on her."

Yes!

**

I could see Jenna's car parked in front of Warren's double-wide when we arrived, but Lightning hailed us from the corral when we passed his mobile. "Hey, something spooked the horses last night, and they knocked part of the corral loose," he called. "Would you have time to give me a hand?"

"Sure," Mac called back. "I'll take Ivy on over to where Jenna is and be right back."

So Mac dropped me off at Warren's place. The front door was open. I said, "Knock-knock," and Jenna called me to come in. She was just getting her computer set up on the desk.

"I thought hooking it up might be complicated, but it looks as if all I have to do is plug into the modem."

"You're feeling better today?"

"Oh, yes. Much better." She smiled. "The chicken soup must have been what did it."

"You have some research for your book to do on the internet?"

"Well, that and some other things. After Mike left last night, I started looking through Dad's old income tax records. I have to admit I've always been curious about that IPO thing on which he made so much money."

"I guess we'd all like to know how to do that."

While we were talking she fastened a cord from the computer into the modem and turned the computer on. "Hey, look! It works!"

She sounded surprised but not nearly as surprised as I would have been if I'd tried something like that. In my experience, if technology can figure some way to give you a cyberspace sucker punch, it will gleefully do so.

"The thing is," she went on, manipulating keys as she spoke, "I couldn't find anything anywhere about some big stock market windfall.

But one tax return from several years ago does show Dad received a huge amount of money for . . . something."

Oh no. Did that mean he'd blackmailed someone out of some impressive amount of money and dutifully reported it? Could he have tried to coerce more money out of that person and gotten himself killed for the effort?

"How huge?"

"Over two and a half million dollars."

Wow! Blackmail apparently paid a lot more than what was in my "found money" jar of pennies and nickels. The figure was even larger than the amount Sable would get from insurance now that Warren was dead.

"It looks like some kind of government payment," Jenna added. "Though I can't imagine why the government would be paying Dad anything."

A government payment? Not blackmail, then. Unless he'd figured out some way to blackmail the government.

"You think there'll be something about it on the internet?"

"Not his payment specifically, of course. But maybe . . . I don't know . . . something about government payments in general? What it might be for? I can't think of anywhere else to look."

"Could he have received a big final payment from Craigmont when he left them, a severance package, something like that? Companies do that, I understand."

"I suppose that's possible. Dad worked for Craigmont for a long time, and head accountant was a fairly important position in the company." Her expression brightened. "Could the payment look as if it came from the government because they were handling distribution of the funds in the bankruptcy?"

I had no idea, of course. But it seemed doubtful to me that with all the creditors a company must have in a bankruptcy that a current or former employee would be entitled to two and a half million dollars.

Jenna's phone made that peculiar noise again, something between a guitar in pain and an underwater drum. Grunge music was definitely an acquired taste. She pulled the phone out of her pocket and grimaced at the screen. "I suppose you get really black marks as a daughter if you block calls from your own mother." She gave a big sigh and tapped the screen. "Hi, Mom."

This time she gave me a little wave and, perhaps anticipating more of yesterday's rant and rave, moved into the living room to talk to her mother.

I hesitated a moment and then sat down at the computer. Doing that sometimes makes me feel almost powerful, as if I have the whole world at my fingertips. Maybe the whole universe! Would a satellite connection give more information than we'd gotten with the connection at the library? I flexed my fingers and typed Mike Redstone's name into the search line.

I studied the results. Offhand, it looked like the same list we'd gotten on the library computer. Then I heard Jenna returning and hastily clicked the back arrow. I didn't want her to know I was checking up on Mike. I typed in the first name that came to mind.

"I was wrong. Mom isn't coming right now. She's talking about a trip to Paris. Though she'll probably have to wait until the insurance money comes in."

Even if Sable hadn't been on good terms with Warren, taking a fun trip on the proceeds from his death struck me as rather ghoulish. Kind of like sticking out your tongue at someone while dancing on his grave.

"Your mother and her husband will both go?"

Jenna frowned. "I don't know. Actually, I think they may be having . . . problems. They got in a big fight when we were in New York. There was some kind of glitch with Hayden's credit card on the hotel bill. Sometimes I wonder if, after she gets all that insurance money . . ." She let the thought trail off and jumped back to the prospect of Mom coming here.

"I think Mom's afraid that if she comes here they *will* arrest her. Can't you just imagine Mom in jail?" Jenna smiled as if she found the prospect entertaining, although she quickly quelled the smile and turned serious. "Though she didn't do it, of course, and I hope the authorities don't waste time investigating her instead of going after the real killer." She peered at what I'd typed in the search line. "What are you looking for? Oh, Craigmont. Good idea."

I vacated the chair so she could slide into it. She was definitely more expert at this than I was, but she only had to click on "Search" and a screenful of listings instantly came up.

"You've never looked up the company before?" I asked.

"No, I never had any reason to. But look at all these sites the search brought up!"

She bounced through them, spending only a short amount of time on sites related to movies or TV shows Craigmont had produced, including Lightning's old westerns. They'd indeed had some big successes, including their early horror movies, but the later ones had apparently floundered.

She spent more time on sites that involved the Craigmont bankruptcy. They had gone out with quite a splash, and there were numerous articles about the demise of the company, including comments from various celebrities about "the terrible loss to the industry." But their downfall apparently came from more than bad movies. The company had made various investments totally unrelated to the movie business . . . perhaps because their movies were on the skids . . . and the major owner had wound up in prison from a huge tax-evasion scheme on big income from Alaskan oil investments, Texas real estate, and a questionable business in Thailand. The money had been hidden through a complicated scheme involving several other companies apparently created solely for the purpose of concealing the outside income.

As head accountant for Craigmont, would Warren have known about those investments? Had he been involved in the scheme to conceal the money? Or were the investments and concealment made outside his area of accounting? I hadn't seen his name mentioned in any of the articles.

"Was this man who went to prison someone you knew?" I asked.

"I didn't know him. But the head of the company, maybe this guy, had a big home theater, and I remember Mom and Dad going to pre-release screenings of some Craigmont movies there." She opened another page. "Oh, here's something more about him. He died while he was still in prison."

"You didn't know that?"

"I may have at one time, but if I did I guess it just slipped through the cracks."

All very interesting, but did it have anything to do with Warren's death? Could the big payment have come from the company as his share of the unreported gains? But that surely wouldn't have come as a government payment. And if he was both helping conceal and making money off the hidden deals, wouldn't he have wound up alongside the man who went to prison?

All very murky.

I heard the pecking at the back door again, and I took Jenna around to introduce her to the roadrunner. She was delighted to give him more hamburger balls from the refrigerator and immediately named him Harry.

She laughed. "Or Harriet, as the case may be."

I had the feeling the roadrunner wouldn't lack for food from now on.

Mac came in a few minutes later. He and Lightning had finished repairing the corral. Jenna thanked us for coming over to check on her but said she'd be fine now until Mike got back from San Diego. "But I'm always glad to have you two come over anytime."

158

The rough, dusty road back out to the highway was not conducive to conversation, and I waited until we were back at the motorhome to tell Mac what we'd found on the internet about Craigmont. He came up with a possibility that hadn't occurred to me.

Chapter 15

IVY

You've heard the term whistleblower?" Mac asked.

"Whistleblower." I repeated the word as I took off my shoes and dumped sand out of them. I seem to collect a shoeful of sand if I barely step outside the motorhome. "That's someone who supplies the police or government with information about someone else's illicit activities."

"Right. Like someone giving information about the money Craigmont concealed. The government might have uncovered the company's maneuvering through an audit or series of audits, since several companies were involved. But someone may have supplied them with dollar figures and a road map. And names." He sat down on the dinette bench seat, and Koop instantly jumped into his lap. "There's a financial reward for that."

I turned to look at him. "You're saying Warren may have given the government information about Craigmont's concealed income, and they gave him a *two-and-a-half-million-dollar* reward?" I find that level of money almost incomprehensible. I still get a little thrill out of finding a stray quarter on the sidewalk.

"I've heard the government can be quite generous with those awards. And who'd know the incriminating details of concealed income better than the head accountant for the company?"

"But if Warren helped conceal the income, wouldn't he have been guilty of something too?"

"Maybe he didn't help conceal it. Maybe he just discovered that it was being concealed. Or maybe whistleblowing takes care of whatever guilt might be involved."

I dropped onto the bench seat across from Mac at the dinette. "And this is what sent Craigmont into bankruptcy. Paying the government all they owed for taxes and interest and penalties on the concealed income. It must have been millions."

"That and making some box-office-flop movies. And then the top man in the company going to prison might have been a finishing touch."

"Would he have known Warren was the whistleblower?"

"I'd guess the government does all it can to conceal a whistleblower's identity in order to prevent retaliation," Mac said. "But to an insider in the company, it may have been obvious where the government got their information."

Obvious to someone with a big motive for revenge. A big motive for murder. But the man who went to prison couldn't be Warren's killer. "I don't remember the date, but the man who went to prison died there. So he couldn't have killed Warren."

"But maybe someone else, or several someones, took a big hit when the company went down," Mac suggested. "Someone who *isn't* dead."

A whole new universe of killer possibilities!

"But it doesn't look as if Warren was scared enough to actually go into hiding," I said. "He did move out to Deadeye, but he was using his real name."

"But he lived quite cautiously. He apparently cut off contact with everyone he'd known at Craigmont. He didn't make any friends around here, and he avoided anyone who asked nosy questions."

"Like Betsy," I said.

"He also lied to his daughter about where his big windfall of money came from."

"I wonder why he did it?" I mused.

"Why he reported the company's concealed income or why he lied to Jenna about getting a big award for doing it?"

"Both, I guess. But a basic reason for lying about it would be to protect himself from retaliation, don't you think? Better to tell no one the truth than to offer it selectively and risk the truth getting out. He probably thought that if Jenna knew, her mother might squeeze the information out of her, and from there it might go anywhere."

"That, and the fact that while there might be a certain heroic element in being a whistleblower—righteously telling the truth and bringing a lawbreaker to justice—there are other words for what he did. May have done," Mac corrected, because so far this was all conjecture on our part.

I remembered the condemning word when I was a kid. "Tattletale."

"Right. Stool pigeon. Even backstabber or traitor. As to why he blew the whistle to begin with, maybe he knew a big award was possible and did it simply for the money."

True. Warren apparently spent most of his days since Craigmont making money on the stock market. He didn't seem to have much else going on in his life. But there could have been other, less greedy reasons.

"Maybe he was trying to protect himself," I suggested. "Maybe he figured that even if he hadn't been a part of Craigmont's concealment scheme, if the government eventually found out about it on their own that he'd be caught up in it. That he might even wind up in prison."

"Maybe he wanted a share of the concealed income, and they wouldn't share," Mac said.

"Or maybe the company did him wrong in some way, and he did it in retaliation for what they did to him."

So many possibilities. Although we could be making another of those grasshopper-on-steroids leaps. "We don't know for sure Warren was a whistleblower," I reminded him.

"No, we don't," Mac agreed. "Maybe the government just had some extra money lying around . . . after all, what's a few million to the government? . . . and decided to give it to some upright citizen as a gesture of good will."

Yeah, right.

I had to think we were on to something here. *Whistleblower* explained so much: Warren's big windfall of money, his retreat to Deadeye and not wanting Lightning to bring in some new movie production, his attributing his financial windfall to stock market expertise. His death.

This now seemed to put Mike and his red cord, Lightning and his claim to the entire Deadeye property, and Jenna's mother and her eagerness to latch onto Warren's insurance money in the shadows as more remote possibilities.

In the spotlight was someone who knew what Warren had done and wanted to get even. The top man at Craigmont, who'd wound up in prison, was obviously the big loser, but he was dead. Someone else within the company who'd also suffered a big loss that wasn't apparent in the articles we'd seen about Craigmont's downfall? Or perhaps someone outside the company, an investor or lender? If the lender was an institution, maybe someone within that company got in desperate trouble for making such a loan?

Could we find out more if we delved deeper on the internet?
**

I felt uneasy asking Jenna about using her satellite-connected computer to look up more information about whistleblowing and Craigmont and her father, so we drove back to the library in Yuma.

There we learned that there was actually a government Whistleblower Office, part of the IRS, and a two-and-a half-million-dollar award was certainly within possibility. The payment was based on a percentage, up to 30 percent, of what the government collected in taxes, interest, and penalties from the guilty person or company. Awards in the thousands were common, but we found instances of sixteen and seventeen million, even one whopping award of fifty million. Persons receiving those awards all unnamed, of course.

I wondered if Warren, before the top man at Craigmont went to prison, had thought of blackmailing him, offering his silence for a share of the illicit money, then going ahead with the whistleblowing when the threat of blackmail didn't work. But blackmail was only Sable's suggestion; maybe Warren had never even considered it and made a good-citizen decision that a company shouldn't get away with such unlawful activity.

Had it been honesty that got him murdered?

We found a site that identified the main people at Craigmont at the time the company went under. It wasn't a publicly owned company with stockholders. The man who went to prison was both primary owner and president of the company, and there were several other people with indeterminate-sounding titles. A biographical paragraph told about how Lawrence Grantham worked his way up to being major owner of the company. He had a wife, a son, a yacht, and a big home in Malibu. A formal portrait showed a husky man with red hair and a good-humored smile. All the family assets had been sucked into the Craigmont collapse.

Warren Langston wasn't important enough to be listed among the Craigmont big shots, none of whom except Grantham had gone to prison. We did a separate search on Warren's name but again got entangled in information about people who weren't him, plus Langston products, streets named Warren, even a line of Langston rodent traps.

We bought some groceries and then stopped at Dateland for another date milkshake on the way back to the motorhome. It was after dark by the time we got there. I was fixing a meat loaf and baked potatoes for supper when Mike's van pulled up. He got out carrying something and headed for our door. Mac opened it for him.

"Jenna said you might be leaving in the next day or two, so I wanted to bring it over before you left," Mike said.

"Hey, great!" Mac said. "C'mon in."

Mike's broad shoulders and muscular figure seemed to take up most of the space in the motorhome. Or maybe it was that a *killer* seems to take up an unusual amount of space. Because, even though I'd shifted my main suspicions to someone connected with Craigmont, seeing Mike again somehow brought that ominous red-cord connection to the forefront.

Mike held out the framed painting. "I hope you like it. I usually use plain wooden frames that I buy, but I decided to try making a frame from the hollow skeleton of a cholla cactus for you. I got the inspiration from that cholla-skeleton cross in the church."

The painting showed a roadrunner doing what the name suggests, running down a sandy desert road, a comic yet somehow dignified creature, with a mound of boulders in the background. Mike had signed his usual "Redstone" in red down in one corner. The cactus frame, with the distinctive pattern of round and elongated holes in the cholla skeleton, fit the desert scene perfectly.

"Mike, I love it! Both the painting and the frame. We're looking for a home where we want to settle down permanently, and this will be the first thing we put in it."

Mike grinned, looking even more boyish than usual, obviously pleased with my delight in his work. He gave the painting a last look.

"Actually, I'm getting kind of fond of my roadrunners. Maybe they're not such bad art as I've always thought."

"I like your roadrunners. Maybe you should expand to other desert creatures."

"Lizards?" He grinned again. "Scorpions?"

"I was thinking more along the line of coyotes or wild donkeys."

"Maybe I will."

I got money from my purse for the payment we'd agreed on and held it out to him. "Oh, but it should be more, shouldn't it? Because you made the special frame."

"No, no, that's fine. I just wanted it to be special for you."

Actually, he looked embarrassed and lifted a hand, as if he were about to push my hand away and say both painting and frame were a gift. I quickly tucked the money in his shirt pocket before he could do that. I gave him a spontaneous hug and thanked him again.

Then I felt a little strange. Was I hugging a killer? Oh, surely not. Not likeable, nice-guy Mike. Probably, if I asked, he'd have a perfectly reasonable explanation for the switch from red cord to red ribbon.

Yet, feeling uncomfortable, I backed off and asked him if he'd gotten his mother moved over okay.

"Yes, she's set up in the RV park in Tacna. She and her cat. It's a stray that moved in just a few weeks ago, but she said she couldn't leave it behind. I pulled her trailer over with my van, but she had to drive her car, and with the accident and all, she's pretty well worn out from the trip. But she says she's coming to hear the band play Friday night. She's never heard us."

"We might be interested too," I said impulsively.

Mike looked doubtful. "We're playing at a bar just outside Gila Bend. It's called the Laughing Ferret." He smiled. "Very high-class place. The drinks come in tin cans and the restroom doors say 'Hobs' and 'Gills.' That's the ferret equivalent of gentlemen and ladies."

"Oh." I guess I sounded a bit taken aback.

"But you don't have to drink, of course. If you'd like to come, you could have a, you know, Coke or something. Or just sit there and listen to the music."

"We like 7UP," Mac said. We'd done some snooping in a bar before, and 7UP was always our go-to drink.

"They have pizza too," Mike added.

"Can you tell us more about grunge music?" I asked. "Do lots of people come to hear you?"

"Grunge isn't as popular as it was back in the '80s and '90s, so we never know what kind of an audience we'll have. Sometimes it's standing room only, sometimes you could throw a dart in any direction and not hit anyone. Grunge music is kind of a fusion of punk rock and heavy metal."

What did that tell me? Not much, since those terms meant about as much to me as *hobs* and *gills*.

"Will Jenna be there?" Mac asked.

"I think so. Well, I'd better get going. Nice to see you guys again."

"Say, why don't you stay and have dinner with us?" Mac suggested. "Ivy is making her great meat loaf, and there's plenty to eat."

Mac's unexpected invitation gave me a jolt. I liked Mike. I didn't think he could be a killer. I was almost sure he wasn't a killer—

Working word in that thought: *almost.*

But I was saved from having to wonder if we'd be sharing meat loaf with a murderer when Mike said, "Thanks, but Jenna is expecting me. And the band still has a practice session tonight."

"Hey, wait a minute," Mac said. "I have something I want to give you."

He disappeared into the bedroom and came back with one of several extra Bibles we had packed in a storage container back there. We'd picked them up at a yard sale somewhere. Mac handed the Bible to Mike.

"We thought you might like to have this."

For a moment Mike simply looked startled by the gift. "I don't have much time to read." He sounded doubtful.

"It doesn't take much time to read a verse or two. And there's no better reading to start with than the Bible."

"Okay, well . . . maybe I will." He flipped the Bible open. "I might try to find some of the verses the pastor talked about in his last message. They were interesting. But I'll probably never be able to find them."

"There's a concordance in back. You look up a word, and it tells you all the places to find it."

I hastily grabbed some chocolate chip cookies from the cupboard and stuffed them in a plastic bag. At the door I handed the bag to Mike and also asked an oh-so-casual question. I really needed a reassuring answer. "I noticed you changed the cord on your little yarn roadrunners in the van to a red ribbon." Rather lamely I added, "It was such an attractive red cord."

"Oh yeah. It, uh, broke, so I had to use something else."

So there it was. A perfectly reasonable explanation. Although somewhat less than reassuring. The cord had been very sturdy looking . . . strong enough for tying up a dead body for transport . . . and I strongly doubted it could have broken unless he'd had a heavy-handed gorilla riding with him.

Had Mike realized I'd recognized the red cord and gotten rid of it? Did he now also realize I thought he was dodging the truth?

Apparently unconcerned, he lifted the Bible in a little wave and called another thanks as he went out to the van. "I hope we see you Friday night." He smiled wryly. "Although you might want to bring ear plugs."

Mac waited until the van pulled away before he closed the motorhome door. We looked at each other.

"So, what do you think?" I asked.

"About ear plugs or Mike?"

"Both."

"Ear plugs? Nah. It'll take more than a little loud music to make me need ear plugs." He smiled but then turned more serious. "About Mike . . . I think Mike isn't a very good liar."

"And he apparently felt the need to *try* to lie about the red cord," I said. "What do you think about Friday night?"

"I think we should give it a try. Though I may regret not taking Mike up on his ear-plugs advice. With both Mike's mother and Jenna there, who knows what kind of interesting information might turn up?"

I nodded. Okay, I was up for a couple of hours swigging 7UP at the Laughing Ferret and listening to a fusion of punk rock and heavy metal.

Although I'd better figure out if I was a hob or a gill.

Chapter 16

IVY

We arrived at the Laughing Ferret about 7:00, apparently earlier than most grunge enthusiasts. We'd asked Magnolia and Geoff if they'd like to come along, but Magnolia had twisted her neck trying to do some facial exercise she'd seen in a magazine and was keeping a cold pack on it. Mike and the band were just setting up their instruments. Several of Mike's roadrunner paintings, with For Sale signs, decorated the entryway. Another sign by the small stage supplied the band's name: The Dogfoot DingosI thought Dingos was a misspelling, but I guessed they can spell a band name any way they want to. A can for tips stood next to the sign.

The light was dim, but I could see that all four guys wore plaid flannel shirts, ripped jeans, and heavy combat boots. Two guys wore caps with the visors turned to the back; Mike and another guy had black stocking caps. They all looked, well, *grungy*. Even a little sinister.

I'd wondered what I should wear on this occasion and had finally settled on boots and the jeans grandniece Sandy had sent me a while back. Mac liked the jeans, although the oversized, fanciful design on the rear pockets still made me feel as if I were walking around with a glittery octopus twined in a Christmas tree on my backside. But I figured I'd be sitting down most of the time anyway.

Mike's mother and Jenna were at a table off to one side. Jenna stood and waved us over. She was in sync with ripped jeans of her own, but Mike's mother wore a dark pantsuit. The style was a bit outdated, but it looked elegant on her slender figure. Although my experience with fashion doesn't go much beyond Walmart and Penney's, I thought the pantsuit also looked quite expensive, maybe even designer-brand expensive. Maybe a good thrift shop find?

"Good to see you again, Leanna." I reached across the table and gave her hand a squeeze. "Though I'm sorry to hear about your fall."

Mike's mother smiled, but I sensed a certain reserve in the smile. Or maybe she was just tired. "Good to see you too."

A waitress, also in jeans *du jour*, with enough rips to make a mother worry about cold drafts and pneumonia, came to the table. We ordered our 7UPs, Jenna chose white wine, and Mike's mother asked for a margarita.

Leanna was not a talkative woman, but we managed to keep some small talk going. I asked about the trip over from San Diego and how she was doing after her fall. She touched the back of her head and murmured something about staples. Jenna and Leanna had come in Jenna's car so she could take Leanna home in case the evening turned out to be too much for her. Jenna also said Harry the Roadrunner had come back looking for more hamburger.

No startling new information in any of that.

Mike came over, said a welcoming *Hi* to everyone, and asked if we'd like to try a pizza. He recommended the Underground Ferret. No one else expressed an opinion, so I said, "That would be great," and he went over to talk to the waitress. He picked up a guitar when he went back to the stage.

Our drinks arrived, and yes, they were in tin cans. Although the cans were labeled with brand names, they weren't—thankfully—actually old used tin cans; the names were painted on. Mine was Nalley's Chili, and

Mac's said Pink Salmon and showed a big fish. Crystals of salt clung to the rim of Leanna's margarita in a corned beef hash can.

Then the music—I use the term loosely—started. The guy in the other stocking cap was the lead singer—again I use the term loosely—and I couldn't tell if he was wailing about a lost love or some bad fish he'd eaten. I winced at the discordant guitars and thunderous drumming. We needed more than ear plugs. This called for shooter's earmuffs and an insulated helmet. My hands edged up to clamp over my ears.

Then I swallowed hard and determinedly decided to try to be more open-minded. Lots of people apparently liked this music. I put my hands back in my lap and managed to quit wincing. I could see Mac was also trying. We held hands and after a few minutes I kind of became accustomed to the noise, rather like getting used to the taste of Kalamata olives. Yucky at first, but eventually quite tasty. The energetic—and limber—younger people on the small dance floor obviously enjoyed the music.

The pizza arrived during a short pause between songs. The young waitress set the giant-sized platter in the center of the table. "Would you like a plate, Mrs. Redstone?" she asked.

Mike's mother didn't acknowledge the waitress's question. She just kept sipping her drink. "Mrs. Redstone?" the waitress repeated with a light touch on Leanna's shoulder.

Leanna gave a little jerk. She straightened in her chair, as if she'd just realized the waitress was talking to her. "Yes, yes, that would be nice. Thank you."

And Jenna said, "Plates for everyone?"

I usually just set pizza on a napkin to eat, but plates were fine. We all nodded. But I wondered about Leanna. Did she have a hearing problem? Or maybe the music had affected her hearing; even being open-minded, I still felt as if my ears had been attacked by an army of pecking roadrunners.

No, a hearing problem wasn't it. Leanna had heard the question. She just hadn't realized it was directed to her. Almost as if being addressed as "Mrs. Redstone" was unfamiliar to her. Odd.

I'd been a little wary of what "underground ferret" might mean in a pizza, and the best I'd hoped for was something with pepperoni or hamburger, not totally inedible. But this pizza turned out to be unexpectedly sophisticated and quite delightful. Artichokes, spinach, and ham in a creamy sauce on a thin crust.

We scarfed down the pizza during the next couple of songs, and then I decided it was time for a trip to the restroom. I'm not a let's-all-go-to-the-restroom-together kind of person, so I got up to find the restrooms without inviting anyone to come along. On my way, the waitress came up behind me.

"Hey, your bling-on-the-butt jeans look great on you," she whispered. She also gave me a smile and an approving thumbs-up.

"Uh, thank you." I felt a little strange about a compliment that included the word *butt*. I was just grateful she'd whispered instead of shouting it out. Then, grabbing the chance, I said, "You've met Mike's mother before?"

"No, just Mike, from when the band played here a couple months ago." She gave a melodramatic sigh. "Awesome guy. But, unfortunately, he's taken, isn't he?"

So, she'd just assumed Leanna's last name was Redstone. What else would it be? Just because she hadn't answered to "Mrs. Redstone" probably only meant she was distracted by the music and her injury.

Still, it seemed peculiar. I couldn't think of any connection between her possibly having a different name and Mike possibly being a killer, but I had a sneaky thought that her driver's license would show if her name was something other than Redstone. Her purse was under the table, and when I returned from the restroom I could just lean down and pretend to tie my shoelace—

No, no, no. These boots don't have shoelaces, and getting into her purse might even look as if I were trying to grab money out of it. Or, bending over, I could have a muscle cramp and find myself stuck in that position. To say nothing of the questionable ethics of snooping in a friend's purse.

Junk that idea.

I was relieved to find that the restrooms had further identification on the doors. Under "Hobs" was a cartoonish picture of a mustachioed ferret wearing a cowboy hat and tie. The "Gills" ferret had shiny red lipstick, a glittery necklace, and flirty eyelashes.

I was definitely a gill. I was short on the shiny lipstick and eyelashes, but I did have glitter on my backside. When I went back to the table, Mike was at the mic. He looked over at us and smiled. "This next song is dedicated to my great friends Mac and Ivy." He identified us with a little wag of the guitar. "Thanks for coming."

And then, with Mike singing, they played a very decent rendition of the old Whitney Houston song "I Will Always Love You." Mac gave me a nice kiss on the cheek, and there was an unexpected round of applause.

We sat through several more songs before Jenna whispered that Leanna was getting tired and she was taking her home now. There were two pieces of the enormous pizza left, and we collected several napkins for Leanna to wrap them in. She gave me a little wave as they left.

Grunge wasn't my new favorite form of music, but we decided to stay for a couple more songs. It was during the second song that my foot hit something under the table. I peeked under there. Leanna's purse! In the fuss of getting the pizza wrapped so the grease wouldn't leak through, she'd forgotten it. By now Leanna and Jenna would already have left, but we could take the purse over to Mike.

I straightened in my chair, hit with a different thought. I'd contemplated this earlier, rejected it, but here it was: opportunity! Or was this a temptation I was supposed to avoid?

I touched the purse again with my foot. I clamped my boots around it so it wouldn't drift away.

Opportunity won.

I ducked my head under the table and unzipped the purse. I riffled around inside and found a wallet, unfolded it and felt around for the window for a driver's license. Yes, there it was! I could almost make out the photo. But a head under a table in a dimly lit bar is not exactly prime sleuthing territory, and I couldn't read the name. I bent farther down . . . I could almost make out the name now . . . but I was also instantly aware that my bottom was sticking up like some old western movie can-can dancer. A glittery-bottomed dancer. And I felt a back cramp coming on—

I hastily jerked upright in the chair before I was trapped in the rump-up position.

Mac touched my back. "Are you okay?"

"I'm fine. I . . . I think I'll go to the restroom again."

I tucked the wallet under my loose blouse and, trying not to look like someone who'd just snitched a wallet, headed for the *Gills*. Once inside, I stepped into a stall and opened the wallet. There with the picture of Leanna on the driver's license was a name. Not Redstone.

But it was a name, not too common a name, that I'd seen somewhere recently—

Then I remembered.

Back at the table I managed to duck down and stuff the wallet back in the purse. A minute later I pulled the purse onto the table. "Oh look, Leanna forgot her purse," I said brightly.

Between songs, we took the purse over to Mike, and Mac dropped a few bills in the tip can.

MAC

All the way out to the pickup, Ivy gave off that buzz of energy she gets when she's holding something in. In the pickup, I didn't start the engine. "Okay, what is it?" I asked.

"Did you notice that Mike's mother didn't respond when the waitress addressed her as Mrs. Redstone?"

"No, can't say that I did."

"At first I thought I might have imagined it, or maybe the music had affected her hearing, but when I looked at the driver's license in her wallet—"

"You looked in her wallet?" I was startled. "When?"

"I, uh, sneaked it out when I found her purse under the table. I looked at it in the restroom."

It's a good thing Ivy is an honest LOL because sometimes I think she could have been rather successful at various less-than-lawful occupations. Including, at the moment, pickpocket.

"And what did you find?"

"The license shows that her name is Leanna Grantham."

"Grantham? That sounds familiar—"

"Yes. It's the name we found on the internet. The name of the majority owner and head man at Craigmont, the man who died in prison after being sent up on the big tax fraud scheme."

We both contemplated the significance of that for a minute.

"You think Leanna was his wife . . . and Mike his son?" I asked.

"The information we found on Lawrence Grantham said he had a wife and son. His photo showed a healthy head of red hair, just like Mike's. Leanna's pantsuit tonight looked too expensive for a woman working in a hairdressing salon."

The pantsuit comment was a non sequitur for me, but I caught what Ivy was getting at. I thought of an alternate possibility.

"Aren't there places that sell designer clothing secondhand at reasonable prices?"

"There are. I thought of that too. But the pantsuit could also be something she's had for several years, something that came from back when she led a more affluent life as the wife of the head of a film company."

I hadn't noticed Leanna's pantsuit, but then Ivy added the thought that had also instantly barged into my mind. "A son whose father died in prison might be . . . bitter about the man who helped put him there," she said.

I nodded slowly. "Murderously bitter."

We drove back to the motorhome, and I was fairly certain Ivy was thinking the same thing I was: neither of us wanted Jenna's father's killer to turn out to be Mike. Someone from Warren's past at Craigmont, someone totally unknown to us, would be much more preferable.

But, as Ivy has said before, a killer is who he is, not who we'd prefer him to be.

IVY

In the morning we talked it over while eating oatmeal with cinnamon and raisins for breakfast and reached a reluctant decision. Although I kept reminding myself that we didn't have to get up on a pedestal and bluntly shout *Your boyfriend is a killer!* We could simply tell Jenna what we'd found, perhaps show it to her on the internet, and see what she thought. Her relationship with Mike appeared to be quite serious, and it wasn't fair to hide what we'd learned. It might even be dangerous for her, because if Mike was capable of one murder . . .

I went over to see Magnolia and ask how her neck was now. I found her wearing a brace, leftover from some previous neck problem. Typical of Magnolia, however, she had the brace wrapped in a flamboyant purple-and-red scarf so it looked more like a decoration than a medical device. She said, with the thought that heat might work better than cold, they were going into Yuma to find a spa where she could soak up to the neck in a hot tub.

So Mac and I headed out to Deadeye. Lightning's pickup was parked at his mobile, Jenna's blue car at her little trailer. But when we pulled up, she called to us from the door of Warren's double-wide and waved us over there.

"Do you have a few minutes?" Mac asked her when he opened the gate. "We'd like to talk to you about something."

"Sure. C'mon in." She stood back at the door to let us in. "I'm trying to get back to writing this morning, but I'm having writer's block. I think my mind needs a jump start to get it going."

I doubted the jolt we had to offer would be an uplifting jump start.

She led us into the living room and offered tea and Oreos she'd found in a cupboard, but we both declined. Somehow, enjoying tea and cookies when you're informing a woman her boyfriend may be a murderer seemed a bit insensitive.

First Mac gave her a general recap on what we'd found about Craigmont's demise and the principal owner's imprisonment and subsequent death.

"We had a, umm, thought on how this might be connected to that impressive chunk of money your father received," I said.

"The money that didn't come from some big stock market thing as he'd told me it did."

"Right," Mac said.

"Does it confirm what my mother said, that Dad may have been blackmailing someone?"

"We think what it suggests is that the money may have come from the government as a reward for information Warren supplied about a rather large amount of concealed income at Craigmont."

Jenna played lightly with her long braid as she considered this possibility. She didn't seem startled by it. "If anything was going on with finances at Craigmont, Dad would have known about it." She nodded to herself. "When I was a kid, I once skipped lunches at school so I could spend the money on some books meant for readers above my age. Dad called me into his home office and told me exactly what I'd done. And after that, for weeks I had to give him a written account of every penny I spent. With receipts." She paused and nodded again. "Yeah, if Craigmont was into anything sneaky, Dad would have found out about it."

My first thought was to wonder if she'd wanted to read books above her literary intellectual level or if she wanted a peek into something X-rated. I remember when I was a girl— Skip that. Irrelevant. But while I was thinking that, Jenna's thoughts apparently went elsewhere. She jumped up as if what we'd told her had just gotten through to her.

"He lied to me! Dad flat out lied to me about all that money! Maybe he was even in on helping them conceal it!"

Well, yes, that was certainly a possibility. But at the moment there was more to be concerned about than that.

"How about we take a look on the internet at the Lawrence Grantham who went to prison for the . . . irregularities at Craigmont," Mac suggested.

So Jenna booted up the computer she'd installed in her father's office, and Mac gave her the URL of the website. I hadn't noted it before, but he had. And there was Lawrence Grantham's photo, same as before. Except now I saw even more than before. Jenna instantly saw the resemblance too.

"He looks like Mike!"

"We think he's Mike's father." I hesitated. "Mike's mother's name isn't actually Leanna Redstone. The name on her driver's license is Leanna Grantham, although she may not be using that name now that

179

she's over here with Mike. But we think Mike's name is probably Mike Grantham."

I was relieved that she didn't question how I knew what name was on Leanna's driver's license. Instead, she caught her breath, shocked again. "Mike lied to me about his name?"

Yes again. But again there was more to be concerned about than another lie.

Jenna spent another long minute studying the photo until finally she said, "And *my* dad got *Mike's* dad sent to prison."

"That was apparently a side effect of the information Warren may have supplied the authorities about Craigmont's concealed income," Mac said. "But he didn't necessarily do it with any *malice* toward Lawrence Grantham."

"And now you think Mike killed my father as payback for what he did to Mike's father."

I thought about telling her about that incriminating red cord in Mike's van and around her father's body, but I let it go. That would all come out eventually. This was enough for now.

Fury suddenly twisted her face. "But you're *wrong*. Mike didn't do it. I know Mike. I . . . I love him!"

A strong defense. But she said the words with a touch of surprise, as if this might be the first time she'd admitted loving him, even to herself.

"He couldn't have done it. You're just . . . twisting everything! How do you know his mother has some other name on her driver's license? Did you snoop in her things and *look*? What right did you have to do that?"

Well, she'd hit on an awkward detail about the acquisition of this information. Sneaking a wallet out of a left-behind purse might be effective sleuthing, but it wasn't exactly friend-to-friend admirable.

Mac stood up and nudged me with his hip. Half of me wanted to stay and argue with Jenna; the other half just wanted to run from her fury. Actually, I felt a certain admiration for her outburst, for standing up for Mike. She wasn't going to accept all this simply because we said so.

Mac put his hand on my back and edged me toward the door. Jenna looked ready to pick up the computer and throw it at us.

"Yes!" she stormed. "Go. Get out! I won't listen to any more of this."

We hurried out to the pickup. Jenna didn't slam the door behind us. She just planted herself in the doorway and stood there, arms crossed, staring wrathfully at us. An avenging angel in ripped jeans.

Chapter 17

IVY

"Well," Mac said as we followed a roadrunner down the rough road in the pickup, "that didn't go too well, did it?"

"We can't really blame her for the hostile reaction. She's in love with Mike."

"Love is blind?"

Could be. "So, where do we go from here?" I asked.

"On a honeymoon?" Mac suggested.

A honeymoon. Yes. Eventually. But—

Before I could say anything, Mac echoed what I was thinking by adding, "But if we leave now, I'll feel as if we're abandoning Jenna. And, even if she's angry at us now, I think she may need us."

"She did suggest we leave," I reminded him. A rather forceful suggestion. I sighed. "But you're right, even though she certainly doesn't think so now, she may need us."

We went on back to the motorhome. Once again we showered the road dust away and then took BoBandy and Koop out for a walk before lunch. This time we actually saw one of our neighbors in the RV park. A middle-aged man, wild haired and bearded, dressed in something burlap-bag-looking, and carrying a walking stick big enough to whack dragons. Probably harmless, but I'd rather not meet him in a dark alley at midnight.

But then he surprised us by giving an enthusiastic response to my tentative wave and coming over to tell us his name was Tall Cactus and he'd been away on a pilgrimage to Boise, Idaho. This struck me as an odd place for a pilgrimage, but then he gave me a nice bag of Idaho potatoes and I felt a little guilty for being suspicious of him. I'd taken "pilgrimage" to mean a religious mission of some kind, but to Tall Cactus it apparently meant potatoes.

That evening we shared potato soup with Magnolia and Geoff, and the next morning Magnolia came over to tell us they'd decided to go over to the Tucson area for a few days. For once, it wasn't genealogy she had in mind; she'd been reading about Biosphere 2, an environmental research area where a team of people had spent a year or so living in an enclosed area shut off from the rest of the world, and she wanted to see it.

This sounded interesting, but Mac and I looked at each other. No, we weren't ready to leave yet. So we headed for church while they were readying the motorhome for a road trip. They'd said they'd probably come back in a few days.

Mike and Jenna weren't in church, which I regretted. After church, the space next to us in the RV park empty now, we had lunch and were lingering over tea and looking at maps of Baja again when my cell phone rang.

Jenna identified herself and then without preliminaries said, "I want to apologize for my outburst yesterday. I know you meant well telling me about Mike, and my rude reaction was way out of line."

All I could think to say was, "I know it was a shock—"

"I just got another shock. Mike called a few minutes ago. He was in his trailer working on a painting today, and two deputies from the sheriff's office had just left. They'd been there questioning him for over an hour. Apparently he's a suspect."

The sheriff's office must be working overtime if they were out questioning a suspect on Sunday morning. Which probably meant they'd just uncovered the same information we had about Mike's connection to Warren. I had no idea how they'd done it, but probably not by digging around in someone's purse while listening to grunge music with a glittery-bottomed rump stuck up in the air. I said a cautious, "Oh?"

"I asked him why they were questioning him, and he said he had something he needed to tell me. He's coming over. I'd guess he's going to tell me the same thing you did, about who he really is."

I felt a sharp jolt of alarm. "Would you like us to come over and be there when—"

"No! Of course not. The police might think Mike could have killed my father, but he didn't do it. I *know* he didn't! We just need to . . . talk about the situation. He's coming on his bike and we're going for a ride."

"Did they question his mother?"

"I don't think so. He didn't mention that. They probably have no idea she's here."

Maybe. Maybe not. Even though the sheriff's department wasn't advertising their activities, they were obviously keeping busy, definitely not shirking on the investigation.

"They'd have no reason to question her anyway," Jenna added.

Probably. Although devastated and bitter wives have been known to be rather vengeful too. Son and mother working together?

"Look, I'll call you again after Mike and I talk, okay?"

"Where are you going on the bike?"

"To those big rocks off to the east of here. We've been there several times. There are a few trees and a little pool of water. Desert animals come there to drink. There are more of them than you might think." Sounding as if it were a sudden inspiration, she added, "It's a nice spot for a lunch. I'll make some sandwiches to take along." I thought that was good-hearted of her, attempting to turn what she apparently expected might be an awkward exposé of lies Mike had told her into a pleasant picnic. But if Mike really was a killer—

"Well, uh, have fun," I said lamely and tapped the Off button.

Mac lifted his eyebrows, and I told him what Jenna had said. "I suppose everything will be okay. He just wants to talk to her."

"So he says. But maybe Jenna knows something incriminating that connects him with her father's murder. Something she doesn't even realize she knows. And when they talk, he realizes there's big danger here. So he decides, *Well, it's too bad, she's a wonderful girl and all that, and I really like her, but—*"

Another lift of eyebrows as he let me fill in the unpleasant possibilities.

"She could wind up buried in the desert somewhere, like her father."

"Right."

"*If* he did something to her father. We don't have any proof," I reminded him.

I was still resisting believing Mike was a killer, but I didn't want that resistance to close my eyes to the danger here. If Mike had just said to Jenna, *We have to talk,* it wouldn't be so worrisome. But taking her to some isolated spot out on the desert alone . . .

"Maybe we should run over there again," I said. "We could be there when Mike arrives. Just in case."

"Maybe the time Jenna needs us has come sooner than we expected," Mac agreed.

So we jumped in the pickup again and roared—at least as much of a roar as our little pickup can make—out to Deadeye again.

No bike was parked outside Warren's double-wide. I felt an uptick of hope. We'd gotten here first, before Mike. We jumped out of the pickup and ran through the gate and up the steps. Mac pounded on the door. No answer.

Without hesitation he threw the door open. "Jenna!"

Silence. No Jenna. Then we looked out the window that showed the boulders off to the east. A plume of dust rose between us and the rocks. No, we had not gotten here before Mike.

"Can we follow them?" I asked.

Mac hesitated only momentarily. "We can try."

We ran back to the pickup. Mac wheeled it around Warren's double-wide and then drove along the end of the clearing, looking for a way through the creosote bushes and rocks and cactus.

He peered over the steering wheel at some faint markings on the ground. "Is that a road?"

Well, no, it wasn't really a road. But there were old, dim tracks leading into the desert, and one side showed the fresher single tire track of a motorcycle.

Mac followed the tracks. Creosote bushes whipped the sides of the pickup. Cholla cactus thrust a bristly arm into the window. A big bird circled in the sky ahead of us.

Vultures are carrion eaters. Somehow it doesn't feel like a good sign when a vulture is considering how soon you may reach snack stage. The plume of dust had faded now. Had Mike and Jenna reached their destination? We were going too slow to raise any dust of our own. Maybe Mike wouldn't realize we were following him.

Good. We'd sneak up and surprise him.

We floundered on. One side of the pickup went up as a front tire climbed over a rock. Mac swung the steering wheel, trying to avoid hitting the rock with a back tire too. Didn't make it. The back wheel lifted and the pickup tilted precariously before it made a teeth-rattling thunk back to level. We dodged bushes and cactus and bigger rocks. We roused some little desert birds that took to the air in panic. We crossed a dry creek bed, down one crumbling bank, up a steeper bank on the far side, tires spinning ominously. If we got stuck out here—

No. Mac managed to back up a few feet, then stormed up the bank. I wasn't sure we were even on the old tracks now, but the big tan

186

boulders were closer, even bigger than they looked from a distance, and odder shaped. I could also see a couple of small trees. And yes, there was a bike parked in the shade of a boulder shaped like an upright French baguette.

Mac stopped the pickup beside the dusty motorcycle. A couple of motorcycle helmets hung from the handles. Desert silence immediately surrounded us. Then we heard a faint hint of music.

We followed the sound around the baguette-shaped boulder and between several other tan boulders shaped like everything from a Volkswagen Bug to an oversized puffball. And there was one that Mac would no doubt call just a lumpy rock, but I saw a definite silhouette in it. That singer. What was her name? I was too fearful of what we might find at any moment, however, to really appreciate the picturesque boulders. Mike burying Jenna's body in a secluded spot of sand? Mike lying in wait for us?

I felt in my pocket for a weapon. Usually my pocketknife is in my purse, but sometimes I stick it in my pocket. Hopefully this was one of those times—

No. Now my pocket held one tissue—used—and one peppermint candy in a tattered wrapping.

Did Mike have a gun?

Some old saying warns *Never take a knife to a gunfight.* We were in an even more worrisome situation because a peppermint candy is undoubtedly even less useful in a gunfight.

Mac apparently wasn't worried about weapons, however. He charged ahead and I followed. And there, up ahead, was the tiny pool of water Jenna had mentioned, a paloverde tree beside it.

Also there were Mike and Jenna, sitting on a bench-like rock and eating sandwiches, cans of Pepsi beside them. The music came from a cell phone sitting on the rock between them.

An idyllic scene of young love. Or was it music to kill your girlfriend by?

Although Mike didn't look murderous at the moment. I couldn't see any bulges that suggested he was carrying a gun or a knife. He unwrapped another sandwich and looked our way.

"Well, this is an unexpected pleasure," he said, the sarcasm heavier than the motorcycle boots on his feet. "What brings you out this way?"

How to respond to that? *We just happened to be in the area* was a little flimsy. I said, "We, umm, missed you in church this morning."

"I was busy answering questions from a couple of detectives. Perhaps you sent them?" he inquired with polite malice.

"No, but we're here now because we're concerned about Jenna," Mac said.

"You're worried I might kill her the way you think I killed her father?" Mike took a chomp of the sandwich. Ham and cheese, I could see now.

Before I could say that we didn't necessarily *think* he'd killed Warren, that we were just considering all possibilities, Jenna said forcefully, "I told you you didn't need to come. Everything's fine. Mike was just telling me what you told me, that his father was the head of Craigmont and went to prison on tax fraud."

"And that my name is really Mike Grantham, not Mike Redstone. Pepsi?" he added with that same polite venom. "There are a couple more in the saddlebags."

We ignored the offer, and Mac pointed out another discrepancy. "You also told Jenna that your father was a banker and you dropped out of college when he had a heart attack and died."

"Well, partly true. Dad wasn't a banker, but he did have a heart attack and died, and I did drop out of college. The collapse of Craigmont took every asset my parents had. I was hanging on part-time at college with the money I made with a weekend band. And then, before Dad died in prison, he told me he was certain the company's head accountant had collaborated with the IRS to bring both him and the company down. He thought the collaborator had gotten a big reward for doing it."

Mike's double use of the "collaborate" word somehow made it sound as if Warren was the one who had done something underhanded and unethical, not his father. Jenna wasn't nodding agreement, but neither was she protesting this harsh view of her father.

"So you dropped out of college, vowing vengeance against the man you considered responsible for your father's death," I said.

"That's phrasing it a bit melodramatically, but yes, it was something like that," Mike agreed. "It took me quite a while after my father's death to find out where Warren had gone after he left Craigmont, and even then I didn't have a specific address for him. I decided I'd use a different name while I looked for him so he wouldn't accidentally hear the name Grantham and know I was after him."

"Under the cover of being a simple roadrunner artist and player of grunge music," Mac filled in.

"But I didn't kill Warren," Mike declared. "I don't care how it looks, or how much motive you or the sheriff think I have, I didn't kill him."

"Do your buddies in the Dogfoot Dingos know your real name?" I asked.

"No, I met them here. And I only started painting roadrunners using the name Redstone after I came here. Mom has always used her real name over in San Diego and on her job, but we decided it would be best if she also used Redstone here."

Except when you've been Grantham for as long as Leanna had, it's rather difficult to get used to another name. I know. I had a little difficulty moving from Ivy Malone to Ivy MacPherson. It's probably especially difficult when someone unexpectedly addresses you by that different name when you're drinking a margarita in a noisy bar.

"But when you met Jenna you decided you couldn't do something harmful to her father after all?" I asked.

189

"I'd decided that even before I met Jenna." Mike glanced over at her sitting silently beside him, gaze apparently stuck on her sandwich. "I still think my father would be alive if he hadn't been in prison when he had a heart attack. He didn't get proper care there." He swallowed. Hard. "But I didn't kill the man who was responsible for his being there."

I didn't point out that the bottom line was that Lawrence Grantham, by doing a shady coverup of a large flow of income, was himself responsible for his being in prison. Jenna kept her gaze on her sandwich.

"I know Dad broke the law with what he did. But he was a great guy, a great father," Mike said. It was a first admission that his father hadn't been totally innocent in all this. "Good friends called him Lefty because he was left-handed. I used to try to use my left hand so I could be more like him. Mom always called him Larry. Before he died, I promised him I'd always take good care of Mom."

The little details somehow showed how they'd once been a close-knit family, and I felt a pang for his loss. I could also see he was doing his best to take care of his mother.

"But I finally had to admit to myself that I'm not a killer no matter how bitter I felt about Dad's imprisonment and death."

"But you did find out Warren was living out by Deadeye and came out to confront him," Mac said. "That's how you met Jenna."

"No. I came out to Deadeye because I'd heard there was an old desert town out here, and I thought it might make a good background for some roadrunner paintings. It wasn't until I met Jenna and she told me her name and showed me around Deadeye that I realized her father was the man I'd come here to find."

"Mike did not kill my father," Jenna stated almost fiercely. "Even if he did . . . mislead me about a few things."

"So if you didn't kill him, who did?" Mac challenged.

Mike hesitated for a moment, and I was almost certain he had someone in mind. But then he simply shook his head and said, "Who knows?"

So, if he did have someone in mind, it wasn't information he planned to share with us. Why not? He took a couple more bites of his sandwich, as if the conversation was over.

But I had an incriminating point to add. "The cord used to wrap Warren's body was the same as the cord you used to tie those two little roadrunners in your van."

Jenna shot Mike a dismayed look. He gave a dismissive shrug without looking at her.

"And then, when you realized I'd recognized the cord, you changed it to a red ribbon."

"I told you. The cord in the van broke. I don't know where it came from. Maybe it was in one of the bags of old stuff I hauled off to the dump for an elderly woman when I was painting her garage. Or I might have gotten it at one of the gift shops that handles my paintings. Or maybe I just picked it up off the ground somewhere. Then, when it broke, I replaced it with that piece of red ribbon I happened to have. The ribbon probably come from one of the gift shops too."

TMI, I thought. Way too much information.

"So it's just coincidence that the cord you used on the little roadrunners in your van just happened to be the same kind of cord that was around Warren's body when we found it," Mac said.

"That's right. Coincidence." Mike's statement had a stubborn that's-my-story-and-I'm-sticking-to-it sound. Then an equally stubborn attack. "What makes you so sure it was the same? Did you actually compare them?"

"No, of course not," I said. But I was as sure of it as I was that something was crawling up my leg under my jeans. I felt panic crawling with it. Scorpion? Desert mouse? Some deadly desert species hitherto unknown to science?

I jumped and stomped and shook my leg as if I were inventing a new grunge-music dance. Mike grabbed my arm and saved me from a tumble to the ground. An ant dropped out of my jeans. It was the size of a couple of pinheads.

"Thank you," I muttered to Mike, and Mac said, "You okay?"

"I'm fine."

Mike ignored my impromptu dance and resumed his position on the rock. The ant wisely disappeared into the sand.

"Perhaps you mentioned the cord to the detectives investigating Warren's death and that's why they came to question me?" Mike suggested.

"No, we haven't said anything about that to them." Mac paused a moment for emphasis. "Yet."

"I have to go in to the sheriff's office and talk to someone else there tomorrow," Mike said. "Perhaps you should hurry and tell them before then so they'll be ready to slap me in handcuffs."

"You could tell them yourself," I pointed out.

"Right. I could even see if I have any more of the cord left to show them, couldn't I?"

Jenna rewrapped her half-eaten sandwich. Although she had loyally defended Mike, her stricken expression now said that doubts were surfacing. But in spite of those doubts, she determinedly moved over and sat closer to him.

"I'm going in with him," she said. "I can't locate the lawyer who wrote Dad's will. I think he must be retired or dead. I'm going to see if I can get into that file cabinet they took out of Dad's office. There must be a copy of the will in there."

"I hope that works for you," Mac said.

In an abrupt change of subject, Mike suddenly said, "I want to thank you for the Bible you gave me. I looked up those verses that interested me. One of them was in the book of Hebrews, about God never forsaking you."

"There's also a verse in one of the Psalms along similar lines: 'God is our refuge and strength, an ever-present help in trouble,'" Mac said. "And another from . . . somewhere. 'Cast all your anxiety on him because he cares for you.'"

I was surprised and pleased. Since Mac came to share my faith, he and I study the Bible together regularly, and it's nice to know the essence of what we study is really sticking. Even if he can't always pin down the location of a verse yet.

"But I suppose all that good stuff is just for people who don't commit any sins," Mike said, his tone dismissive.

"We all commit sins," Mac said, and I was again gratified by his comment. But I was also wondering if Mike was thinking that killing Jenna's father was probably a sin that shut him out of God's love and care forever. I know that the extent of God's forgiveness can be amazing, but given Jenna's troubled expression, I had to wonder how forgiving her human love might be.

"I'll do some more reading," Mike muttered.

I tossed him my lone peppermint candy before we retreated back the way we'd come. The sand here among the boulders was softer than out in the open, though I couldn't identify the many animal tracks scrambled together. We should bring BoBandy out here sometime. He'd love chasing around in the sand and boulders.

"It's encouraging that Mike is actually reading that Bible we gave him," Mac said as we rounded the baguette-shaped boulder.

I nodded. Yes, encouraging. "Unless . . ."

"Unless?"

"I hate to think it, but maybe he's just trying to butter us up."

"Make us think he's such a good guy, reading his Bible and all, that he couldn't possibly be a killer? Yeah, could be," Mac agreed, although he didn't sound happy about it.

We bumped and bounced back across the desert, and when we passed Warren's double-wide, we saw Lightning doing something at the pump house. Mac backed up and swung closer to where Lightning was leaning against a shovel, watching us.

"Hey, we haven't seen much of you lately," Mac said.

It looked as if Lightning had been uncovering the pipe leading from the pump house to Warren's double-wide. Trying to figure out how to divert the water from this deep well over to his place? The thought occurred to me that even though I hadn't given Lightning much thought lately, he was still right up there as a suspect in Warren's murder.

"Been keeping busy. Lots of things going on with the company that's going to use Deadeye as the site for their next project."

"Have you talked any more to the detectives investigating Warren's death?" I asked.

"Yeah. I had to go in to the office and sign the statement I'd made. Though I think they're just a bunch of Mickey Mouse losers trying to make it look as if they know what they're doing when all they're really doing is spinnin' their wheels."

"You might be surprised how much they're doing," Mac said.

"That so?" Lightning looked interested and, I thought, a little wary. "Well, I hope they don't do nothin' to mess up my deal with Hamilton Productions. It's comin' along nicely. Probably start filmin' this fall." He held up his arm and looked at his watch. "I'll be leavin' in a few minutes to go back over there for a day or two."

"You need someone to feed the horses for you?"

"Nah. I'll put out enough feed for them for a couple days." Then, as if it were merely an afterthought, he added, "You think those deputies are zeroin' in on any suspects in Warren's death?"

"The sheriff's office is pretty close-mouthed about what they're doing," Mac said.

In an apparent change of attitude toward the "Mickey Mouse losers," Lightning nodded approvingly. "That's good."

He didn't ask what we'd been doing wandering around on the desert, which made me wonder if there was some distracting worry behind the nod of approval. I also wondered if he knew about Mike's connection with his old movie company.

I do a lot of wondering, don't I?

We'd just waved goodbye to Lightning when Mike's motorcycle roared up and skidded to a stop at Jenna's trailer. Jenna slid off and they exchanged what looked like heated words, and then the bike roared away.

"What was that all about?" Mac asked.

I wondered too. Jenna was still standing where Mike had dropped her at the trailer. "Should we stop and ask if she's okay?"

I momentarily thought Jenna was going to turn her back on us when we pulled up beside her, but she simply stood there as if her feet had frozen into the ground.

"Is something wrong?" I asked when I got out of the pickup.

"Mike got a phone call. His mother is in custody. She just confessed to killing my father."

Chapter 18

MAC

"*Confessed?*" Ivy squeaked.

"I wanted to go with him, but he wouldn't let me," Jenna said.

Which explained the heated words.

"But he's supposed to call me after he finds out what's going on," she added.

"Look, why don't you come over to our place while you're waiting for him to call?" Ivy suggested. "You can have dinner with us—"

She touched her stomach. "I couldn't eat anything!"

"And maybe, if Mike hasn't called yet, stay the night with us. Lightning is leaving in a few minutes and you'll be all alone out here."

I didn't think she'd do it. She hadn't objected to being alone here before, and at this point we probably weren't her favorite people. But, after looking around with a vague expression, as if everything around her was strange and unfamiliar, she unexpectedly nodded. She didn't even go into the trailer, just followed us to the pickup. Which emphasized how stunned she was by this.

Back at the motorhome and an enthusiastic welcome-home greeting from BoBandy, Ivy asked Jenna if she'd like to shower. After a ride across the desert on a motorcycle, she was even more windblown and dusty than we were, messy strands of dark hair falling out of her usually neat braid. She shook her head.

"I don't want to miss Mike's phone call."

So we sat there in rather awkward—dusty—silence until Ivy mentioned that we were planning to go down to Baja when we left Prosperity. Jenna seemed relieved to talk about something other than Mike and his mother, and we carried on a rather extensive, if stilted, conversation about Baja and the Sea of Cortez. Koop jumped into Jenna's lap while we talked and BoBandy snuggled at her feet, as if they both knew she needed comforting.

Somewhat later, Ivy started dinner. Taco night. Ivy cooked and seasoned the meat, and I chopped onions and tomatoes and lettuce. Jenna helped by grating cheese. While we were eating, Jenna got the call from Mike. She got up from the table and went over to the sofa to take it.

When she returned to the table, she said, "He doesn't know much more than he did before. He couldn't get in to see his mother. I told him I was here, so he's on his way to pick me up."

"You're still welcome to stay here tonight," Ivy said.

Jenna murmured something that sounded much like Ivy's "umm" when she's stalling for time.

I had four of the great tacos and Jenna managed to finish one. Ivy washed the dishes in our tiny sink. Jenna dried. She peered out the window every few minutes, looking for Mike, and well after dark, his motorcycle roared up. Jenna headed for the door, ready to run out to him, but Ivy restrained her.

"Let him come in. He must be tired. Maybe he needs something to drink."

So Jenna just opened the door, and a minute later Mike came inside. He looked chilled to the bone. At the time he'd dropped Jenna off at her trailer, he hadn't been dressed for a long bike ride in the dark.

He plunked down on the sofa, and Jenna sat close to him.

"You look as if you need coffee," Ivy said. He nodded and she poured a cup for him. He grabbed it and didn't ask for sugar or cream. "You didn't get to see your mother?"

"No. There are regulations about not having visitors right after being taken into custody. They said I could probably see her tomorrow."

"Perhaps the first thing you should do is get a lawyer for her," I suggested.

Mike just sat there in silence, his usually smooth brow now wrinkled in worry and thought.

"Did . . . did she really do it?" Jenna's voice wavered.

More silence from Mike, which struck me as peculiar. Was he horrified by what his mother had done? Disbelieving? Worried about her mental state?

"No, she didn't do it," he said suddenly. "She only confessed because she's trying to protect me. She thinks I did it."

Not a surprising thought on his mother's part. Ivy and I'd certainly had similar suspicions since finding out Warren had gotten the big-bucks reward for reporting on Craigmont. And then Mike hit us with the bottom line.

"And she's right. Because I did do it. I killed Warren."

He spoke calmly, as if he were merely announcing that he'd eaten the last cookie in the jar. Jenna didn't move, just sat there as if turned into a statue. Ivy and I exchanged quick glances.

Mike suddenly stood up. He looked at me, then Ivy. "You know it too. Ever since you saw that red cord, you've known it."

"I-I don't believe it," Jenna said. "You didn't . . . you couldn't . . ."

"You want to know how I did it? Okay, I'll tell you. You were gone, on that trip to New York for your mother's birthday. I drove out and knocked on Warren's door. I went there on purpose to kill him. Because of what he did to my father. I'd just been waiting for a good opportunity."

"A good opportunity was while I was gone." Jenna's voice was flat.

"Yes. I asked him if he'd unlock the gate to Deadeye so I could get my van in there to set up some photos."

"Why didn't you just kill him right there at his mobile?" Ivy asked. "Why get him out on the street at Deadeye?"

"Because I-I didn't want Jenna to come home and be the one to find his body." He didn't look at Jenna as he said it.

"You had a gun and shot him?" she asked.

"No. I-I strangled him." That brought a sob from Jenna, but Mike ignored it. "I used a piece of leather cord."

Which explained why there wasn't any blood within the one-legged outline Magnolia had drawn in the dirt.

Mike swallowed. "I figured I'd just leave his body there on the street and Lightning would find it later. But then, minutes after I'd killed him, your friend Magnolia came waltzing down the street. I hid, but when she went back to the motorhome, I picked up his body and carried it over to the back fence and . . . threw it over."

That explained Warren's cell phone dropped outside the fence.

A strangled sob came from Jenna as she heard about this rough treatment of her father's body, as if Mike were discarding no more than the old rags the deputies thought Magnolia had found.

"Why?" Ivy said. "If you planned to leave the body there, why did you change your mind and move it?"

"Because I-I panicked. My van was still over at Warren's mobile. I couldn't drive the van away without going past the motorhome that was parked out at the gate. I knew they must be calling 911 or the sheriff's office, so while they were doing that I went back and moved the van around behind Warren's mobile where it would be harder to see. Then I just stayed there. Fortunately for me, when the deputies came and searched for the missing body, they didn't look outside the fence and they didn't come around to where the mobiles are."

He paused and took a deep breath.

"Then, after both the deputies and the motorhome were gone, I went back and retrieved the body. I got a blanket from Warren's closet and wrapped his body in it and tied that red cord around it to keep the blanket in place. Then I-I drove back to my trailer and waited some more, and then in the middle of the night I drove out to Prosperity and buried the body in one of those old holes there. I figured it wouldn't be found for months, if ever, and there would be less investigation now if Warren was just missing than if a body was found."

"What about that postcard from Las Vegas?" Ivy asked.

Mike looked startled, as if he'd forgotten the postcard, but he had a quick explanation. "I figured that would make it look as if he went missing from there. Which would keep the investigation away from here. Where his body was buried."

"But how did you send it from Vegas?" Ivy persisted.

"I-I took a quick trip up there. I bought the postcard, and I knew Warren always printed, so that's what I did on the postcard."

"You helped me look for Dad's Jeep at the airport, and all the time you knew it wasn't there!" Jenna said. "You suggested maybe he'd flown out of some other airport. When all the time you knew he was dead and buried out on the desert!"

Mike ignored her and turned his gaze to Ivy and me. "But then you two had to go messing around out there and find him."

"How inconsiderate of us," I muttered.

"Out there at the boulders, you were quite definite in saying you *hadn't* killed Warren," Ivy pointed out.

Mike shrugged. "I didn't know then that my mother would come up with some wild idea of confessing. I can't let her take the blame for something I did."

"You know we have to go to the sheriff with this information," Ivy said. "Unless you intend to kill us too?"

"No. I-I killed the man who was responsible for my father's death. I don't have anything against you. But you don't need to turn me in. I'll do it myself." He clapped his hands against his thighs, making a punctuation mark on the statement, and stood up.

"Now?" Ivy said. "It's getting late and it's dark—" She broke off as if realizing those details were hardly relevant when a murder was involved.

"This is as good a time as any," Mike said.

"Maybe they won't believe you," Jenna said. "Since your mother already confessed."

"They'll believe me. I'll stop by my trailer and pick up the leather cord I killed him with. And the rest of that roll of red cord too." His smile was unnaturally brilliant. "That should convince them."

He went out the door without a backward glance, and the three of us just sat there in stunned silence as the bike roared away. After a while Ivy said, "The sofa makes into a bed. I'll make it up for you so you can sleep here tonight."

"I-I can't do that." Jenna frowned, apparently searching for a reason. "I don't have pajamas or . . . anything."

"I have extra pajamas. They'll be short in the legs for you, but they'll work."

Jenna didn't say anything. I suspected she was torn. She didn't want to stay here with us but she didn't want to be alone back at the trailer. And then her cell phone rang.

She looked at the information on the screen and groaned, but she managed to sound perky when she said, "Hi, Mom."

I couldn't hear what Sable said, but Jenna's dismayed response was clear enough. "You're *here?*" She moved the phone away from her ear, as if expecting a loud response, and that's what she got.

"Yes, I'm *here.* Where are *you?* Your car is here but *you* aren't," Sable blasted through the phone, loud enough for Ivy and me to hear. "I'm sitting out here in the dark and this place is like a tomb—"

"I thought you were going to Paris."

"I want to go, but you know I can't do it until I get the insurance money."

Jenna put the phone back to her ear and walked over to lean against the kitchen stove. "I didn't know you were coming, Mom. You didn't tell me, or I'd have been there at the trailer. I'm over here at Mac and Ivy's place. You remember Mac and Ivy? Their motorhome is in the RV park behind the little Prosperity store."

Now I couldn't hear what Sable had to say, but I could see Jenna's expression. *Just what I don't need, my mother here,* it said. Dismay and frustration. "Just wait there, Mom. I think Mac and Ivy will bring me back to the trailer—"

She lifted her gaze to Ivy, and Ivy gave her a quick nod. But then Sable was talking again, and finally Jenna said, "Okay," and tapped the Off button.

"We'll take you over right away," I said.

"Mom's coming here. She doesn't want to be sitting out there alone. She says she hears wolves howling."

"Wolves?" Ivy repeated doubtfully.

"I often hear coyotes yipping in the night. Mom has apparently turned them into wolves." Jenna gave a humorless laugh. "No doubt the man-, or woman-, eating kind."

We'd heard coyotes too. I rather liked to hear them yipping in the night.

"Mom doesn't want either of us staying out there at the trailer. She says we'll go into Yuma and get a motel for the night, and then I should come back to Scottsdale with her."

"That might be best," Ivy agreed.

"So we'll go in to Yuma and get a motel, like she wants. Tomorrow we'll try again to get the death certificate she's after, and then she can go on home." Jenna's voice hardened. "Alone. I'm not going with her.

I-I guess Mike will be in jail?" She said it as a question not a statement, and Ivy just gave her a wordless hug.

IVY

Sable didn't come in when she arrived, just blasted the horn, and Jenna told us goodbye and went out to the car. What would Sable's reaction be when Jenna told her about Mike? Especially if Sable herself had killed Warren? The sheriff may think he had his killer now, but I had my doubts about Mike's story. It was certainly a detailed and specific story, but I still didn't believe it. I declared as much to Mac as soon as Sable's car disappeared in a flare of red taillights.

"I think he was just making it up as he went along. He's confessing to protect his mother."

Mac tilted his head reflectively. "It's a pretty good story. He even said how he killed Warren, with a leather cord, which is information the sheriff's office has never released."

Yes, that was troubling. How could he have known how Warren was killed unless he'd done it himself? "But there are other parts of the story that just don't hold together," I insisted.

"Such as?"

"Why would Warren go with Mike to unlock the gate out at Deadeye? Warren wasn't that helpful a kind of guy. And all that stuff about going up to Las Vegas to send the postcard." I gave it a thumbs-down gesture. "And out at the rocks, when you asked him if he didn't do it, who did? He hesitated, and I'm sure he had someone specific in mind, but he didn't want to tell us."

"Because the person he had in mind was his mother," Mac said.

I put a pot of water on the stove for tea. I needed tea.

"But Mike apparently has both the leather cord with which Warren was strangled and the red cord that was tied around the body," Mac said.

More troubling points. Very troubling. But I still wasn't convinced of Mike's guilt. Leanna's guilt was another matter, however.

"So what are your thoughts now on who did it?" Mac asked.

My thoughts were muddled, but they definitely swayed toward Mike's mother. Losing her husband and almost everything they'd owned was plenty of motive. It would explain why she'd rushed home when Jenna invited her to lunch; she was uncomfortable lunching alone with the daughter of the man she'd killed. Mike had the leather cord and the red cord because his mother was the killer.

But if Leanna had done it, how had she managed all the body-moving complications? Warren, according to Jenna, was not a big man, but it was still hard to picture rather fragile-looking Leanna lugging him around.

And there were still the other possibilities. The other mother, Jenna's mother. She had a big motive: two million dollars of insurance money. She could have killed Warren while Jenna was still in New York seeing literary agents. She was apparently physically capable of lugging a dead ex-husband around

Or mothers might be getting a bad rap here, I reminded myself. Lightning could have killed his brother in order to acquire all of Deadeye for himself. He'd certainly jumped into grabbing onto the well water quickly enough.

Someone unknown from Craigmont may have done it.

And we'd never actually disproved that blackmail theory. Perhaps, in addition to the big whistleblower payoff, Warren had had a tidy blackmail income. And a very unhappy blackmail-ee.

Suspects galore. The only one I'd really eliminated was Jenna herself.

"I still don't think Mike did it," I said.

Mac didn't say anything, but I could read his mind in response to that. *Stubborn LOL.* What he actually said was, "What are we going to do now?"

And my response was quick. "Find out who really killed Warren."

Chapter 19

IVY

Last night I'd made that bold statement about finding the killer, but this morning my idea box on how to accomplish that looked as shiny and empty as Koop's dish after he's attacked a half can of tuna. So, while Mac took BoBandy for a walk, I baked a big batch of raisin-oatmeal cookies. Afterward we took a sack of them over to the man who'd given us the potatoes. He thanked us effusively and said his next pilgrimage would be to Wisconsin to visit a cheese-making factory. Apparently, his pilgrimages had a great deal to do with food and were perhaps more successful than our efforts to have a honeymoon.

We returned to our motorhome. I'd hoped the diversion would jump-start some ideas, but that didn't happen.

Maybe we should just get on with the honeymoon.

But shortly after lunch, I had a thought on a different subject. "With both Mike and Leanna in custody, I wonder if anyone's taking care of her cat?"

Mike had said it was a stray she'd taken in before she'd come to Tacna. I looked over at Koop, his long, orange body draped over the back of the sofa as he watched out the window with his one good eye. King of his domain. But he'd once also been a stray. So had BoBandy. I had a soft spot in my heart for strays.

"We could go over and check," Mac said.

We found the RV park in Tacna easily enough. It wasn't overflowing, but it was considerably more populated than the Prosperity park. A woman in the office said Mrs. Redstone's trailer was in Space 21. I wondered, if the cat was inside, how we were going to handle that, but it didn't turn out to be a problem. Leanna opened the door as we approached the trailer. She saw my surprised look.

"I didn't expect to be here either, but they released me this morning." She sounded more frustrated than pleased about the release. She was also, I guessed, more annoyed than pleased to see us. She was wearing a silky, flowered muumuu, but she was barefoot and her hair was sleep-deprived messy. She gave it a fluff with one hand. "I just got up from a nap. Jail is not conducive to a good night's sleep."

"You were released because they have Mike in custody now?"

"I guess that's the reason. A get-out-of-jail-free card."

So, even though I found Mike's story rife with weak points, it had apparently been good enough to convince the authorities.

"But Mike didn't *do* anything! *I* killed Warren Langston." She slapped a hand on her own chest in exasperation. "Me! But I can't seem to convince them of that."

"Did you tell them how you killed him?" Mac asked.

"Why should I tell them?" Leanna gave a defiant toss of the messy hair. "They know how he was killed."

Which said to me that she didn't know how Warren was killed. Mike was right. She'd confessed to protect him. But it hadn't worked, and now Mike had confessed. Was he really a killer with a good-son conscience that wouldn't let his mother take the blame for him? Or had he confessed because he thought his mother had actually done it?

"How did you move the body out of the street in Deadeye? How did you know about the hole he was buried in?"

More questions for which she had no answers.

"I really don't have time for this," she snapped. "I was just ready to leave for Yuma to see Mike when you arrived."

Yeah, right. In a muumuu and bare feet.

"We were concerned about your cat. We thought, with both you and Mike in custody, that it might need taking care of."

"Oh, that's very nice of you." She sounded both surprised and guilty for treating us as if we were here with some nefarious motive. "But she's fine." Leanna half turned in the doorway and looked back at a black-and-white cat snoozing on the sofa. Her trailer was larger than Mike's, but space was still limited. "Her name's Twiggy, because she was so skinny when she first showed up at the trailer park."

A full dish of cat food on the floor suggested the cat might soon outgrow her name.

"It's good of you to take in a stray," I said. "She looks like a lovely kitty. She must be good company."

Unexpectedly, the kind words about the cat seemed to be Leanna's undoing, and her antagonistic attitude fizzled. She grabbed a tissue out of a pocket in the muumuu and dabbed at her watery eyes. "I'm sorry. This has been a difficult time and I don't seem to be coping very well. I appreciate your concern about Twiggy."

"Can we do anything to help?"

"I don't think so, but— Please forgive me for not being more hospitable. Come in and we'll have . . . something."

"We could use a cup of tea."

"Tea. Yes!"

We sat on the sofa with Twiggy, who immediately gave my leg a friendly kneading, and Leanna bustled around making tea. She looked over at me once and smiled. Twiggy's approval had apparently also tipped our approval rating with Leanna from the minus to the plus side.

The tea was the loose kind, not tea bags, and Leanna did it very nicely, bringing us the tea in fragile porcelain cups.

"These cups aren't very practical in a trailer, but I couldn't bear to give them up when everything . . . happened," she said. "They were a wedding gift from Larry's mother. But this is all that's left of the set."

"They're beautiful." Early on, I'd also lost a few breakables in my motorhome life. Forget to make sure a cabinet door is closed tightly when you're on the move and you wind up with a mountain of broken jars, pickles, jam, cornflakes, and M&M's on the floor.

And then we all sat there in awkward silence. It didn't seem like a suitable occasion for small talk. Finally she broke the silence.

"I don't know anything about bail for Mike. Or what to do next. Or *anything*."

"Mike will need a lawyer," Mac said.

"I'm sure he will, but I don't know how to find one." She looked around as if hoping to discover one peeking out from under the sofa. "We had lawyers when Larry needed one. Not that it did him any good. And money may be a . . . problem."

"I think a lawyer will be provided for him if you don't have the funds to hire one."

"Mike didn't do it, you know," she said. "He confessed just to protect me."

"He thinks you did it?"

"Yes. Because I *did* do it. He didn't."

What I got out of all this was that Leanna had confessed because she really believed Mike had killed Warren. Mike confessed because he believed his mother had done it.

Admirable family loyalty there, but a misplaced loyalty. Because as of right now I didn't think either of them had done it.

"Mike is a good son," Leanna said. "A good person. He was very angry and bitter at Warren Langston, and so was I. But Mike isn't a killer."

"And you are?"

"Yes. I just need to convince them of that."

I didn't feel inclined to provide her with what Mike had said about how *he'd* killed Warren. His statement, that he'd killed Warren by strangling him with a leather cord, felt too specific to be made up. He'd said, in fact, that he could produce the leather cord. If the authorities were unconvinced, they'd surely have turned him loose as quickly as they had his mother. From what I've heard, puzzling as it seems, the police often receive false confessions.

"I feel bad for Jenna in all this," Leanna added. "She's a sweet young woman."

"She may have visited Mike this morning. Or at least tried to visit him. She and her mother stayed in Yuma last night."

"Her mother! She's here?"

"Yes, she drove down from Scottsdale yesterday. Do you know her?"

"We were never close, but when Warren was head accountant at Craigmont we socialized with them occasionally. Before they divorced."

There was nothing at all derogatory about Sable in Leanna's words, but somehow a hint of negativity seeped through. As if she realized that, she hastily added, "She's a former model, as you may know. Very beautiful. It's good of her to come. I'm sure Jenna needs all the support she can get at a time such as this."

I was sure Jenna needed support too, but I doubted she was getting much of it from her mother. Sable was as targeted on that death certificate as BoBandy on a Frisbee.

Leanna glanced at the clock on the wall, and I knew she was anxious to get back to Yuma, but I wanted to get in a few more questions.

"Was there anyone else at Craigmont who was particularly bitter at Warren when the company collapsed?"

"A lot of people lost jobs, of course, but I didn't have contact with anyone after Larry went to prison. You're thinking someone else at Craigmont may have killed Warren? But I—I did it." For the first time she sounded less positive in her claim. Apparently, she hadn't considered anyone other than Mike as the killer, but now she saw that if someone other than her son was the killer, she didn't need to claim responsibility.

"We heard there was a rumor Warren may have been involved with blackmailing someone in the movie industry, someone who'd worked with Craigmont at some time. Does that seem possible to you?"

"I never heard anything like that. But I don't suppose it's something either a blackmailer or the person being blackmailed would talk about."

"But if it were true, and the person being blackmailed grew tired of paying off . . ."

I purposely let the thought trail off, so she could fill in her own ending. She did. "That person might have killed him!"

Which said again that she wasn't the real killer. And that she was now seeing ever more clearly that perhaps her son wasn't either.

"Do you have any idea who that might be?" I asked.

She shook her head. "Warren had access to information about people in the company that I certainly didn't."

"Blackmail-worthy information?"

"I have no idea. I've never considered blackmailing anyone." She gave me a speculative glance as if thinking I might know all about do-it-yourself blackmailing.

"Okay. Well, thanks. If you happen to think of anything, would you give me a call?" I scribbled my phone number on a scrap of paper from my purse and handed it to her.

"What's your involvement in this?" she asked, now sounding a bit wary again. "You didn't know Warren, did you? And you're not a deputy or anything."

Okay, good question. We'd never met Warren before we encountered his dead body, and I was no closer to being a deputy than I was to being a gymnast on the high bars. "Perhaps you didn't know it, but a friend of ours first found Warren's body in Deadeye, and then later, after the body had been moved, Mac and I found it buried out on the desert."

I wasn't sure that was a good enough explanation, but it seemed to satisfy Leanna. She nodded, and Mac and I headed out to our pickup. We were both reaching for the door handles when Sable's car pulled up. Jenna jumped out of the passenger's side; Sable exited the driver's side less eagerly. She looked chic and rather glamorous, although not exactly desert-dirt appropriate, in a red tank top, white skinny jeans, and spike-heeled red sandals.

"Is Leanna okay?" Jenna asked. She apparently didn't think to question why we were here. "Mike asked me to check on her."

"She's right inside—"

Jenna dashed to the trailer door before I could say anything more. Sable didn't follow. Mac slid into the pickup, but I stayed outside to see if Sable had anything to say.

"What a mess," she said. I assumed she meant the general situation of the murder and Mike's confession, but the way she looked around the RV park, as if it might be hiding anything from illegal drugs to spike-heel-eating termites, I couldn't be sure.

I detoured the subject of the "mess." "I understand you and your husband may be taking a trip to Paris soon," I said brightly.

"I hope so." She paused to wrinkle her elegant nose as she eyed the weeds growing around a nearby trailer. "Actually, I think I'll try to talk Jenna into coming with me. It would do her good to get away from here."

The way she said it, that she'd try to talk Jenna into coming with *her*, suggested husband Hayden would not be along on the trip.

Curious me, I had to explore that subject further. "Your husband doesn't care for Paris?"

"Well, staying home without me for a couple of weeks would give him more time with his girlfriend." She said it with a certain sourness, but unexpectedly she touched my shoulder and laughed. "Don't look so horrified. I'm just kidding. Actually, Hayden can't take more time off work after we went to New York and then his trip to San Francisco right afterward. Paris with Jenna will be more fun anyway."

Sable was passing off mention of a "girlfriend" as kidding, but I wondered if there might be truth behind the flippant remark. Had Sable killed her ex-husband so she could get enough insurance money to divorce the current husband . . . who was cheating on her?

But I managed to go a more polite route and merely asked, "Will you be staying here with Jenna for a while?"

"I may be here for a few days to help her cope with all that's going on. She did manage to get a look in Warren's file cabinet for the will, and they let her have it. After they made a copy, of course. But I think I'll stay in Warren's place. There's no need for Jenna and me to be cramped up in that tiny trailer of hers when the big double-wide is just sitting there empty."

"You wouldn't be . . . uncomfortable there?"

She laughed. "Why should I? I doubt Warren's ghost is hanging around guarding it."

Probably not. Although, if I believed in ghosts—which I don't—I might think Warren's ghost was stomping around in frustration that Sable was not only making herself at home in his mobile, she was also going to get all that insurance money. And all he got was dead.

"Is the death certificate available yet?" I asked.

"It's available, but . . . can you believe it? . . . there are all these regulations about who can get a copy." She gave an exasperated sigh. "So Jenna had to apply for it. She ordered several copies. They'll come in the mail."

So, was Sable staying to "help" Jenna or so she could grab a copy of the death certificate the instant it arrived? Me, I wouldn't want to get between Sable and the mail. Too much danger of finding spike-heel tracks planted on your back.

"Did you see the death certificate before ordering copies?" I asked.

"No."

Which meant that neither she and Jenna nor Mac and I yet knew the official cause of death. Was what Mike said about strangling Warren actually how he'd died?

I was so tied up thinking about that point that we were in the pickup and heading back to the motorhome before something else Sable had said got through to me. "Hayden went to San Francisco after they got back from New York!"

I'd earlier thought Sable would have had time to jaunt down to Deadeye and murder Warren while Jenna was still in New York, but this opened a different window of opportunity.

Opportunity for Hayden.

Had he actually gone to San Francisco?

Yes, he probably had. Gotta keep that alibi intact, in case one was needed.

But had he also made a murderous detour to the streets of Deadeye?

Chapter 20

MAC

Once we were out on the highway, Ivy told me about her conversation with Sable and her new suspicions.

"Hayden's motive?" I asked.

"To help Sable get all that insurance money. She has expensive tastes, and a golf pro's salary may not stretch to cover all of them. Maybe he has some expensive tastes of his own and figures on grabbing a share."

I nodded agreement with that. "So, do you think killing the ex-husband was something Sable and Hayden did together, something to which she gave her stamp of approval, or did he do it on his own?"

Ivy tilted her head as she considered those questions and came up with her noncommittal, "Umm." She squinted her eyes as we zipped by a dual-wheeled pickup pulling an enormous fifth wheel trailer. She sounded mildly deflated when she added, "Of course, we don't actually know much about Hayden, so this is all just speculation."

"Speculation can be helpful."

"If Warren was actually killed by strangulation, that would fit with what we do know about Hayden," Ivy said. "Jenna says he can't cope with blood, and there apparently wasn't any blood on the street where Magnolia found his body."

"Strangulation would definitely be useful for a killer who can't stand blood."

"But how would Mike know how Warren was killed unless *he* did it?" Ivy paused and thumped her fingertips on her leg in frustration. "This feels like my attempt to learn knitting years ago. When what I wound up with looked like something out of a plugged-up drainpipe. Matted and lumpy. With ugly tentacles."

Well, there's an attractive picture. Although, having unplugged a few drains, I can testify that what comes out looks matted and ugly. Now another entangling tentacle occurred to me. "Could Mike and Hayden have been in on it together? Hayden did the killing with the leather cord, but Mike did the body wrapping and disposal?"

"They both had reasons for wanting him dead," Ivy agreed. "But how would they get together? Had they even met?"

Good question.

Ivy answered it herself. "But even if they had met, would you say to someone you barely knew, *Hey, my girlfriend's old man is a jerk. How about we get together one of these days and get rid of him?*"

"How about we give our brains a rest and get a date milkshake on the way home?"

So that's what we did. We stopped at Dateland and got a big milkshake to share. It didn't answer any of our questions about Warren's murder, but it tasted—to be a bit fanciful—like honey and sunshine and kisses. Although not as sweet as Ivy's kisses.

Later that afternoon we took BoBandy for a walk out in the Prosperity subdivision. It took us by where we'd found Warren's body, and we stared down at the hole as if it might have answers we weren't finding elsewhere.

It didn't. All we saw were scattered rocks and dirt and a stray gum wrapper.

We walked for longer than we intended, and when we got home, Jenna's little blue car pulled in as I was opening the motorhome door.

"I thought you might want to know that I don't know any more now than I did earlier," Jenna said when she got out. "I couldn't get in to see Mike a second time."

"That's frustrating," Ivy sympathized.

"Actually, I guess I'm relieved," Jenna admitted. "Right now, my feelings about him are . . . confused."

"Does he have a lawyer yet?"

"I think they'll probably appoint one for him, but his mother is looking into it. But I did find a lawyer who can handle Dad's will. I have an appointment to see him tomorrow."

"That's good. Your mother didn't go back in to Yuma with you?"

"Mom decided to go on home." Jenna's smile held a hint of guilty satisfaction. "Actually, we got in an argument after we got back to the trailer from Leanna's, and she went off in a huff."

We didn't ask for details, but Jenna volunteered them anyway.

"She wanted to stay in Dad's house, and I questioned whether we had the right to do that. She pointed out I had my computer over there and if that was okay, why not use the whole house? But I still didn't feel right about doing that. I mean, the will says that Dad leaves almost everything to me, but I'm not sure if that includes the mobile. Maybe the mobile is part of the property that belongs to Lightning now, because of their joint ownership. Anyway, she accused me of being ridiculous and stormed off."

"Would you like to stay with us tonight?" Ivy asked.

"Thanks, no, I'm fine now." Jenna paused, then shrugged and smiled again. "Well, not exactly *fine*, but beyond wanting to run screaming into the desert."

"Does Hayden go to San Francisco often?"

This quick change of subject earned Ivy a puzzled glance from Jenna. "Why do you ask that?"

"Your mother mentioned that he made a trip to San Francisco right after they got home from New York, and I just wondered why."

Why wasn't exactly any of our business either, but Jenna didn't offer any objection.

"He's some kind of consultant for a sporting goods company there. Something about checking out their new golf products before they're released to the public. He goes over there a couple times a year. Mom didn't go with him, although she usually does. She likes San Francisco."

But she didn't go this time. So we were back to the thought that Sable had time while her husband was gone to take a quick run down to Deadeye for murder with payoff of a couple million dollars.

IVY

We didn't hear any of Sable's "wolves" howling that night, but we did hear coyotes yipping. Next day we caught up on laundry with Betsy's washing machine, and I got a call from Magnolia saying the Biosphere was very interesting and educational, and she'd just happened to run into a young woman who was a descendant of the Scottish branch of her family. I do believe Magnolia could find family in the middle of a jungle on some lost continent. We called Mac's family in Montana, and I talked to niece DeeAnn in Arkansas.

Family matters taken care of, Mac had a suggestion that instantly appealed to me. I hurriedly put on more sunscreen and made tuna fish sandwiches. I had to donate a couple of bites to Koop, of course. Koop can smell tuna like a heat-seeking missile finds its target. I packed the sandwiches in an ice chest along with cans of 7UP, two tangerines, potato chips, and cookies. BoBandy eagerly jumped in the pickup with us.

We didn't know any way to get to the boulders except the same rough route we'd taken following Mike and Jenna on the bike. Deadeye Heights appeared empty when we passed through, no vehicles in sight, and the track going out to the boulders was fully as rough as before.

But BoBandy's joy when we got there was worth the trouble. He raced ahead of us and was already lapping water in the tiny pool by the time we caught up with him. We ate our lunch in the shade of the paloverde tree and then made a dog-led exploration of the oddly shaped boulders. A wind was blowing out on the open ground, but here among the boulders, the air was a gentle caress.

Does sunshine have a scent? I wouldn't think so, but it almost seemed as if it did here. Along with scents of dry desert earth and creosote bush and wet dog. Because BoBandy joyfully jumped in the little pool and gleefully shook all over us.

We climbed one of the sloping boulders and could see to Deadeye and beyond. We could also see a car with the usual cloud of dust behind it between the highway and Deadeye. Jenna must be coming home from her appointment with the lawyer.

Altogether, a glorious and relaxing afternoon, with nary a mention of murder and who might have done it. BoBandy was, for a change, all tuckered out by the time we crawled back into the pickup.

We got a surprise when we got back to Deadeye Heights. It was apparently Sable's car we'd seen on the road, not Jenna's little car, and the Mercedes was now parked in front of Warren's mobile.

"Do we have any reason to stop and see why she's here?" I asked.

"Other than curiosity?"

Yes, curiosity, of course. But we needed something more socially acceptable than mere nosiness. "To see if she's okay?"

Mac's flick of hand gave that a so-so rating. "Rather generic, but it might work."

So we parked and went to the door and knocked. It took Sable quite a while to open the door. She'd apparently been in the back bedroom. Settling in for a longer stay?

"We didn't expect you back so soon," I said. "Is anything wrong?"

I didn't expect a full-blown explanation right there at the door, but that's what we got. Sable was angry enough to let it all hang out. She crossed her arms across her chest and let loose.

"I couldn't stay there one more minute. I got home yesterday and Hayden wasn't there. He wasn't expecting me, of course, because I'd told him I'd be staying with Jenna for several days, but I thought he'd be home later. But he didn't come home all night. I actually called the police to check if there'd been an accident. They couldn't find any record of an accident. They said if I really thought he was missing I could file a missing person report right away, but it would be better to wait at least twenty-four hours."

"Did you file a report?" I asked.

"I didn't have to. He showed up this morning. He claimed he'd gone to a movie and was so tired that he just fell asleep in the car and slept there all night."

I'm not experienced in what kind of stories cheating husbands tell their wives, but I figured this one needed some work.

Sable confirmed that. "I wasn't about to fall for *that*, of course," she said, her tone disdainful. "I told him I knew where he'd been. Which was with the girlfriend I've suspected he's been sneaking around with for months now."

"Umm," I commented. So Sable's earlier reference to a girlfriend wasn't just lighthearted kidding.

"And I know who she is. It's this Savannah woman who's been taking golf lessons from him. *Golf lessons.*" She rolled her eyes. "I'd have to be dumber than a golf ball to believe that's all they were doing."

Before she could get more specific about their activities, I hastily said, "It's probably good to get away so you can both cool off."

"I'm not about to cool off. I'm going to a divorce lawyer." She looked up. "Oh, here comes Jenna now."

Jenna's car headed for her little trailer but then veered in our direction. She got out and ran to the gate.

"Mom! You came back. Is something wrong?"

Jenna might have spats with her mother, but her concern now was obvious.

I wondered if Sable would repeat what she'd just told us, but all she said was, "I'm fine. I'll fill you in later." She gave us a wary glance, and I suspected she was now sorry she'd unloaded all that personal information on us. "I've been unpacking."

"You plan to stay *here*, in Dad's house?"

"You and I have stayed together in your trailer before, and it's like two sardines in a one-sardine can," Sable snapped. "Yes, I'm staying here. You should move over here too. There's plenty of room."

"Mom, I told you I don't think—"

"Don't be silly, sweetie." Sable looked at us and smiled. "Jenna has a bit of her father's penchant for being as fussbudgety as a little old lady."

On behalf of little old ladies everywhere, my back stiffened with resentment.

I fumed for a moment but managed to swallow a snarky retort about greedy ex-wives, present company included, and merely said, "We'll run along now, but you let us know if we can do anything to help."

Jenna turned and gave us an exaggerated look of someone going down for the third time in deep water, but I figured she and her mother would patch things up as they apparently always did. I also suspected Jenna may as well accept that Sable, like some fast-growing weed, intended to live exactly where she'd planted herself.

Lightning's pickup was now parked near his mobile, and he came out and waved us over.

"I been thinkin' about that friend of yours who says we have a family connection. She still around?"

"No, she and her husband left a few days ago."

"I'm sorry to hear that. I got to thinkin', she got a couple of photos of her and me, but I didn't get any and I wish I had. I'd like to talk to her more about family matters too."

I was surprised, and for Magnolia's sake, pleased. I knew she'd been disappointed that Lightning hadn't been more interested in family connections, and this would make her feel better.

"Magnolia and Geoff may be coming back. I'm sure she'd like to meet with you again."

I called Magnolia that evening to pass along Lightning's interest in taking photos and learning more about their family tree. She exchanged a few words with Geoff and then said yes! They'd be back to Prosperity the following day.

They arrived late in the afternoon, and she was quite excited about this new interest from Lightning. She'd even made copies for him of the ten-page diagram of around-the-world family connections she'd constructed plus an almost hundred-page family history. "Of course this isn't really complete. I'm still working on some of the family branches."

I figured she'd need a wheelbarrow to carry that around once she got done.

I already had a roast in the oven so we all ate dinner together at our place. I didn't have a phone number for Lightning but I called Jenna and she said she'd run over and tell him we'd be there the following morning.

**

Next morning, Geoff loosened up on his resistance to driving the rough road out to Deadeye in his Subaru, so on this trip we all sat inside and arrived at Lightning's place relatively undusty about midmorning, Magnolia in her pink cowboy hat and boots. We found Lightning all duded up in movie cowboy gear, ready for photos. His jeans were tucked into tall boots with yellow leather inlays of lightning bolts, a saucer-sized silver buckle with more lightning bolts at his lean waist, a fringed leather vest with a lawman star fastened to the front, and a big white hat.

Although I also noticed an extra car parked at Warren's double-wide. My vehicle-identification skills haven't improved, but even I could tell it was a red convertible. I really wanted to rush over and find out who it belonged to, although good manners stopped me from being so openly nosy.

Well, good manners plus the fact that Magnolia had a grip on my arm like BoBandy with a bone.

It was a very thorough photo session. Lightning furnished a digital camera. Mac is a good photographer, and they started with photos of Lightning and Magnolia in the corral with the horses. Lightning wanted me in a couple of photos too. I protested that I wasn't family, but Lightning said friends were part of a family.

Then we moved over to Deadeye and got photos in the saloon, the hotel, on the street, and in the church, some including Geoff and me. The toothpaste outline was mostly gone now, blessedly. I doubted he'd want a photo with it anyway, but I wasn't sure. A light wind came up, growing stronger as the day advanced, but Lightning wasn't giving up yet. Several times he grabbed the camera himself and got photos of the four of us. He even rolled back the rug, opened the mine-shaft trapdoor, and got us all looking down into the dark hole.

Eventually a suspicious thought occurred to me. There'd been plenty of time to do this earlier, but Lightning hadn't been all that interested in photos then. But now he was suddenly eager to embrace this newfound family?

Or was it because in a photo, who could tell family from fans? Lightning was apparently a little short of real fans these days, and I could see that with some judicious editing and splicing, the photos could be made to look like a small crowd. Was this really a plan to generate some publicity or provide the movie production company with promotional photos that showed Lightning still had real, live fans eagerly making treks out to the desert to see him?

Still, I didn't see any harm in it, and if our cooperation would help his faded career, fine with me. I presented a stray bit of paper for an autograph, and Mac got a shot of Lightning signing it. I threw in an enthusiastic hug for another photo.

After enough photos to populate several generations of family scrapbooks, we all trooped back to Lightning's place. There, with a glance at the mysterious convertible, I suggested to Mac that we go over and say hi to Jenna and her mother while Magnolia and Lightning talked family. I was pleased that even if Lightning had some ulterior motive for this photo session, he was still willing to give time to "family." Though I thought he looked a bit dismayed when Magnolia pulled out her family history and diagrams and presented both to him with the suggestion that they go inside so she could explain it all to him. Geoff looked as if he'd really like to come with us, but he told us to drive the Subaru over to talk to Jenna and dutifully followed his wife and Lightning into the mobile.

We parked the Subaru beside the open convertible, wind stirring the dust around us. It wasn't until we were right next to it that I realized the vehicle was not unoccupied.

Chapter 21

IVY

A red golf cap covered the face of the person slumped in the convertible.

"Oh, no," I breathed. Another body. A body wearing dark tan slacks and a lighter tan golf shirt.

I was just getting out of the car to check for a pulse when the "body" sat up and slid the cap up to his head of thick blond hair. He was tanned and magazine ad good-looking. He opened the car door and slid out. He was taller than I realized when he was all folded up in the car seat, his body lean and athletic. I retreated to the car and closed the door.

"Hi. I'm Hayden Bromfield." He gave us a dazzling, white-toothed smile and thrust a hand toward my open window. He looked remarkably vigorous for someone I'd thought dead a few moments ago.

I'd have known him even without the self-introduction, which was also the first time we'd heard his last name. He exuded charm and friendliness. The kind of man who'd make you want to sign up for golf lessons even if you couldn't tell a golf club from a hockey stick.

I managed to get a hand out the window and shake his. His grip was exactly right. Firm but not overpowering. He reached farther through the window to shake Mac's hand also.

"We're friends of Jenna," Mac said. "Mac and Ivy MacPherson."

"Ivy. Mac." He treated each of us to a moment of personal attention with eyes of deep-sea blue.

"We've met your wife, but we didn't know you were coming," I said. "Isn't, uh, anyone here?" I asked. Which was likely a useless question, because Sable's car was on the other side of the convertible, so she must be inside. If she and Jenna had gone anywhere together, she'd have insisted on taking her car. Sable had said once that riding in Jenna's tiny car was like being in a thimble on a roller coaster.

"Jenna went into Yuma but Sable is inside. Behind the closed door. At the moment, I'm not allowed inside." He smiled as if there was something delightfully whimsical about his exclusion.

I couldn't think of a suitable response to the cheerful statement, so I used my handy-dandy, "Umm."

"Sable and I had a little misunderstanding and she stormed out of our house in Scottsdale, breathing fire and smoke about a divorce." He managed a slightly woebegone, though not despairing, look. "But I'm not going to let that happen. I'll sleep out here in my car for as long as it takes to get this straightened out. Because I love her."

He sounded so sincere that I was tempted to believe him, but characterizing a night spent with another woman as a "little misunderstanding" struck me as a bit unrealistic. Or just plain sleazy. Or had Sable jumped to a conclusion of husbandly guilt when Hayden actually had gone to a movie and then, weary, spent the night in his car?

I remembered Betsy saying Hayden was much like the preceding husband Warren in his picky, fussbudgety ways, which argued against car-sleeping, but he appeared to have been doing exactly that here. Without even putting the top up on the convertible. Ensuring that Sable could look out and see him suffering for love?

"How long have you been out here in your car?" I asked.

"I left home about four this morning." He wiggled his tongue over those dazzling teeth. "I need to brush my teeth. They feel as if they're covered with moss."

Practical me, I also wondered, if he wasn't allowed in the house, what he doing about bathroom needs? It wasn't a question I wanted to ask a stranger, but I did ask, "Have you had anything to eat?"

"No, but I'm hoping Sable will let me come in for lunch. Perhaps you could act as a go-between and talk her into lunch and a friendly discussion about our situation?"

Mac leaned across the car seat. "And that 'situation' would be—?"

"Clients sometimes think they're entitled to more than golf lessons when they sign up with the club professional." Big, put-upon sigh. "Which can lead to misunderstandings."

"Women clients, you mean?" Mac asked.

Hayden gave him a you-know-how-it-is nod of brotherhood between two attractive males. "Exactly. And then Sable reads more into a strictly business relationship than is actually there."

I glanced at Mac. Was he believing all this? Was I?

I'm well aware of the Biblical injunction against judging others, but I figure a little skepticism isn't necessarily judging. And I was definitely skeptical of good-looking, smooth-talking Hayden. Were those spectacular blue eyes his own or colored contacts?

Then I had a flutter of guilt. Was I unfairly holding his good looks and smooth speech against him? Should we try to persuade Sable to at least talk to him?

We were saved from having to make that decision by Sable's sudden appearance in the doorway and then her stomp out to the vehicles. She was wearing loose but shapely sweats and sandals with a high wedge heel. I had to admire her ability to stomp in them. I'd have done a Mt. Everest–sized tumble to the dirt if I'd tried that.

"I suppose you've been telling Mac and Ivy some half-baked story about how you've been unjustly maligned?" she said. A gust of wind grabbed her hair, and she smoothed the dark strands back in place.

"I'd never accuse you of unjustly maligning anyone, my darling."

She crossed her arms over her chest. "You're full of hogwash, you know that?" she said, a statement which I figured was fairly accurate. "How long do you intend to sit out here and play misunderstood martyr?"

"Sweetie, I love you even when you're all riled up," Hayden said. "And I can sit out here for as long as it takes for you to realize how much I love you." He swept a hand up to clutch the area of his heart.

About all I could give him credit for in those declarations was that he didn't actually use that old cliché *You're beautiful when you're angry.* I didn't want to encourage Sable in divorce plans, but I had to admit I was relieved she wasn't succumbing to his silver-tongued blarney. A reconciliation needed something more solid than the sugar-coated confetti Hayden was throwing at her. I rather expected her to snap back with some version of *And I can happily let you sit out here until the next ice age moves in.*

But she didn't say anything at all, just stood there with her arms crossed over her chest, until finally she muttered, "Really, how long do you intend to carry on this farce?"

He gave a big sigh. "I suppose I'll have to give up eventually." He rubbed his tanned jaw, which had just the beginning of a blond shadow of unshaved whiskers. An attractive shadow, of course. "I'm going to need a shower and a shave. And a bathroom. And something to eat."

"You should have thought of that before you—" She broke off and glared at him, and I thought she was going to end the sentence with something about a woman named Savannah. Instead, what she said was, "Before you charged down here like a . . . a chicken with its head cut off."

The unappealing expression was so out of character for sophisticated Sable that we all gaped at her in astonishment.

"I don't believe I've ever heard you use that expression before," Hayden said.

"I haven't had to deal with you acting like a philanderer before."

Really? I'd guess Savannah wasn't Hayden's first rodeo. To say nothing of the fact that he was still right up there on my could-be-a-killer list.

"I'm sorry. I really am. Look, if you won't let me come inside, will you at least let me take you to lunch?"

"And lunch would be where? You see any five-star restaurants in the vicinity?" She put a hand like a visor over her eyes and scanned the horizon. "I don't even see a greasy spoon in shouting distance."

"We'll fly to New York if you want. Paris. The moon. Anywhere." He flung out his arms to take in all the known universe.

Sable laughed. "Oh, Hayden, you really are full of hogwash. I suppose we could go in to Yuma for lunch, just so you won't starve. But I'll have to change clothes."

So Sable went back inside, and what I was thinking as I studied Hayden was MOM. Motive. Opportunity. Means.

Hayden had the Motive for murder: two million dollars of insurance money to keep Sable supplied with trips to Paris, five-star restaurants, and wedge sandals. Perhaps to keep himself in convertibles too.

The Opportunity: a detour on that trip he took to San Francisco.

The Means? Was the leather cord that Mike said Warren had been strangled with something like a leather shoelace? I looked down at Hayden's feet. No lace-up shoes there. Just a pair of high-end, suede loafers—

But hey, they were loafers with a cord woven through metal eyelets around the upper edge of the shoe and tied in front. A leather cord? Yes!

No cord appeared to be missing on the shoes, but that was an irrelevant detail. He could have a dozen pairs of these shoes providing an ample supply of leather cords for murder. Or replaced a missing one.

Which then gave me the problem of Mike providing a leather cord to authenticate his confession. How could he have the murder weapon if Hayden had used a cord from his own shoes to kill Warren?

I tried to think of a quick question or two to throw at Hayden while we waited for Sable, something brilliant but innocuous that would bring out incriminating information without giving away my suspicions, but all I came up with was a muttered, "Nice shoes."

"Thank you. They're very comfortable."

"When I like a particular kind of shoe I sometimes buy several pairs."

"That's a good idea," he agreed without saying if he ever did that.

"Are the laces leather?"

"Yes, I believe they are."

Did you strangle Warren Langston with one of them?

Mac got me out of this dead-end exchange by saying, "Do you and Sable like Mexican food? A place called the Red Bull in Yuma has very good enchiladas."

"Thanks." He gave Mac a wink that was apparently meant to join him in some kind of man-to-man conspiracy. "Hey, maybe we could all get together for dinner. I barbecue a killer steak."

His use of the word *killer* made me cringe, but then a thought hit me. "Maybe you'd like to take a tour around Deadeye?"

"Sounds interesting. I was here once with Sable to see Jenna, but we didn't go over to the town." He grinned. "Most of the time I was too worried that Warren might be hiding somewhere with a rifle aimed at me. We never managed one of those sophisticated modern arrangements of the ex- and current husbands being good ol' buddies."

"Someone apparently felt very unbuddy-ish toward him."

"Yes. A real shocker, isn't it? And almost as big a shocker that Jenna's boyfriend has confessed to doing it."

"Yes. He seemed like such a nice young man," Mac said.

"Apparently he put on a good act. I know Jenna's taking it hard, but it's a good thing she found out what kind of person he really is before she got even more involved with him. We're hoping she'll come up to Scottsdale and stay with us for a while."

Hayden sounded as if he'd fully accepted Mike's guilt. His cell phone gave a manly sound of a trumpet blaring.

"Excuse me." He pulled a cell phone out of his pocket and walked over and planted a foot on the rail fence around the yard, his back to us.

Suspicious me, I wondered if this was Savannah inquiring about a "golf lesson," but I couldn't hear anything, of course. But surely she wouldn't call him, not knowing but what he might be with Sable when the call arrived. Or maybe she wouldn't mind that happening. Maybe she was hoping something would happen to cause a big break.

I'm really not familiar with how these under-the-radar relationships work.

When he turned back to us a few moments later, he dropped the phone back in his pocket and said, "Sorry for the interruption. Another of those irritating robocalls."

Sable came out the door dressed in white capri pants (or did they call them something else these days?), white halter top, and the red, spike-heeled sandals I'd seen before. I guessed she could do a world-class stomp in them too, if she wanted, but at the moment her walk was more of a runway strut. Hayden's eyes followed her appreciatively.

"Would you rather go in your car?" Hayden asked her. "You'll get all windblown in the convertible." He smiled. "And still be more beautiful than any other woman on the road."

Sable could have suggested the simple solution of putting the top up on the convertible, but she chose a different response. Tilt of head.

Toss of lush mane. Flirty smile. "We can go in my car. I appreciate your thoughtfulness in suggesting it," she said in queenly tones. Then she came down to earth. "But you're still full of hogwash."

Hayden grinned and bowed. "At your service, beautiful lady."

They got in Sable's Mercedes and drove off like two young people happily setting off on a first date.

"What do you want to bet that by the time they come back he isn't sleeping in the car anymore?" Mac said.

We watched until they disappeared beyond the low hill between the mobiles and the entrance to Deadeye. The rising wind whipped a miniature tornado of dust from the clearing and swept it over the convertible.

"He should have put the top up before he left," I said. "But I guess he had other things on his mind."

"I suppose we could do it."

"You know how?"

"It isn't, you know, rocket science or brain surgery."

He opened the car door, but before he found the control, another gust of wind whipped a plastic bag from somewhere and plastered it to the inside of the windshield. I opened the door on the passenger's side and slid inside to scrape the bag off the glass. At the same time Mac found the control and the top rose over me. I sat there a moment, enjoying the unfamiliar and luxurious softness of the leather seats and the brilliant shine of the teak dashboard. I could become accustomed to this kind of luxury.

Then I had a different thought. Here I was in Hayden's convertible, Hayden and Sable long gone. Would it hurt to take a peek around?

I opened the glove compartment and tentatively poked at the contents. Everything was neat and tidy. Registration and insurance papers. A carton of breath mints. A small flashlight. Two road maps.

I got on my knees and turned around to look in the cramped space behind the seats.

Legal search warrants are not conducted on a fishing-expedition basis. The search warrant had to name something specific connected to the case. What was I searching for?

Although those constraints obviously didn't apply here. This wasn't exactly a legal search and I didn't exactly have a formal search warrant. No rules applied.

I leaned over farther and started digging.

Chapter 22

MAC

"Ivy, what are you *doing?*"

Actually, I could see what she was doing. Practically standing on her head as she rummaged through the space behind the seat of the convertible. I was just a little startled that she was pawing through somebody's belongings the minute the owner was out of sight. She muttered something I couldn't hear and came up with a pair of cleat-soled golf shoes.

She sniffed the shoes and wrinkled her nose. "He must douse them with male cologne."

She dropped the shoes back into the space behind the seat and dug deeper. This time she dragged up a duffel bag and unzipped it. I could see socks, underwear, and a couple of golf shirts as she poked around in the contents. She dug deeper in the bag and came up with a toothbrush holder and an electric shaver. Not exactly incriminating items.

"You're searching Hayden's car?" I asked finally.

"We'll never have a better chance."

"What are you searching for?"

Ivy paused in her digging. "It's like going to a yard sale or flea market. You don't know what you're looking for until you find it."

A fishing expedition, then. Legal searches do not operate this way. A legal search warrant requires that a specific item or items connected with the crime investigation must be named. I learned that from Ivy herself.

This was obviously not an official search, however. This was an LOL with a red-convertible-sized curiosity. But even though I sometimes feel as if I'm diving into a deep-sea herd of sharks—or den of killers—when I'm with Ivy, we do things together.

So I said, "May I be of help?"

"You can look under the driver's seat. I'll look under this side."

She scooted backward out of the car. I felt around under the driver's seat. Under the seat of our pickup, I could undoubtedly find any number of items. Old Snickers wrapper. Squashed cup from McDonald's. Peanut shells. If I was lucky, maybe a few lost coins. But here, picky-fussy Hayden's under-the-seat space was as pristine as if the vehicle was on a new car lot.

On her side, Ivy came up with a vehicle manual and a see-through plastic pouch of shiny, unused-looking tools. Then she dug farther back and came up with another pouch. This one was leather, fastened with a drawstring pulled tight.

With a quick glance around, apparently to make sure Hayden hadn't unexpectedly returned, she yanked on the center opening of the pouch and pulled out a cell phone.

"He talked on a cell phone earlier. We saw him put it in his pocket. Why would he have a second phone hidden under the seat?" I asked.

"To talk or text his girlfriend without using his regular phone because Sable might peek at that one and see who he's been talking to," Ivy said. "So he has this second phone that he uses exclusively for the girlfriend. And he keeps it in this bag which looks nothing like a cell phone holder."

I suppose for a man my age, I'm rather naïve. That kind of complicated deviousness to hide a relationship would never occur to me. Although having a clandestine relationship would never occur to me either.

"I read it in a true-crime book," Ivy said by way of explanation for her own knowledge. "Man had wives in two different cities. Separate phones, even set up on different phone systems, to talk to them."

"Did it work?"

"He made a mistake and called one of them by the wrong name on the wrong phone. The wives got together to murder him and then, realizing he'd been dividing his time between them, thought it only fair to divide his body. Though the process was a little messy and ruined a couple of good butcher knives. And both wives found the law frowned on this type of 'fairness.'"

I didn't let my thoughts wander into either the fairness or messiness of body distribution, although it did occur to me that even a two-phone system of infidelity has its shortcomings. "Are we going to see what's on this phone?"

Ivy pressed a few spots on the screen. "It's password protected."

Hayden was taking no chances with his phone system, though that didn't necessarily protect him from angry wives and/or girlfriends with butcher knives. Ivy replaced the phone in the pouch, then tucked the pouch far back under the seat where she'd found it. She also pushed the manual and tools back where they'd been.

"Now what?" I asked. "Do we confront Hayden about having two phones?"

"Two phones suggest Hayden may be a sleazy husband, but does it have anything to do with Warren's murder?"

"Maybe we should go see Mike and discuss murder and leather cords and confessions."

So, after we got back to the motorhome with Magnolia and Geoff, that was what we did.

IVY

Getting in to see Mike was not as simple as walking into the county jail and asking to see him. There was protocol, which included filling out of forms and waiting. Much waiting. But finally we were led down a hallway to a cubicle facing a window with phones on both sides of the glass. The surroundings didn't actually smell grim or distressing, but a scent of strong disinfectant wafted up from the floor, and the air held an unsavory hint of old stew, heavy on the onions and cabbage. A uniformed guard led Mike in, and he sat in the chair on the other side of the glass.

He looked as if he'd put in an all-nighter studying for college exams. And then flunked. Saggy eyelids. Tornado-tousled red hair. Puffy lips. I was reminded of what his mother had said about jail not being conducive to a good night's sleep.

He picked up the phone on his side of the glass and I picked up ours. I wasn't sure how much time we had, but I figured not enough for small talk about sleeping conditions. I went straight to the point.

"We talked to your mother. She still claims she killed Warren, but we think she confessed because she thought you did it and she was trying to protect you."

I held the phone away from my ear, and Mac and I leaned our heads together so we could both listen.

"Yes, you're right. She did it to protect me, and I appreciate that. But I decided I had to take responsibility for my own actions. I killed Warren. I believe you already know the reason."

"Yes, you had a strong motive. But we don't think you did it. We think you confessed to protect your mother because you think she really did do it."

We both spoke with an unnatural formality, as if the grammar police might be listening. Maybe a glass wall, phones, and nearby guards do that to you. But now Mike's blue eyes flared out of the cautious zone.

"It's really none of your business," he snapped. "This is a family matter."

"But she couldn't have done it," I pointed out. "She doesn't even know how Warren was killed. She isn't physically big enough to haul Warren's dead body around. She isn't familiar enough with Prosperity to find that hole to bury him."

He hesitated a moment, as if these points about his mother made uncomfortable sense. But then, not giving an inch, he said, "That's right. Just like I said, she didn't do it. I did."

I couldn't think of any convincing argument to prove he didn't do it. I made a different attack. "Do you realize you're not only putting your own future on the line by claiming you did it, you're also protecting the real killer."

Mike opened his mouth as if to argue that point, but he scowled and shut it without saying anything.

"Maybe you and your mother should have had a serious discussion about murder and murderers before you both rushed to confess," Mac said.

"You think I should have said something while we were having lunch?" With sarcastic emphasis Mike added, "Maybe, 'Hey, Ma, I've been wondering, did you go out to Deadeye and kill Jenna's father the other day? And pass the salt, would you please?'"

"That might have been better than simply assuming she did it."

"Your confession was apparently quite convincing, since they're still holding you after releasing her," I said. "And if you keep insisting you did it, we may never know who the killer really is."

Mike hesitated a long moment before asking warily, "But if my mother didn't do it . . . who did?"

"As long as you're sticking to your quite-believable confession, the law enforcement authorities don't have much incentive to find out," I pointed out. "Have you heard anything about bail?"

"I don't think bail is a consideration when there's a confession."

Long silence. I waited to see if Mike would fill it.

"Most of what I told them in my confession was true," Mike finally said reluctantly. "I did move the body from where it was lying there on the street in Deadeye. I did drop it over the back fence. I did move it over to Prosperity and bury it under rocks in that hole."

"You're saying you found Warren there on the street and he was already dead. Strangled with a leather cord. But you did move the body."

He didn't confirm or deny my statement. "I was going out there every day to feed the horses while Jenna and Lightning were both gone. Warren was there, of course, but Lightning would never ask him to feed the horses."

I encouraged him by affirming what he was saying. "Jenna was in New York. Lightning was in LA trying to drum up movie business."

"I noticed the gate into Deadeye was partly open when I went by, but I didn't think anything about it at the time." Mike shifted uncomfortably in his seat on the other side of the glass. He wiped one hand on the orange prison garb, then looked at the hand as if expecting the orange might rub off. "I fed the horses, and then I got to thinking, Warren had always been . . . well, not exactly hostile to me, but definitely not very friendly. Even though I was angry and bitter at him for whistleblowing on Dad, I figured, for Jenna's sake, I should try to put it in the past and get on better terms with him. So I decided I'd go over and offer to mow his little patch of grass or see if he needed anything from Yuma. He didn't go to town very often."

"He seemed to avoid contact with people," Mac said.

"He was afraid someone who'd suffered from what he'd done would come after him to get even," Mike agreed. "His actions were no doubt right from a legal and ethical standpoint when he turned whistleblower. The company was concealing a huge amount of income, and Dad was responsible."

Mike sounded as if he'd come to terms with that fact, but it still wasn't easy to think of his dad as a law-breaking tax evader.

"Warren's Jeep was parked out front, and I knocked on the door. When he didn't answer I figured it might be because he just didn't want to talk to me, but then I remembered that open gate into Deadeye, and that seemed kind of odd. So I walked over there, going the back way through the fence instead of around by the gate."

"Why?"

"Because I wondered if he was over there . . . doing something."

"Doing something?" Mac sounded as blank as I felt. "What could he have been doing?"

"Warren was dead set against Lightning getting movie or TV productions going in Deadeye again. Jenna thought it was just because he didn't want a lot of people milling around, but I knew it went deeper than that. He didn't want someone to show up and recognize him. So I thought, with everyone gone, maybe he'd decided to take care of that by sabotaging the place some way. Burn it down or something."

"You really thought Warren might do that to his brother?" Mac asked.

"I figured a man who'd snitch on his friends like Warren did might do almost anything."

"But you didn't find Warren sabotaging the town."

"No. What I found was Warren's body. I moved it enough that I could see he'd been strangled with that leather cord. It was still tight around his neck." Mike took a steadying breath. "I right away figured Mom had killed him. She'd stopped in to see me the day before, on her way to Lake Havasu, so I knew she'd been in the area."

"You really thought she could have strangled him?"

"She was so angry and bitter about what Warren did. Same as I was, and we both blamed him for Dad's death. At one time I'd planned to kill Warren myself, and I'd heard Mom actually say she'd like to kill that man."

"But people say things like that without really meaning them in the literal sense," Mac pointed out. "Like, 'My brother's gonna kill me when he finds out I wrecked his new bike.'"

"I know. It also seemed unlikely Mom could overpower and strangle him. But I really thought she'd managed to do it."

Thinking his mother had turned killer wasn't a totally unreasonable thought. People have been known to exhibit extraordinary strength in extreme situations.

"How did you think she got him to go out there to Deadeye?"

He shook his head. "I was wondering that when I was standing there by the body and heard a vehicle coming. I looked around the corner of the building and saw a motorhome and then a woman getting out and coming toward me."

"Magnolia."

Mike nodded. "I didn't want to be found standing over the body, so I ducked inside one of the buildings and watched. I saw her find the body and then hurry back to the motorhome. I knew she must be calling the sheriff or 911, so I ran back out and picked up Warren's body and carried it to the back fence and dropped it over."

"Why?" I asked.

"Because I . . . I thought the authorities would come and they'd figure out Mom had killed him . . . and she'd be in prison for life. Or worse. I couldn't let that happen. I figured if they didn't find the body . . ." He shook his head. "Not very clear thinking, I suppose, but that's what I thought and what I did. Then I ran back to my van at Warren's place and moved it around back where it wouldn't be seen so easily and just sat there and tried to figure out what to do. After dark, I went back and carried Warren's body to my van. I intended to wrap it in an old blanket I had in there. But the blanket was all dirty and greasy and wrapping Warren in it just didn't seem . . . right."

"So you went inside his house and got a clean blanket?"

He nodded. "And I cut the leather cord from around his neck."

"Why?"

"I don't know. I just kept thinking this was Jenna's dad, and it just didn't seem right to leave it there. It made his face look all bloated and kind of . . . discolored."

"What about the red cord you tied around the blanket to keep it in place?" I pictured again how neatly the body had been wrapped and tied. With care.

"I had that in the van. It wasn't even mine. One of the guys in the band had used it for tying up a gift for his girlfriend. It was really stupid of me to use it again to tie those little roadrunners together, wasn't it?"

It was. But Mike didn't have a killer's mind-set about taking care of every possible connecting clue.

"Anyway, after the body was wrapped, I put it in Warren's Jeep and drove out to that old Prosperity subdivision where I knew there were various places I could bury him. I didn't want to use my van because I figured the blanket might leave incriminating fibers. I put the body at the bottom of one of the holes and covered it with rocks. I didn't want coyotes or vultures getting to the body. By then I was figuring if it was never found, or at least not found for a long time, the authorities would think he just took off and went somewhere and wouldn't be looking for him. Even Jenna thought he might take off without telling her."

"Even if Jenna and her father weren't close, didn't you think this was going to be very difficult for Jenna? Her father missing, wondering if something had happened to him. And then to have him found buried out on the desert under a pile of rocks."

He nodded, his face a map of misery.

"But you'd promised your dad you'd take care of your mother," Mac said.

Another nod.

Stuck between a rock and a hard place.

"So after I buried the body, I drove the Jeep into Yuma and parked it in back of that mechanic's shop where I thought it would just sit for a while. There were various other cars there, and I figured it wouldn't be vandalized or stolen there." He shook his head, as if his own actions now baffled him. "Isn't that something? Worrying about the Jeep after I'd just buried Jenna's dad."

"And then what? You were in Yuma, without a vehicle once you'd gotten rid of the Jeep, and your van was still out at Warren's place."

"I waited until early morning and then hitchhiked a ride out past the Deadeye turnoff and hiked to my van and drove home. I told the old couple who gave me a ride in their motorhome that I was homeless but I'd found an old shack to live in out on the desert. They insisted on giving me five dollars." He swallowed. "I donated it to the church the first time we went there with you."

"But later, with Jenna, you drove to the airport 'looking' for the Jeep," I said. "When it wasn't there, you suggested maybe he'd flown out of some other airport."

"Yeah. I was just full of helpful suggestions, wasn't I?"

Did I believe he was telling the truth now? Yes, I did. What Mike had done, moving and burying a body already dead, wasn't exactly admirable. It was also illegal. There were laws about that sort of thing. But I thought it was the truth. Mac and I exchanged glances, and his little nod told me he also believed Mike.

"What happened to the leather cord that was around Warren's neck?" Mac asked.

"I took it home and hid it in some junk under my trailer. I thought it might have come from Mom's hiking boots. I didn't want the authorities to get hold of it and connect it to her. I should have just dropped it out on the desert somewhere. But I didn't. I turned it in when I confessed."

"What about that postcard from Las Vegas that Jenna received?"

"When it arrived, I thought Mom must have sent it. That she'd figured, like I did when I buried the body, that it would delay any investigation. Or send the authorities off on a wild goose chase around Vegas."

"Something else you and your mother never talked about," I said.

"Yeah. Well, murder isn't a topic that a mother and son tend to discuss," he muttered.

"Perhaps it's time to tell the authorities all you've told us," I said.

He hesitated before finally saying, "I'll think about it."

I wondered if they'd believe this new version of events. His confession had been believable because a good portion of it, how he'd moved and wrapped and buried the body, was the truth. There was the bottom-line hard evidence of the leather cord and the red cord he provided to clinch the confession.

Evidence that might be difficult to refute now.

"Do you have a lawyer?" Mac asked.

"I was in court for a preliminary hearing of some kind. They asked then if I needed a court-appointed attorney, and I said I did."

He stood up on the other side of the glass wall. We stood too.

"I appreciate your coming," Mike said.

"And you will tell the authorities the full story?" I asked.

"I'll think about it," he repeated.

"Pray about it," Mac suggested.

"I'm not sure I'm in a position to ask God anything."

"Give it a try anyway," I said. "You might be surprised."

I knew the reason for Mike stubbornness. He had to find out for certain whether or not his mother had killed Warren before he changed his confession. Because he'd promised his dad he'd take care of her.

Chapter 23

MAC

We picked up hamburger, fresh fruit, and vegetables that Betsy didn't have in her little store at Prosperity and then drove on out to the motorhome. We found Magnolia making up a scrapbook of family photos and clippings to give to Lightning. Geoff was off talking to our potato-pilgrimaging acquaintance. I divided the hamburger into several portions and wrapped them in plastic for our small freezer.

"Should I keep one package out for dinner?" I asked Ivy.

"I'm thinking we should accept Hayden's invitation. I feel like a good steak," she declared.

"I think it was more of a maybe someday invitation than an actual invitation for tonight."

Ivy smiled. A serene smile. Or maybe I was mistaken. That might be a sly smile. "I'm taking it as an invitation. I'll make a salad for our contribution."

"You don't mind eating steak cooked by a possible killer?"

"It should be safe enough. He hasn't any reason to put rat poison or insecticide in our food."

No, not yet. But if he figured out our senior-snoop magnifying glass was targeted on him . . .

"I want to find out more about Hayden Bromfield," Ivy said with determination.

So she made a crisp Caesar salad, bagged some cookies, promised BoBandy and Koop a walk when we got home, and off we went. When we arrived at Deadeye Heights, Jenna's little car was parked at her trailer, and Sable's Mercedes and Hayden's convertible were at the double-wide. The convertible was empty, I saw when we pulled up beside it.

I knocked, and Hayden opened the door. I guessed seeing us was a surprise, but his charm didn't falter for more than a mini-second. He gave us a big smile. I spotted the duffel bag that had been in the convertible, which I assumed meant he'd graduated to inside status.

"Hey, guys, good to see you. Great tip about enchiladas at the Red Bull, Mac."

Ivy stepped forward. "I brought a salad to go with the steaks."

"Steaks?" Hayden blinked. "I guess that, uh . . . slipped my mind. We didn't get a chance to do any shopping while we were in town."

Ivy sailed in as confidently as if we were honored rather than unexpected guests. "I think the freezer is quite well stocked," she said as she deposited the salad on the kitchen counter.

Sable hadn't yet made an appearance, but now she came in from the hallway leading to the bedrooms.

"So nice of Hayden to invite us over to share steaks with you," Ivy said with enthusiasm. I don't think she's ever considered trying to crash some White House event, but I suspect she could pull it off.

"Yes . . . indeed." Sable spoke as if she must have missed something in the day's schedule of events. She gave Hayden an inquiring glance, and he returned a minimal shrug.

"Will Jenna be coming over too?" Ivy asked, all bubbly innocence.

"No, I don't think so. Mike was allowed another phone call to Jenna. He's now saying he didn't kill Warren, but apparently he hasn't convinced the authorities and they're still holding him. Jenna is very confused. She says she doesn't know what to believe now."

"We don't think Mike did it," Mac said.

"Jenna took Hayden for a tour around Deadeye and then said she was going out for a hike to clear her head." She smiled wryly. "I'm afraid that may take some time."

"I think the situation with Mike may be about to change. Some new information has surfaced," Ivy said. I spotted her surreptitious side glance to see if this announcement had any effect on Hayden.

A hint of surprise, maybe even a bit of uneasiness, ruffled Hayden's tanned face. He'd no doubt been delighted by Mike's unexpected confession, so this wouldn't be happy news. But he managed to say, as if he were quite pleased, "Hey, that's great! Maybe the experts decided it was just an accident or something."

"No, I don't think there's any doubt about it being murder. But I believe this new information may exonerate Mike."

"But Mike confessed, didn't he?"

Ivy gave a guileless smile. "Yes, he did. But perhaps this new information will make that irrelevant."

"Must be some spectacular information, then. Do you know what it is?"

"I think we'll just have to wait and see what happens next."

If Ivy was trying to rattle Hayden, I couldn't tell if she'd succeeded. Except for that brief hint of uneasy surprise when she'd mentioned "new information," he remained the picture of affable goodwill.

"Well, hopefully it's good news for Mike and his mother. Now about those steaks—"

He headed for the freezer and said a cheerful "Ta-da!" as he pulled out two packages of rib eye steaks. "These look great."

IVY

Hayden couldn't, however, find a barbecue grill tucked away in the garage or anywhere else. Apparently Warren had not been a barbecuing person. Hayden nuked the steaks in the microwave to thaw them and turned on the oven broiler to heat. He fussed about a lack of proper spices to season the meat, but a mouthwatering scent of steak sizzling under the broiler soon filled the room.

Sable set plates and silverware, which included Warren's elegant teak-handled steak knives, on the counter separating the kitchen from the dining room. I was relieved we weren't going to be sitting at that parking-lot sized dining room table. We'd have needed an Uber to move the food around.

Sable found a package of dinner rolls in the freezer, and I removed the plastic wrap from my Caesar salad. Hayden casually selected a bottle of wine from Warren's wine rack and located an opener to extract the cork. I'm no expert in opening wine bottles, but this opener looked as if it might take an engineering degree to use it. He poured a red stream into a gracefully curved glass, then swirled, sniffed, and tasted, as if he were quite the wine connoisseur.

"I hate to admit it, but I'm impressed with Warren's taste in wine. This has a masterful complexity with a marvelous integration of polished and oak tannins. A great balance of cherry, apple, plum—" He took another sip and swished it around his mouth. "Even a hint of pepper for an earthy sensibility. And a perfect soft finish." He dipped his head and tipped the glass in deference to the former husband's expertise.

What I had to admit was that I sometimes found wine connoisseurs a bit pretentious, and Hayden struck me as zooming way beyond the pretentious level. He was right up there in hogwash territory.

Although I also had to admit when we ate that the steaks were very good, thoroughly cooked without being overdone. I remembered what Jenna had said about Hayden's aversion to underdone meat. Hayden offered us some of the wine he'd opened, but both Mac and I declined. I was surprised when Sable also declined. I had the unexpected feeling that she was a little uncomfortable with how Hayden was making himself at home with Warren's possessions.

I launched into my getting-to-know-more-about-Hayden project with a subject I expected he'd be eager to talk about. "We aren't golfers, so I'm not sure what a golf pro does. Perhaps you could tell us."

Hayden did that, with enthusiasm and in considerable detail. I encouraged him by asking how he'd gotten into a golfing career, which he also covered quite thoroughly. Without prompting he segued into his side career of consulting for a sports equipment company.

In spite of a lot of words flowing out of Hayden, so far my efforts to elicit *helpful* information were right up there with getting Koop to tell me why he has a fanatic dislike of smokers.

Without expecting much, I asked if the consulting entailed much travel, and Hayden said it was only a couple of trips a year to San Francisco.

"Don't forget all those 'conferences' in Las Vegas and Dallas," Sable said.

Hmm. Definitely an undercurrent of resentment in the way her tone put snarky quotation marks around *conferences*. Although what I was also thinking was that the postcard that made it look as if Warren was alive and gambling had been sent from Vegas . . .

Hayden was not inclined to modesty when he talked about his accomplishments . . . how he'd won various golfing awards before deciding to settle down as a golf pro, how he'd been instrumental in increasing the membership at the golf club there in Scottsdale, how he'd turned down an offer at a prestigious Georgia golf course because he and Sable didn't want to leave Arizona . . . But he made no revealing slipups about a girlfriend or murder. I finally asked what his ambitions and plans were for the future.

"Oh, I just want to grow old with Sable by my side." He reached over and gave her hand an affectionate squeeze. "Maybe do some traveling to places we've always wanted to see."

Poster boy for The Ideal Husband. Give the man a gold star. Although I also had another thought: more hogwash. The man was full of it.

Sable was also looking at him with what I was reasonably sure was skepticism. Hayden may have made it to inside status, but he hadn't completely won her over.

We had cookies and coffee after the steaks, and then I said I thought I'd run over and see how Jenna was doing after her walk. Sable asked Mac if he'd like to see Warren's collection of unusual paper money.

"I'm assuming you don't mind my inviting your husband into the bedroom," she added with a conspiratorial wink, and I assured her I was fine with it. They were headed down the hallway, Hayden following, when I went out the front door.

I couldn't see any light in Jenna's trailer when I got outside, but I walked over anyway, thinking perhaps she was sitting outside to think. Surely she wouldn't still be out walking in the dark. It seemed too early for her to have gone to bed. However, when I got there, I decided that must be what she'd done.

I paused to look up at the stars. A glorious desert night, with an incredible array of stars filling the sky with the centerpiece of a slender curve of moon. A Psalm echoed in my mind. *The heavens declare the glory of God; the skies proclaim the work of his hands.* Oh yes! How many stars? A gazillion, at least. And how many more were out there somewhere, known only to God? The faint moonlight silvered the cholla cactus and gave even the lowly creosote bush a fairytale elegance. I picked out the Big Dipper, with its guiding line to the North Star, amazed, as I always was, by the size and magnificence of the Lord's creation. But instead of being intimidated, I somehow felt closer to him out here under the stars. Wasn't it astonishing that in the midst of all this magnificence, he cared about each one of us here on earth? *Thank you, Lord!*

A shooting star arced across the sky. A comment from God about my thoughts? Nah. Couldn't be. But . . . who knows? The Lord works in mysterious ways. I thanked him again.

I wandered on down to say hi to Lightning's horses and then headed back to the double-wide.

As I got closer, I could see through the window that Sable and Mac were still looking at the paper money in the bedroom. Sable had taken one of the frames off the wall and was showing Mac how glass on both sides made viewing both front and back of the bills possible. No sign of Hayden, however. Perhaps he was back in the kitchen guzzling more of Warren's masterfully-complex-with-a-soft-finish wine. He'd made a fair dent in the contents of the bottle during dinner.

Then as I passed the convertible, I saw in the glow from the house lights something lying on the seat. The cell phone pouch! And then I heard the murmur of a muted voice on the far side of Sable's Mercedes. I strained mightily to hear, but I couldn't make out the words. I tiptoed around the back of the convertible, then slithered over to crouch in the dark shadow behind the Mercedes.

Hayden saying, ". . . wearing that new nightgown I bought you?"

Silence, then more suggestive conversation about the nightgown and a planned trip to Las Vegas together. A couple of low, intimate laughs from Hayden. "Yeah, it'll be a great 'conference.'"

Hayden's extramarital antics made my stomach roil. I also felt uncomfortably voyeuristic listening to a conversation with what must be girlfriend Savannah.

Okay, I'd just creep away before they got into something even more X-rated. But then I paused with only one tiny creep-step taken as Hayden said, "No, hon, I can't leave yet. You know I have to stay here until I get this business with my uncle's estate settled."

Uncle's estate?

What kind of story was he telling this girlfriend?

Silence from him as she made some response.

"I know, hon. I miss you too—" Another silent space as she apparently cut in. "No, of course I'm not *enjoying* being here with her. This is business, not some fun vacation." He managed to sound indignant, even a bit wounded, that she would think he would enjoy time away from home with his wife. "She's staying with her daughter, and I have a motel room."

I felt an unexpected flurry of indignation. The girlfriend having an affair with a married man wasn't exactly operating on solid moral ground, but he was lying to both of them! No more honest as a boyfriend than he was as a husband. More silence as she apparently gave him an earful about something.

"Tessa, hon, don't be upset," he soothed. "I know it's difficult, waiting to be together, but it *is* going to happen—"

Tessa? Cheating on girlfriend Savannah as well as wife Sable? Maybe the guy needed three phones.

Silent space before he said, "No, don't do that—" Now he sounded alarmed. Was she threatening something? "Sweetie, you know I love you and as soon as—"

Cut off again. Hayden might be charming and smooth-talking, but his double life—or was that triple life?—obviously had some speed bumps. I figured if he left Sable for this woman he'd also better worry that he'd never get to finish a sentence. But it sounded as if his worry at the moment was that she might walk out on the relationship.

"Hon, I don't know yet how long it will take to settle the estate and I can collect what I have coming. I know it's frustrating, but we just have to be patient."

Their relationship must be on hold until Sable's big insurance payment came through, and I suspected patience was not one of Tessa's strong points. But why wait for the money? That would be Sable's money, not Hayden's. Did he plan to grab some of it in a divorce? I'm not familiar with divorce and property settlement laws, but I doubted he could do that.

But the fact that it was Sable's money he was waiting for was obviously not the story he was telling this woman.

"It won't be long after the money comes through until we can be together. I promise."

I couldn't hear Tessa's response, of course, but I suppose you don't put a clandestine conversation with a girlfriend on speaker phone.

"Everything's going to work out fine," he said, still in soothe mode. "Don't worry about it. You just think about a new bikini for our trip to Vegas. We'll be doing Cancun and the Bahamas before long."

I didn't get it. He and this girlfriend had a future together planned for when the insurance money came in . . . though he'd obviously told her it was an inheritance he was about to receive, not Sable's insurance money . . . but how was he planning to glom on to that money? Perhaps he could get Sable to put it into a joint account of some kind and then—

A different and much more alarming possibility about Hayden's devious plans slammed into my mind.

"There's going to be plenty of money for us to enjoy life together. I promise that too. My uncle was loaded." He paused as Tessa apparently said something. "No, don't worry about Sable. I'll take care of Sable."

Murder. *That* was how Hayden planned to "take care of Sable."

Another alarming possibility hit me, this one more immediate. If Hayden caught me back here listening to his conversation with a girlfriend about a nonexistent inheritance from a dead uncle, and —

I duckwaddled from the shadow behind the Mercedes to the shadow at the back end of the convertible, aware as I crossed between the two vehicles that I made a moving shadow of my own under light from the skinny moon. I remembered the old fun of making animal shadows with your fingers. No fun involved here. My shadow now was an LOL version of the hunchback of Notre Dame, or maybe a two-legged tank. Would Hayden somehow see that shadow . . . and *me?*

Invisibility, don't fail me now!

At the last second before reaching the shadow of the convertible, just when I thought I'd made it safely, I stumbled. My forehead hit the rear of the convertible. *Bong!* Pain ricocheted from my forehead to the back of my head and down my neck. I reeled dizzily. The stars spun and twirled overhead like some celestial carnival ride. My head bong echoed in my ears, loud enough to disturb small animals hiding out on the desert, maybe even send vibrations to those distant stars. Cataclysm.

I cringed silently. Invisibility may not have failed me, but it obviously hadn't made me noiseless. No point in trying to hide now. Better to announce my presence. My *just-arrived* presence. I hastily belted out a line from an old hymn. "Nearer, my God, to thee . . ." Familiar as the hymn was, pain and dizzy disorientation chased the next lines out of my head. So I just shouted out the same line again. Louder. "Nearer, my God, to thee . . ."

Hayden popped up on the far side of the Mercedes.

"Hey," I said as if seeing him was a big surprise. Actually, at the moment, I saw two of him, menacing figures ballooning to monster-sized proportions. "Hey, are you enjoying the starlight too? I'm sorry if my singing disturbed you." Both of you.

Was that all he'd heard, my singing? Or had he heard the earlier head bong and realized I'd been listening? I was glad we'd already eaten the steaks. If he realized what I'd heard, he might have good reason to season them with rat poison now.

"I was just getting some fresh air," he said. "It seemed a little stuffy inside."

The sense of disorientation was, blessedly, beginning to fade and the two figures shrank into one closer to normal size. I rattled off an explanation for my presence.

"Jenna must have gone to bed already, but I walked on down to see the horses. A night like this under the moon and stars makes me feel so close to the Lord that I couldn't help singing about it." I threw out my arms and again belted out that only line I could remember at the moment. "Nearer, my God, to thee . . ."

See, Hayden, just a harmless LOL singing in the night. Not hearing a word about you murdering your wife so you could inherit her pile of insurance money.

Chapter 24

MAC

It was an impressive collection of paper money, everything from confederate bills to silver certificates to counterfeits, some convincingly realistic, some, like the two-dollar bill with a picture of Spider-Man on it, definitely just for fun. I thanked Sable for showing me, and we went back to the living room just as Ivy came in the door, Hayden right behind her.

"We were both enjoying the fresh air and the stars." Ivy sounded a bit breathless. "I was even singing my joy."

"A beautiful evening," Hayden agreed. "So inspiring."

So how come they both sounded as phony as the million-dollar bill that had been part of Warren's collection of improbable counterfeits?

"I didn't see Jenna," Ivy added. "She must have gone to bed early. That's what we should do too, don't you think, dear?" she said to me as she dashed over to the counter and picked up our empty salad bowl.

Ivy has a few lovable names for me, but "dear" isn't one of them. What did her use of the word mean? She fingered her head with an odd caution, then pulled a strand of hair forward.

"Oh, it's early yet," Hayden said, surprising me. I figured he was ready to sweep us out the door with a large broom. "I've done all the talking, and we hardly know anything about you two. Let's have some coffee."

I started to say sure, let's do that. Hayden hadn't revealed anything incriminating yet, but maybe there was still a chance. But I caught Ivy's minuscule shake of head, accompanied by a wince, and instead said, "Thanks, but we really should be getting home. We still have to take our dog out for his nightly walk."

"Our cat too," Ivy added brightly. "Koop loves to take walks." She edged toward the door. "Thanks for the great steaks."

"Maybe we can do this again before Sable and I go home," Hayden said.

"Maybe we can," Ivy said, but it sounded like what she really meant was no-way-José, not in this lifetime. Then, in a surprise about-face, she said to Sable, "I was thinking about going into Yuma tomorrow to do some shopping. Maybe get some new sandals. Would you like to come along?"

"Oh, Ivy, thanks, but I think I should stay around here. Jenna—"

Hayden flung a hand to his head as if in shock. "I can't believe it. Sable turning down a shopping trip?"

Sable gave him a cut-the-baloney look. "I want to do whatever I can to help Jenna cope with all this. She and Mike were apparently more serious than I realized, and this has really hit her hard."

"Well, uh, okay," Ivy said. "Maybe we can do it sometime before you leave, then."

Outside, once we were in the pickup, I gave Ivy a puzzled look. "How come we just rushed out of there as if Warren's ghost was after us with his fancy steak knives? I was thinking we might still learn something useful about Hayden. And since when have you taken up girly shopping trips?"

"I did learn more about Hayden. A lot more. When I was outside I heard him talking on that extra cell phone to his girlfriend."

"I'm afraid his having a girlfriend isn't news to anyone."

"No, but it may be news that he's planning to kill Sable so he can grab all that insurance money and live happily ever after with the girlfriend. Except it's a different girlfriend than the Savannah that Sable mentioned. Now he has a Tessa."

"You overheard all that?" I asked, startled.

"I heard him tell this Tessa that they will be together as soon as he receives an inheritance from the uncle's estate that's he's taking care of here, and there'll be plenty of money for them to enjoy together." She gave one of those unladylike snorts that always surprises me. "An uncle's estate. When alligators fly."

"Hayden is a great steak cooker, but it sounds as if he might need an Excel spreadsheet to keep track of all the lies he's telling."

"Yes. And I think Sable is in danger. That's why I tried to get her to go shopping with me tomorrow, so I could warn her. I think, as soon as the insurance money comes in, Hayden is planning to kill her just like he did Warren, so he can grab the money as an inheritance." Ivy spoke in an almost-whisper as if afraid Hayden had superhero powers and could hear what we were saying even out here. She leaned forward to watch as he pulled drapes at the window. "And I'm afraid Hayden may have realized I was listening to him on his cell phone. I stumbled and hit my head on the convertible. It sounded like a demolition derby."

I peered closer at the strand of hair she'd pulled across her forehead, and I could see now that an impressive bump had formed there. "We need to get you to the emergency room—"

"No, I'm okay." She wiggled her shoulders and twisted her neck from side to side. "I was a little dizzy and disoriented at first, but I'm over that."

"I really think we should have that bump looked at." I carefully pulled the concealing strand of hair aside. "It's starting to discolor"

Ivy again rejected my concerns. "I'll take some ibuprofen when we get home."

I had a better idea. We'd skip going home and go directly to the emergency room. But I'd save that news for later.

"So this is how I see it," she said. "Hayden killed Warren so Sable could collect the big insurance payoff. Now he plans to kill Sable so he can grab the money himself."

I nodded. "Sounds like a plan to me."

Which meant Sable was definitely in danger and we needed to warn her, although the danger wouldn't come until after she received the insurance payoff.

But *we,* if Ivy was right and Hayden knew she'd overheard his conversation, were in danger right now.

Time to get out of here, before Hayden came out snapping a couple of leather cords in preparation. I started the engine. I'd like to do a quick wheelie and disappear in a cloud of dust, but the old pickup does not do a flamboyant spin and squeal of tires. It's more like me: sturdy and reliable, but not exactly race-car flashy. I put the gear in reverse and edged backward.

Too late. Here came Hayden out the door and down the walkway.

IVY

Hayden put a hand on the door. He looked more downhearted than threatening. Could I have misinterpreted what I'd heard? He was carrying the duffel bag that had been inside when we went in.

"I thought you'd already left," he said.

"We were just talking about how good the steaks were," Mac said. "And what a great evening we had."

"Yeah, great," Hayden echoed. He cocked his head as a coyote yipped somewhere out on the desert. "Sound really carries on a night like this, doesn't it?"

An innocent comment? Or maybe a subconscious revelation that he knew I'd heard his conversation with Tessa?

"Are you, uh, going somewhere?" I asked.

"At the last minute, Sable decided I wasn't welcome inside after all." He managed to sound downhearted about the rebuff. "So I'm headed into town to get a motel for the night."

He could make an alteration on that spreadsheet of lies. At least one part of what he'd told the girlfriend, the part about staying in a motel, would now be true.

"I'll come back out in the morning and try to make Sable see that I know I've made mistakes but I want to do what's right now." Noble determination in his voice; man with an honorable mission.

"Umm."

"You folks go on ahead. I'll follow you out to the highway. That way you won't be eating my road dust."

Thoughtful of him, but I couldn't escape an uncomfortable feeling that his concern was wallowing in hogwash territory again. "But then you'll get all dusty," I said. Maybe I was in hogwash territory too, because I wasn't really concerned if he got up to his armpits in dust.

"I'll put the top up on the convertible."

So we headed out. Still no lights in Jenna's trailer. I hoped she'd get a good night's sleep. Looking back, I could see Hayden putting the top up on the convertible. About halfway out to the highway, we met Lightning's pickup coming in. Mac edged our pickup off as far as possible so Lightning could squeeze by. He waved and gave us a thumbs-up as he passed. I didn't see any lights from Hayden's convertible behind us.

At the highway, Mac started to turn toward Yuma, but I stopped him. "No, no emergency room. I'm fine. It's barely hurting now."

Mac grumbled but I stubbornly crossed my arms, and he headed across the highway. At the motorhome, we found a note on our door saying Geoff and Magnolia had gone into Yuma for dinner and a movie. Rather a long drive for that, but as we got older, Magnolia had adopted a "just do it" attitude. No sitting around in a rocking chair waiting for the just-right time to do something.

We got the usual ecstatic welcome home from BoBandy, and even Koop was quite demonstrative with much head rubbing and purring. I gave them each a few bites of steak I'd saved from dinner, gave myself a couple of ibuprofens, and changed to ratty old jeans and a pink sweatshirt with a blue paint stain in the shape of a unicorn's head. Although Mac had never been able to see the unicorn in the stain, of course.

"I still think we should take you to the emergency room in Yuma." He gingerly felt my bump again. "Head injuries can be more serious than they seem at first."

"Let's take our walk and see how I feel by then. We also need to decide what we're going to do with the information we have."

It was really getting chilly outside so I pawed around in the closet and dug up a heavy old jacket I hadn't used since we left Montana. I picked up Koop to carry him outside. We left the lights on and hadn't gotten more than a few feet from the door when a figure stepped around the end of the motorhome.

"You can put the animals back inside," Hayden said.

"But we're going for a walk," I protested. A wasted protest since I now saw that Hayden was carrying a powerful persuader.

The gun gleamed in the glow of light from a motorhome window.

"What's this all about?" Mac asked. "I thought you were going into town to get a motel."

"I am. I just decided it would be prudent to take care of this little matter first. I'm sure Ivy has told you all about the conversation she overheard when she sneaked up on me. Which you're no doubt planning to broadcast to Sable and everyone in the sheriff's department as well."

I started to protest that I hadn't sneaked up on him. Lying goes against my principles, but this seemed to warrant a temporary modification to that policy. Maybe I should apologize too. *I didn't mean to do any sneaking or overhearing. It was all just an unfortunate coincidence.*

Hayden, however, gave me no time for either fib or apology.

"Put the animals back inside," he repeated. This time he emphasized the order with a jerk of the gun. "They'll be safe in there."

He was concerned about BoBandy's and Koop's safety? Doubtful. More likely he just wanted them out of the way for whatever he had in mind. I remembered Jenna saying that both her mother and Hayden had taken shooting lessons when there was a serial-killer scare in the Scottsdale area. He appeared ready to make use of those lessons now. But Jenna had also said Hayden had a real problem with blood, and gun wounds surely came with a bounteous supply of blood. Maybe he figured there'd be less blood if he removed the animals from the scene so he wouldn't have to shoot them too.

Not an encouraging thought, because it must mean he was planning to shoot someone. Or maybe he had a leather cord in a back pocket and intended to use that when the time came. Or maybe he'd figured out some other non-bloody means of disposing of us.

My mind seemed to have a ready supply of disagreeable possibilities. Actually, I couldn't think of even one agreeable possibility for this situation.

Mac opened the door and boosted BoBandy, over his protests, inside. I set Koop on the floor. Mac closed the door and turned around.

"Better lock it," Hayden advised. "You never know what kind of lowlife might be wandering around out here ready to take advantage of an unlocked door."

I couldn't tell if Hayden was being facetious or if he really didn't see the absurdity of warning about a possible burglar when he surely had even more nefarious plans.

Mac locked the door, and Hayden said, "Now start walking. Toward the old office building."

Mac hesitated and then spread his feet and crossed his arms over his chest. "Ivy bumped her head quite hard. I need to take her to the emergency room."

I was agreeable to that now. "Yes, that's right. I may have a concussion." I made a dramatic fling of hand to head.

Something spurted at my feet at the same time as a muffled noise came from the gun. He'd shot and barely missed my toes!

"You wouldn't have bumped your head if you hadn't been snooping around," Hayden said. "Let's go."

I glanced across at the potato-pilgrimager's trailer. A dim light but no movement there. The shot hadn't made much noise. Hayden must have a silencer on the gun. Except silencers don't make a gun really silent. They're more accurately called suppressors, just dulling the sound considerably, as this one had done. They can be used on some—but not all—handguns.

Great information I'd read somewhere. Useless as a wig in a windstorm right now. Mac grabbed my hand and we walked. The about-to-set moon still made faint shadows that moved with us. Very pretty. Even a bit romantic. Unfortunately, all wasted ambiance when a man is holding a gun on you.

Hayden had left the convertible behind the unused office where we couldn't see it from the motorhome if we'd looked, and Betsy couldn't see it from the store. I guessed he'd driven in with the lights turned off. Hayden opened the car door and motioned us inside with the gun. I had the impression he rather liked using that authoritative gesture.

"We can't both fit in there," Mac protested.

"I suppose I can make it so only one of you sits up here. The other one can go in the trunk—"

Mac got in and pulled me down on his lap. Sardines in a can had it roomy compared to us. Hayden circled the car and got behind the wheel. He drove with his right hand, his left holding the gun across his body, barrel pointed in our direction. I doubted he had much expertise with left-hand shooting. Most people don't. But he wouldn't need any expertise to put a bullet hole in one or both of us in here.

We drove past the little store and across the highway to the Deadeye road. I'd bet Betsy had a shotgun in there. She'd probably rush out and blast him if she knew what was going on out here. But she didn't know.

We bounced and rattled on the old dirt road. My head hit the top. Twice. Not a good night for my head. It throbbed in complaint. Mac's bony knees, which I'd always found rather attractive, now felt like steel doorknobs under me. My elbow caught him in the nose.

Why was Hayden taking us back out to Deadeye? He meant us ill will, that was obvious. He couldn't leave us alive to thwart his plans now. A sideways jolt and Mac's head cracked against mine. *Ouch.*

The why-take-us-out-to-Deadeye question hit me again. *No, no,* I chastised myself. *Why* didn't matter. *Don't bother to think about it.* What mattered was figuring out how to stop him. There were two of us, only one of him. Surely that was a big advantage.

But he was the one with a different and much more powerful advantage. The gun. We had . . . what? I hopefully felt in my jacket pocket. A scrunched-up Kleenex. A couple squares of tinfoil-wrapped chocolate, crumbly with age. A rock I'd picked up at some time no doubt because it was pretty. That's the trouble with *pretty.* Useless when what you need is big and sharp.

There is something really undignified about being taken to your death site crammed in a car like circus clowns.

Lord, we need some help here!

We reached the gate at the entrance to Deadeye. It was locked. Did he expect us to crawl through the barbed-wire fence? Hope flickered. Between us, maybe we could overpower him while he was crawling between the wires—

"Get out," he said.

Hayden was out and standing beside the door on our side before we could even untangle ourselves from each other and stumble out.

Perhaps he guessed what I was thinking about taking advantage of him while crawling through the fence because he lifted his hand with a ring of keys dangling from a finger. He smiled.

"Warren was so organized. He kept all these spare keys hanging right by the garage door."

"Didn't you use his keys to get into Deadeye the day you killed him?"

He didn't bother to deny what I was saying. "I put them back. So now I'll just drop you off here and be on my way to find a motel in Yuma for the night."

"Drop you off" sounded innocent enough. But common sense told me this was about as innocent as a guillotine. With the blade raised for action.

Mac grabbed my hand. Hayden unlocked the gate and motioned with the gun for us to start walking over toward Deadeye's main street. He followed. I couldn't *see* the gun with him behind us, but I could *feel* it aimed at our backs. Like a drill-to-the-center-of-the-earth laser.

It was still a beautiful night, the stars still magnificent. I didn't feel much like singing, but I did send up another prayer.

We turned the corner and marched past the striped pole of the barber shop. A few faint lines of toothpaste still clung to the ground. They didn't make any identifiable shape now, but Hayden said, "That's where your friend made an outline of the body, isn't it? With toothpaste. That was weird, you know, really weird. She must be a very strange person."

Look who's talking.

"How'd you know about that?" Mac asked.

"Sable mentioned it."

"How did you get Warren to come out here so you could strangle him?" I asked.

Hayden didn't need to answer, but maybe he was proud of what he'd done. "Same way I'm getting you here. With a gun."

He apparently hadn't been concerned about leaving Warren's house unlocked.

"Why not just shoot him at the house?" Mac asked.

"I have an unpleasant reaction to blood. An allergy kind of thing." Hayden spoke in a blustery tone, as if he wanted to be sure we knew this was an uncontrollable physical reaction, like an allergy to peanuts, not a weakness unbefitting a macho male. "I didn't want to have to deal with a big bloody mess in there."

"But once you got out here, you realized shooting him was going to make a big bloody mess here too," I said.

No response from Hayden, and Mac said, "So you yanked that leather cord off your shoe and strangled him."

"Does your girlfriend know you killed Sable's ex-husband and now you plan to kill Sable herself to get hold of the insurance money?" I asked. I knew the answer, of course. He was telling the girlfriend an entirely different, dead-rich-uncle story.

Apparently, he'd had enough of this conversation because now he growled, "Shut up."

"But you couldn't really tell her that, could you? It might make a woman feel just a teensy bit antsy, hooking up with a man who killed a previous wife."

"She's never going to know—" Then he interrupted himself. "I told you, shut up. Just *shut up!*"

Now I felt the actual jab of the gun in my back. The bump on my head turned up the volume on the throbs.

I shut up. We marched on down the street. I had no idea where he was taking us. We passed the Deadeye Mercantile, the hotel, and the saloon. When he stopped us at a familiar building, my insides plummeted like a falling elevator. No, he couldn't know what was under this old telegraph and assay office building . . . could he?

He came up beside us and pulled a penlight out of his pocket. Using his left hand, he shone the light on the closed door. He kept the gun in ever-ready position in his right hand.

"Open the door," he said.

Mac reluctantly stepped forward and opened the door. I hadn't heard it creak before, but now it gave an all-too-appropriate *Inner Sanctum* screech.

"Inside."

We went inside. Hayden closed the door with a shove of his hip and flicked the light around the room. It looked the same as before. Telegraph equipment on the counter. Assay equipment and rocks in the corner. The old carpet covering the trapdoor to the mine shaft below.

The roving beam of light stopped on that section of the carpet, and I knew my momentary hope about his not knowing what was down there was wasted. Jenna must have showed him the old mine shaft when she gave him a tour of the town.

"I should have left it uncovered," he muttered.

"Hindsight is always twenty-twenty," I said primly, which earned me another growl and a vicious, "If you don't shut up—"

In the glow of the penlight, I could see his finger on the trigger. Shutting up now.

"Pull the carpet back," Hayden said to Mac.

Mac hesitated, no doubt trying to think of some way to work this to our advantage, but he finally pulled the carpet out of the way. The outline of the trapdoor stood out like a road sign. What did Hayden have in mind? Shooting us and letting our bodies fall into the mine hole? No bloody mess to give him an "allergic" reaction that way.

"Open it."

"How? There's no handle."

Hayden muttered an expletive that covered the general situation and Mac's incompetence in particular. He flicked the beam of light around the room again. "Jenna used something when she opened it—There, over by the wall. That piece of metal."

Mac headed for the sharpened rod with alacrity. Hayden caught his mistake just before Mac reached for what would be not only a trapdoor opener but also a handy-dandy weapon.

"No! Leave it alone. I'll do it."

Hayden crossed over to the sharpened rod. Then he had a dilemma. One hand held the flashlight; the other hand held the gun. It would take both hands to use the rod to force the trapdoor open. He'd have to set both flashlight and gun down, but he couldn't risk doing that.

But neither could he let Mac open the trapdoor because that would place the metal rod in his hands.

"We don't really need to see into the tunnel," I said helpfully. "We've already seen it."

But Hayden was not without a certain nasty resourcefulness. He carefully positioned the small flashlight on the counter so that the beam targeted one side of the trapdoor, angling and bracing it with one of the glittery rocks. He set the sharpened rod on the edge of the trapdoor and took a step back. He put the barrel of the gun against Mac's back.

"Okay, now you, *very carefully* pick up the rod and pry the trapdoor open. One move to do anything else and you get a bullet in the back." Then, apparently thinking I might do something unexpected—although at the moment I couldn't think what—he told me to go stand in the corner.

Stand in the corner? Like some misbehaving pupil?

"Now," he said.

I went and stood in the corner. From where all I could do was shoot venomous eye-arrows at him. Fully as effective as shooting frozen peas at an attacking tank.

"Now get the trapdoor open." He prodded Mac with the gun.

Mac worked industriously at the door, prying and digging. The door had come up easily enough when Lightning did that, but Mac seemed to be having considerable difficulty. Self-engineered difficulty, I suspected.

Apparently Hayden had the same suspicion. "Stop faking it." A flash of flame erupted from the gun and the instant muffled boom was still loud enough to rattle my bones. Bits of wood flew as the bullet slammed into the trapdoor.

Mac grunted as Hayden immediately jammed the barrel of the gun deep in his back again.

"Next bullet goes in you," Hayden warned.

Mac resumed prying on the trapdoor, and a minute later it came up.

Hayden picked up the penlight with his left hand and aimed the beam into the hole below. I didn't step up to look. If I got too close maybe he'd decide to save a bullet and just shove me in.

"Okay, down the ladder," he said to Mac.

Uh-oh. Obvious now what he intended. Put us both in the black hole, replace the trapdoor and carpet, and leave us there. Our pickup was back at the motorhome. No reason for anyone to look for us here. Would our yelling for help be heard? Doubtful. On most days or weeks no one even came to Deadeye. Even if someone did come, I wasn't sure our voices would be heard from as far below ground as we'd be after he pulled up the ladder.

How long would we last without water or food? With the trapdoor shut, maybe even air would be limited. A slower death than a leather cord around the neck, but eventually just as effective.

And quite bloodless. If a movie company ever started production here, we might be found then. Skeletal or mummified. Maybe it would give some writer a great script idea.

But Mac wasn't moving. Again he planted his feet and crossed his arms over his chest. "I'm not going anywhere," he said flatly.

"I think you are." Hayden smiled. The penlight in his hand gave enough reflected light to give his teeth a vampirish gleam. "I'm counting to . . . let's see . . . five. That's a nice round number. If you're not on that ladder by five, I'm shooting her." He jerked his head at me.

I knew it was an effective threat. Mac might be able to stand up to the danger of a bullet in himself, but not one in me.

"I-I'll bleed all over," I threatened. "I'll make a bloody mess. It will make you really sick and weak."

It wasn't exactly a terrifying threat. About as effective as threatening to squirt some of Magnolia's body-outlining toothpaste on him.

Hayden laughed. "Well, I haven't shot anyone yet, so I really don't know what kind of reaction I'll have. But I've come to realize I'm just going to have to accept a little blood in these unpleasant situations in which I find myself."

A virtuous man making the best of a bad situation. Very admirable.

"If you're allergic to the sight of blood, maybe you should take time to take an antihistamine first," I suggested.

"Good one, Ivy," Hayden said. He gave me a nod of appreciation for what he considered a remark of levity. "I'm really sorry to have to do this, you know. You seem like nice people, and, Ivy, your salad and cookies were very good. But you're just a little too nosy."

Now, I decided, would be a great time for white-hat-hero Lightning to gallop in with spurs jingling and guns blazing.

I listened carefully, but I heard nary a hoofbeat nor a jingle in the silent desert night.

All I heard was Hayden saying to Mac, "Down the ladder. *Now.*"

Chapter 25

IVY

Mac reluctantly put a foot over the edge of the opening and felt around for the top rung of the ladder.

"Hurry up. You're wasting time."

Mac found the rung with one foot and cautiously moved the other foot down beside it. He shifted his weight back and forth. "The ladder is really shaky."

A shaky ladder was probably the least of our worries, but Hayden stepped closer and flicked the narrow beam down the length of the ladder.

"It'll do for what I have in mind," he said.

I looked around frantically. Mac slowly went down two more rungs. Only the top half of his body showed above the floor of the old building now. If I could get to the counter, grab that rock Hayden had used to brace the flashlight—

I made a cautious move toward the counter.

Minuscule as my movement was, Hayden spotted it. He swiveled the gun toward me but before he could fire it, I grabbed the rock and threw it. And missed, of course. Let's face it: I throw like a girl.

But the momentary diversion was enough for Mac. He reached out and grabbed Hayden's ankle with both hands and jerked.

The penlight flew in one direction, the gun another. Hayden *oofe*d when he slammed into the floor. The beam of light shot at the ceiling, then rolled wildly.

I jumped for the gun, but it tumbled out of my reach. Into the dark hole. I spotted the rod Mac had used to pry the trapdoor open and went for that instead. Mac stormed out of the hole and I whacked wildly with the rod. The penlight rolled into a corner where all it lit up was a spiderweb.

My aim with the rod was as poor as my rock throwing. I clobbered the floor—hard enough to send *sproings* shooting up my arm. I moved over and this time hit the edge of the hole, then something softer. I thought it was the folded-back carpet, but a yelp from Hayden told me I'd finally hit metaphorical pay dirt. I whacked again. Hayden cursed and grabbed for the rod—

A dark blur of movement. Mac jumping on Hayden. Wrestling, thumping noises, bodies rolling on the floor, hard breathing. I got a better hold on the rod and lifted it for a strike—

But I didn't know where to strike because Mac was somewhere in that tangle of arms and legs.

"I've—got—him—" Mac panted.

More thumps. An *oomph*. A flailing leg knocked the rod out of my hands. I heard a clatter as it tumbled down the ladder.

I grabbed the penlight out of the corner and aimed the beam at the noises. Mac had Hayden straddled mid-center, his hands spreading Hayden's arms wide and clamping his hands to the floor. In spite of that, Hayden still twisted like a two-legged snake, feet thumping the floor. I dropped the light and threw myself on his flailing legs. I managed to squirm to a sitting position on his knees, my back to Mac. The double weight on Hayden finally stopped his movements, but it didn't stop him from screeching until he momentarily ran out of breath and changed to angry grunts.

Okay, we had him. Momentarily, anyway. Now what? The penlight must have fallen into the hole with the gun and the metal rod . . . an earthly black hole pulling everything around it into its depths? Only a faint glow escaped the hole to send eerie shadows around the room.

We were also at an impasse as far as doing anything.

With Mac holding Hayden's hands outspread and our combined weight holding him down, Hayden could do no more than squirm and wiggle and wheeze threats and curses. But neither could we do anything. The two of us together were barely holding him down. Without our combined weight on him—and right now I was glad I'd put on a few pounds—he could very well rise up and shove, drag, or toss us into the old mine shaft.

Outwait him? I couldn't think of anything else to do, but I also couldn't think of what favorable outcome would be accomplished by waiting.

It didn't seem likely someone would arrive with snacks.

We just sat there until, with a renewed burst of energy, Hayden bucked and twisted again. I could feel Mac struggling to keep from being tossed aside. I'd never thought of golf as a muscle-building exercise, but maybe it was more effective than it looked. My leg started to cramp, but I didn't dare take any weight off Hayden's knees.

I used the only weapon I had, which was that undersized rock in my pocket. I wrapped my fist around it and thumped him energetically on the shin. Not a particularly effective weapon, but we LOLs work with what's available. My hits did earn a nasty condemnation from Hayden about my family origins and current undesirable attributes.

So we sat there some more, and I tried to figure out some way around this impasse. It had to come to some sort of end eventually. We couldn't spend the rest of our lives just sitting here like some TV reality show gone wrong. Hayden no doubt had a longer life expectancy than we did. But how did we end it without finding ourselves dumped in that dark hole?

I also became aware of another uncomfortable problem. Once acknowledged, the need grew like a rising tidal wave. I squirmed restlessly.

I tried to whisper my need to Mac, but with our backs to each other, he couldn't hear me. I repeated the words, but all he said was, "What?"

I finally spoke them out loud, and in the silence they came out like a bullhorn announcement. "I need to use a restroom."

"I, uh, don't think Deadeye has restrooms," Mac said.

I couldn't get up and leave anyway, because that would free Hayden's feet and legs.

"There aren't any restrooms," Hayden said. "When they made Lightning's movies here years ago they brought in portables. Or used self-contained trailers."

"How do you know this?" I asked.

"I asked Jenna when she was giving me the tour of the town. Practical matters such as this tend to occur to me. So you'll just have to go out behind the buildings and—"

I groaned. We were sitting here in the near dark, discussing restroom facilities with a killer.

"I'll hold it," I muttered.

So we sat some more. Again I tried to think where this impasse was headed and how to get around it. Again all I could think of was trying to outlast him.

We sat. Hayden wiggled and twitched. The tidal wave within me grew larger. Hayden said he also needed a restroom. Mac remained silent on this subject. I felt something crawling in my hair. Something that slithered up out of that dark hole? Spider? *Tarantula?* I swatted at it. I was still holding that little rock. It felt a lot larger when I hit myself in the head with it.

So we waited. Sometimes I thought Hayden was weakening; sometimes I thought we were. Could we shove him over a few feet and push him into the hole? *Any suggestions, Lord?*

The door burst open. I blinked against a sudden glare of light.

"Okay, you slimy varmint—" Lightning's voice.

Slimy varmint?

Even in my rather battered, breathless condition, that struck me as needing a better script writer.

Lightning charged in, a gun in each hand. Jenna rushed in behind him, her flashlight showing the way.

Hey, Lord, great idea!

"Don't shoot! It's us, Mac and Ivy! And Hayden." I straightened my leg, trying to ward off another oncoming cramp.

Lightning lowered the guns. "Ivy? What's going on? And Hayden? What're you doing here?"

"Hayden killed Warren," I said hastily, before Hayden could speak. Jenna targeted me with the flashlight. "He's planning to kill Sable too. And he was about to put us down in the old mine tunnel and leave us there!"

"Don't listen to that old woman!" Hayden yelled. "She's bat crazy."

A *bat crazy old woman?* Hey, now, I might be a nosy little old lady, but not—

"I just stopped to check on why the gate was open and these crazy old people jumped me!" Hayden managed to sound so reasonable, so baffled about why we were sitting on him. "Get them away from me!"

"He had a gun on us," Mac said. "It fell down the mine shaft—"

A bucking-bronc move from Hayden lifted us both. "I don't know what's wrong with them!" he yelled. "First they came to the house claiming we invited them to dinner—"

It didn't seem like a good time to nitpick about whether we'd been invited to dinner so I just cut in with, "He followed us back to the motorhome and forced us at gunpoint to come back here. So he could stuff us down the mine tunnel and leave us to die there."

"Okay, both of you git off'n him while I figger out what's goin' on here."

Whatever Lightning's script was, it was apparently written in old-time-sheriff dialect. He spun one gun into a holster and lifted the other gun in the general direction of all three of us. I scrambled away from Hayden, and Mac followed. He pulled me a safer distance from the mine shaft.

Hayden started to get up, but Lightning targeted the gun on him.

"Don't move. Don't anybody move agin till I find out what's goin' on."

"I told you," Hayden yelled. "I was just going to town to get a motel for the night—"

"No, you weren't," Jenna interrupted. "The car was coming in from the highway, not going out."

"Everybody'll git a turn to talk," Lightning said. He turned to me. "Ladies first."

I liked that part of the script. "How did you know to come rescue us?" I asked.

"I'm the one who needs rescuing!" Hayden yelled. "These people may be old but they're dangerous!"

I decided to take that as a compliment.

"I came and got him," Jenna explained. "I saw the car lights coming in from the highway and then stop at the gate. I'd been out walking for hours trying to get my head straight about Mike. Then I saw someone marching two people away from the gate. By then I knew it was Hayden's convertible, and I thought maybe someone else had taken it, and that person was holding a gun on Mom and Hayden. So I went and got Lightning."

Rescued by mistake. Whatever, I'll take it.

"What you saw was Hayden holding a gun on Ivy and me," Mac said. "But, like I said, the gun is down at the bottom of the mine shaft now."

"Jenna, shine that light down in the hole. See if there's a gun down there."

Jenna cautiously stepped around all of us and knelt by the hole. It seemed to swallow up the light as she aimed the beam downward.

"Yes. There's a gun. I can see it." She stuck a foot over the edge. "I'll go down and get it."

"I don't think you should touch it. Hayden's fingerprints are the only ones on it now," Mac said. "Fingerprints may be important in what's going on here."

Jenna looked to Lightning for instructions.

"Yeah, that might be right," Lightning said.

Probably old-time western sheriffs didn't have to be concerned about fingerprints, and it seemed we might be stuck in an old-western time warp here.

"I'm going to call the sheriff," Jenna said.

I think Lightning started to protest that *he* was the sheriff, but Jenna pulled out her cell phone. Lightning came out of his old-western-sheriff persona far enough to say, "See if you can get Deputy Carstairs."

Apparently the probability that a real law officer would show up was enough to tell Hayden he might be in big trouble here. He jumped to his feet and went for the gun now dangling from Lightning's hand.

Hayden grabbed the gun and jerked it out of Lightning's hand. He was younger and probably stronger, but he hadn't counted on the experience of an old two-gun western sheriff. Even a movie version of one. Lightning whipped his second gun out of the holster and fired a left-handed shot while Hayden was still trying to get the gun he'd grabbed into shooting position.

I yelled what seemed appropriate. "Yee-haw!"

It wasn't a fatal shot. It wasn't even an accurate shot. Well, maybe that's not true. Maybe Lightning was aiming for Hayden's toe. Because that's what he hit.

Hayden howled and crashed to the floor, gun crashing with him. A surprising amount of blood poured out of the missing chunk of his loafer. He kicked it off.

A loafer with a leather cord laced around the top. He cradled the bleeding foot in his hands and rocked back and forth.

"You shot my toe off!" Blood oozed around his hands. "I-I think I'm going to be sick."

"You killed my brother, didn't you? You're lucky I didn't plug you in the heart."

"He did it so Sable could collect Warren's insurance, and then Hayden planned to kill Sable so he could get the money to spend with his girlfriend," I filled in quickly. "He took a detour on his trip to San Francisco to come here while both you and Jenna were gone. That's when he killed Warren."

"It's their word against mine," Hayden said. "And they're crazy. Both of 'em! *Crazy*. I need an ambulance."

Lightning pulled a red bandanna out of his pocket and tossed it to Hayden. "Wrap your foot in that." He retrieved the gun Hayden had taken from him and jammed it back in the holster. Then, to Jenna, "Did you get the sheriff's office?"

"They're sending someone."

And then we waited again. I slumped down against a wall, and after a while Mac joined me. We knew what Hayden had done here, what he'd done earlier to Warren, what he planned to do to us and then to Sable. Could we make the law enforcement authorities see that?

Hayden made occasional complaining noises about his foot, but with the flashlight not directly on him he couldn't see the blood, and his "allergic reaction" didn't go beyond a general moaning and groaning.

Lightning stayed upright, as any self-respecting, two-gun western sheriff no doubt would. He kept one gun in hand and a sharp eye on all of us. Jenna stood for a while, but then she came to our wall and slumped down beside us. I whispered to her about my increasing need for a restroom.

"We'll go out back of the buildings. I'll go with you," she whispered back.

So we both stood up, and Jenna explained my need to Lightning.

"Yeah, okay," he muttered. He sounded embarrassed. Ladies in his old movies probably never needed restrooms.

Jenna left the flashlight with Lightning, and I followed her outside and around to the back side of the buildings. A faint starlight lit the way. I relieved myself of that growing tidal wave and made use of the crumpled tissue in my coat pocket.

"Mike didn't kill your dad," I said before we started back to the street side of the buildings.

"But he did some other . . . not-good things," Jenna said.

True. There were various things that might keep him in trouble. It's definitely not good to carry off and bury a dead man even if you had nothing to do with his death. He tampered with evidence when he removed the leather cord from Warren's neck. All of which had muddied the police investigation. I had no idea what all Mike might legally be charged with, but the half-truths and outright lies he'd told Jenna had made the situation more painful and confusing for her.

Jenna and I went back inside. Eventually two deputies arrived in a squad car. One of them, I saw from the nametag on his uniform, was the Deputy Carstairs Lightning had requested.

"Hey, you old coot." The deputy slapped him on the back. "What're you up to now?"

With the real lawmen here now, Lightning abandoned his old-western-sheriff script and joined the script-less world. "I'm not sure," he admitted.

Then we all tried to get in our version of events

Jenna: She'd been out walking on the desert, saw the car come in, then someone marching two people into Deadeye at gunpoint, and ran to Lightning for help. And now she needed to go see if her mother was okay.

Hayden: He was on his way to get a motel in Yuma, realized he didn't have his wallet, and came back to find it. The alteration in this story was apparently to take care of Jenna's observation that when she'd seen the car lights, they were coming in, not going out. Then we, the "crazy old people," had jumped him. He demanded our arrest.

Mac and me: Hayden had followed us to our motorhome, forced us at gunpoint to come here, and tried to force Mac into the mine shaft. With our additional accusations about Hayden strangling Warren with the leather cord from his shoe and planning to murder Sable for the insurance money. We wanted Hayden arrested. He was trying to kill us.

Lightning: Hayden had tried to grab one of his guns, which was why he shot him in the toe. Beyond that he was just trying to figure out what was going on.

Except none of it came out that clearly or well organized. We were all yelling and accusing and explaining and demanding. That went on in what seemed an endless shouting match but probably didn't last more than two or three minutes before Deputy Carstairs thundered a command for everyone to shut up.

After the deputies lined us all up against a wall, one deputy went down in the mine shaft, retrieved the gun, metal rod, and penlight, and bagged all as evidence. The other deputy went out to the squad car, returned with a camera, and took photos of everything. We all had to empty our pockets—and holsters—which turned up my crumbly squares of chocolate, Mac's wallet, Lightning's guns, and Hayden's wallet. Which I was pleased to see contradicted his story of coming back to find it. Jenna's pockets were empty.

After some discussion between the two deputies, done in low tones so we couldn't hear, Deputy Carstairs told Jenna she could go check on her mother and Lightning that he could go back to his trailer, but both should come in to the sheriff's department in the morning for interviews.

The deputies determined that although Hayden's toe was wounded, it wasn't actually shot off, and he didn't need an ambulance.

Hayden, Mac, and I wound up as a cozy trio in matching handcuffs in the back seat of the squad car.

Chapter 26

IVY

I was put in a holding cell for women. It was already occupied by a young woman in pink short shorts and a leather bustier. She was rubbing one bare foot with a hand, a pair of stiletto-heeled sandals on the bench beside her. The problem with sore feet probably isn't one that first comes to mind in her line of work, but perhaps it's a lesser-known occupational hazard.

She appraised me and after a minute apparently came to a decision about the reason for my confinement. "Shoplifting?"

I guess, in my ratty outfit, I looked as if I might indeed have been on a shoplifting expedition for new clothes. "No, we were just going for a walk."

"How did you get the bump on your head?"

"I stumbled and hit my head on the back end of a convertible."

She gave me a sympathetic nod. "I did that once. Except it was a limousine. Complain about it and maybe you can get out of here to see a doctor. I did that once about a cut on my cheek and I got to spend two nice days in a hospital."

"It isn't hurting all that much now." But I had to wonder about Hayden. Had he finagled his toe wound into a nice hospital bed instead of the metal bunk I was looking at?

She nodded at the paint stain on my sweatshirt. "Nice unicorn."

I appreciated her discerning observation. I'd tell Mac other people could see the unicorn even if he couldn't. She showed me her necklace with a little gold unicorn dangling from a chain, and we had a bonding conversation about unicorns and head-bumpings. She suggested there weren't any unicorns today because they missed the two-by-two gathering for Noah's ark, and I took the opportunity to tell her that, however it happened, the good Lord was always in control. The Lord and I have never actually discussed unicorns, I had to admit.

"But I wasn't shoplifting," I assured her. "We were arrested because my husband and I were sitting on a man in a ghost town. He was trying to kill us by putting us down an old mine shaft, but he told the deputies we jumped him in the dark."

The young woman considered that for a minute and then patted my hand. "Don't you just hate it when that happens?"

I think she still thought I was a shoplifter and had a bit of wild imagination as well, but she was wrong about me, so maybe I was wrong about what I thought she was too. Actually, it had been a very long day . . . was it only this morning that we'd gone to see Lightning for a photo session with Magnolia and Geoff ? . . . and my thinking was getting a little fuzzy.

**

In the morning, after a surprisingly good jailhouse breakfast, I was taken to a one-table, two-chair room for questioning. I was read my Miranda rights, and when I asked about Mac, they said he was also being questioned. I asked about Hayden too, but I didn't get any answer to that.

The questioning was long and intensive, and I added a few answers to questions that weren't even asked. One was my conviction about Mike's innocence and the mistake he and his mother had made about each thinking the other guilty of the murder, which had led to their mutual confessions. I also told them about Hayden's extra cell phone under the seat of his car and suggested there might be some interesting phone calls or texts on it. I suggested they investigate his credit cards and see if there were any gas purchases in this area about the time of Warren's death. The deputy thanked me politely for my input but suggested all I need do was answer the asked questions. But I added one more bit of information about a leather cord like the ones on Hayden's loafers being used as a murder weapon.

There was a fairly long wait after the questioning, and then I was given a printed-out version to read and sign. I was pleased and relieved to find that the printout accurately followed the questioning session and included my various bits of extra information.

I was also relieved that in the late afternoon, someone made the decision to release me. A deputy took me out to a waiting room. Mac jumped up and came to wrap his arms around me.

To my surprise, Lightning and Jenna, who had both been questioned, were also there waiting for me, along with Sable. Plus Magnolia and Geoff! They said Jenna had come to tell them what happened and they'd been waiting around ever since. They also assured us BoBandy and Koop were fine.

It would have been the-gang's-all-here except that Hayden was missing.

And so was Mike.

**

I'd never before realized how exhausting a jail experience could be. Magnolia and Geoff took Mac and me back to the motorhome and we both slept a good share of the next three days.

Jenna came then with various bits of news. Lightning had proudly announced that a movie was definitely scheduled for filming at Deadeye, and he had a part in *The Sheriff and the Aliens*. I presumed he was the sheriff, but I guess we'll have to wait until the movie is released to be sure.

I'd been afraid the case against Hayden, in spite of his trying to stuff us down the mine shaft to kill us, was weak, but there were unexpected reinforcements. Sable had contacted girlfriend Savannah, who turned out to be rather vengeful when she learned she was now an ex-girlfriend, Tessa her replacement. Together they confronted Tessa, who turned out to be quite indignant that the dead-uncle story Hayden had told her was a phony. She'd produced a beige painting he'd given her and said he'd promised to take her to the very spot depicted in the Italian scene very soon.

A painting he'd unwisely taken right off Warren's wall.

Hayden was still incarcerated and, according to Lightning, via confidential information from his deputy friend, who was apparently versed in old-sheriff speak, in a "heap of trouble."

Mike would be released on bail later that day, his reversal of his confession to murder apparently now believed, although he still had various fairly serious, non-murder charges against him. His mother was going back to San Diego.

"What about you and Mike?" I asked Jenna.

"I think we'll be able to work things out," she said.

"Love conquers all?"

She smiled a bit ruefully. "Not completely. But we're working on it."

I patted her hand. "I'm glad to hear that."

**

Geoff and Magnolia decided to spend more time at Biosphere 2 and took off. Deputy Carstairs came to see us again. We told him we'd probably be leaving, and he said our presence might be needed for a trial later on. We gave him our contact information.

On Sunday we went to the Wellton church again. I was a little surprised but pleased to see both Mike and Jenna there.

We went back to the motorhome, intending to stay around for another day or two, but about mid-afternoon we looked at each other with the same thought in mind.

"Let's do it!" Mac said.

"Let's!" I agreed.

So we unhooked everything, fastened the pickup to the rear of the motorhome, took BoBandy and Koop out for a final walk, waved goodbye to Betsy, and headed down the road.

Honeymoon, here we come!

The End

Desert Dead

If you enjoyed *Desert Dead,* I'd very much appreciate a review on the site where you purchased the e-book. (Or on any other site as well.) Watch for the next Mac 'n' Ivy mystery!

E-BOOKS BY LORENA McCOURTNEY:

THE MAC 'N' IVY MYSTERIES (also available in print):
Something Buried, Something Blue
Detour
Desert Dead

THE IVY MALONE MYSTERIES:
Invisible
In Plain Sight
On the Run
Stranded
Go, Ivy, Go!

THE JULESBURG MYSTERIES:
Whirlpool
Riptide
Undertow

THE ANDI McCONNELL MYSTERIES:
Your Chariot Awaits
Here Comes the Ride
For Whom the Limo Rolls

THE CATE KINKAID FILES MYSTERIES (in print also):
Dying to Read
Dolled Up to Die
Death Takes a Ride

CHRISTIAN ROMANCES
Midnight Escape
Three Secrets (Novella)
Searching for Stardust
Yesterday Lost (Mystery/Romance)
Canyon
Betrayed
Dear Silver

The author is always delighted to hear from readers. Contact her through e-mail at: lorenamcc@centurylink.net or on the website at https://www.lorenamccourtney.info

Or connect with her on Facebook at:

http://www.facebook.com/lorenamccourtney

Happy Reading!